Guarded Deputy

fabiola francisco

Copyright © 2023 by Fabiola Francisco

All rights reserved.

No portion of this book may be reproduced in any form without written permission from the publisher or author, except as permitted by U.S. copyright law.

also by
Fabiola Francisco

Scan the QR Code to find Fabiola's other books!

dedication

For everyone who's found themselves in awkward situations.
Embrace the awkwardness and find people who love you for it.

chapter 1
LIZZY

"Guess what I just did? I accidentally sent a text message to a parent instead of you. A message about how much I hate dating and all men are assholes. Yes, I used the curse word. To. A. Parent."

I send the voice message to my best friend and keep my phone in hand while I grab the laundry from the sofa and take it to my room.

My hands are shaking from the major mess-up. If I had a magic wand, I'd use it to go back in time and invent the possibility to unsend text messages.

"Ow!" I drop everything and rub my shin.

Staring at the foot of my bed with offensive anger, I curse the day I bought a bed frame with a footboard. As much as I love decorating, I overestimated the space in my bedroom and now, I risk bruising my legs whenever I'm not careful.

I breathe out slowly, squealing at the pain pulsing through my leg, and rest my foot on the mattress to stare at the bump that's already formed. I massage the area around the growing bruise.

A punctuating knock interrupts my observation, and I freeze.

Who in the world is here?

1

A second knock echoes around my apartment with much more force. Grabbing my phone in case I need to call someone for help, I tiptoe to the front door and peek through the peephole to see if I can pretend I'm not home.

"What in the..."

I swing open the door and stare at the man's face. A man very much dressed as a deputy sheriff.

"Uh..."

"Hello, ma'am, we received a call from your home. Is everything okay?"

"I didn't call you." I shake my head.

"I believe you did." He points to my phone.

"I think I'd know if I called 911." I cross my arms. "Are you actually a stripper? Because there isn't a bachelorette party here."

He coughs, shaking his head.

It's a valid question. The man's arms are defined and his chest is broad. He could probably flex and have his clothes shred from his body.

Maybe not quite like that, but he's built.

"I'm not a stripper. I'm here on duty. You can confirm in your phone's call log. If it was a prank call, you'll have to come with me to the station." His jaw ticks.

"Prank call? What am I, fifteen? No, I didn't prank call 911." I check my phone with shaky hands.

I can see it now...

First grade teacher goes from respectable professional to criminal.

Scanning my call log, I see it. I must've mistakenly called while I was carrying my laundry.

GUARDED DEPUTY

"Oh, no." I shake my head. "I didn't mean to call. My phone was in my hand, and I must've accidentally dialed it." I offer an apologetic smile, but Mr. Hot Deputy doesn't budge.

"What happened to your leg?"

I look down at the bruise and back at him.

"I hit it with the foot of my bed frame."

"I'll have to do a walk through to make sure everything is okay in here."

"Are you serious?"

"Absolutely. Would that be okay?" he asks for consent.

"Sure." I wave my arm. I have nothing to hide. It's not like I'm being held hostage in my own home.

He enters my apartment, and his eyes bounce around the place as he makes sure everything is okay. He's like a hawk, scanning each corner as he walks through my home. When he heads to my bedroom, my eyes widen.

"Wait!" I call out as he turns the knob to my bedroom.

What lies beyond that door is a disaster. Hurricane level mess. Not only did I throw my laundry—more specifically my intimate items, which include the scrappy number my best friend got me as a joke on Valentine's Day—on the bed after dropping it on the floor, but I also have a mess of paint supplies on my desk.

My attempt is futile, though, because Mr. Hot Deputy opens the door and walks in. Mortification hits me like a million-dollar punch, and my cheeks flame. They're probably more red than that dainty piece of lace. Hopefully he doesn't judge, but I stay behind anyway.

My mother always told me to be more orderly or this would happen. I'll never admit to her that she was right.

3

My motto has always been: Love me at my worst and messiest or don't love me at all.

I can't be the only woman in the world who hates putting laundry away and lets it linger around the house for a few days.

Weeks.

Whatever.

"Everything seems to be in order here."

I snort and cover my mouth with my hand so he can't see me laughing. Laughing at inappropriate times is a sport I'd win consistent gold medals in. Too bad it doesn't come with a hefty cash prize.

Instead, it's paid with glares and uncomfortable situations.

"Is something funny?" He lifts his brows.

"No, sir." I stand tall, shaking my head.

His eyebrow imperceptibly arches before he nods once.

This night is going worse than I imagined.

I walk him out of the apartment with a tight smile and expel a deep breath when I close the door. I can just imagine the entire apartment building talking about me calling the cops. Heck, the entire town will probably be talking about it come tomorrow morning.

I, on the other hand, am stuck on who that deputy was. I've never seen him before, and no one is a stranger in Emerald Bay. Our beach town is small, and everyone knows each other—we especially know when a newcomer is in town.

I startle when my phone rings, bringing me out of my thoughts. I sigh when I see my mom's name on the screen and answer.

"Sweetheart, are you okay? What's going on? Why did I hear that Roy was at your apartment?" That news traveled remark-

GUARDED DEPUTY

ably fast, even for our small town. Uncle Roy is our Sheriff, so him showing up to my home while on duty would cause her to be concerned.

I roll my eyes and sit on the sofa.

"It wasn't Uncle Roy, Mom. It was a deputy, and I'm okay. It was a misunderstanding." I talk her off the ledge.

"What kind of misunderstanding gets the police to your house?"

"An accidental call to 911." I cringe because it's a terrible excuse.

"Are you lying to me?"

"No!" I hop to my feet, pacing around my small living room.

"If that man is bothering you, tell me. You should move back home."

"Goodness, Mom. No one is bothering me. I told you it was an accident. My ex is harmless. A jerk, but he'd never hurt a fly."

Sean, my ex, isn't a dangerous man, but he is an asshole who tried to turn me into Susie Homemaker from the 1950s. When I wouldn't quit my job to stay at home and instead told him I was going to apply to grad school, we broke up and haven't spoken since.

"Mom, I promise I'm okay." I switch the call to video so she can see for herself. "Move the phone back," I say when I can practically see her pores.

"Sorry." She laughs and puts some distance between her face and phone. "I'm glad you're okay, then. If you need anything, call us."

"I will." I appease her.

5

All I want to do is heat up some leftover pasta and veg on the couch while I watch TV. Hopefully that helps me forget about the call I made—and Mr. Hot Deputy.

Seriously, who is that guy?

"I'm going to have dinner. We'll talk tomorrow, Mom."

"Goodnight, sweetie."

"Night." I hang up and walk to the kitchen, pulling out the container with my pasta. Serving myself some, I heat it up in the microwave and wait.

My phone beeps on the counter, and I see a text message from my best friend. All she sent were a ton of laughing emojis as a response to the voice message I sent her.

Me: Asshole

Dani: That's hilarious. Who did you send it to?

Me: My new student's mom.

Dani: Oh man. Too bad it wasn't to Emily.

Me: I know. She'd laugh along.

Emily is another friend of mine. Teaching in a small town, you're bound to teach your friends' kids. Unfortunately, I sent the message to a woman who's been living in town for a few months and doesn't know me the way others might.

Me: When I see her, I'm going to hide.

Dani: <laughing emojis>

I love her, but she's a jerk sometimes.

Me: By the way, did you hear about someone moving to town? A deputy?

Dani: No... Why?

Me: Just wondering. Heard something but didn't get details.

Dani: Is that the deputy that showed up at your house?

Me: OH MY GOD. YOU TOO?

Dani: I was wondering how long it'd take you to tell me.

Me: It just happened! I give up. I'm oh-for-two today.

Me: I'm going to sleep.

I'm not going to live this down. I can just imagine the gossip around town.

Lizzy Andrews had a break-in.

No, her ex-boyfriend was harassing her.

Actually, she just wanted to meet the new deputy.

Joke's on everyone—I just have careless fingers and a too-sensitive phone.

chapter 2
LIZZY

I AM SO GLAD the day is over and tomorrow is Saturday. As expected, everyone at work kept asking about my 911 call last night. I'm about to write the situation and tape it to my classroom door so I don't have to repeat myself. Maybe the principal will let me borrow the microphone so I can do story-time over the loudspeaker.

I'm standing outside for dismissal, waiting for all my students to get picked up. Then, I'll be home free.

A few students are left, and I wish I could telepathically tell their parents to hurry up so I can go home. Maybe after yesterday's text message mix-up, I shouldn't be communicating with parents at all, fake telepathy included.

"Ms. Andrews, I need to go to the bathroom."

I look at Jenna, one of my students. "Go quickly."

This is why I urge them to use the bathroom before we leave.

She races off to the bathroom, and I call out, "Walk please!"

"I don't know why I bother," I tell myself as I turn back to my students.

My eyes widen, and my heart drops. *Oh, no.*

Mr. Hot Deputy is walking my way. His eyes narrow when they land on me, and I swallow thickly.

GUARDED DEPUTY

"Are you here to arrest me?" I blurt out without thinking.

"No." He shakes his head.

I mean, delayed arrest isn't a thing, right? I'm innocent.

Some of the other teachers whisper, and I glare at them.

"Sorry, Lizzy, but this is funny," Andrea, the other first grade teacher, says.

"Har, har. Laugh it up." I look back at the deputy. "Can I help you then?"

"Uncle Nate!" Walker, the new student whose mom I texted last night, says.

Wonderful.

"Uncle?" I lift my brows.

"You're Ms. Andrews?" He crosses his arms.

"Yes." I look at Walker. "Sweetie, I need to verify your uncle is authorized to take you home."

Walker looks up at me with his face scrunched up. "Why? He lives with me."

"School rules."

"I'm taking him home." Mr. Hot Deputy glares at me.

"I don't have you down as an authorized person. I'll have to see I.D. and check with the office."

"Are you serious?"

"School rules apply to everyone, even men of the law." I try to joke, but he shakes his head, fishing his license out of his wallet.

I smile at Walker as I grab my walky-talky and page the secretary. I look at the license, reading the name to her.

He even looks good in his license picture. No one ever looks good in those. Is this guy some kind of mythical creature? A vampire from *Twilight*?

Edward, is that you?

11

I keep my eyes on the license while I wait for the secretary to check her notes. Nathan is only three years older than me, too.

Down girl. This isn't some dating site match-up.

He's originally from Dallas. It makes sense since Walker is from there, too.

You're a genius, Lizzy. They may just hire you as a detective.

"He's cleared," the secretary says.

"Oh. Okay, yeah. Thanks."

"Here you go, Mr. Nathan. I mean, Deputy." *Shut up.*

"Have a good weekend, Walker."

"Thanks, Ms. Andrews. You too!" Walker skips away ahead of his uncle, who is staring at me for a beat longer than normal and crossing into awkward.

"I trust you won't make any unnecessary calls anymore."

"Nope!" I hold my phone up. "This bad boy will rest on a table if I need to carry laundry."

He doesn't even chuckle at my bad joke. Tough crowd.

As he walks away, Walker asks him if they can stop by the grocery store to buy ice cream. Nathan wraps his arm around his neck and smiles.

I hadn't seen him smile, and it's a glamorous thing. Dimples pop up on his cheeks, and I'm ready to dive into them.

Dive into them? What in the world does that mean?

"Mr. Nathan?" Andrea says.

"Shut up."

"He's hot," she continues.

I groan and lean against the wall.

"If it makes you feel better, when I was in college, I totally entered my RA's dorm by mistake and caught him naked in the hallway."

"Why was he naked in the hallway?"

"How the hell should I know? I screamed, beat him with a pillow, and then ran. That's when I realized I was in the wrong dorm."

"Oh, my goodness!" My entire body shakes with laughter, tears in my eyes. "Stop it. That's hilarious!"

"I couldn't face him for the rest of my college career. I apologized, but that didn't help kill off the embarrassment."

"I would die." I wipe the tears from my eyes.

"I did meet my then boyfriend because of that situation, though." She shrugs and smiles.

"I guess it worked out, then."

"So don't worry. Maybe you'll meet a guy because of this."

I scoff and shake my head. "This store is closed for business." I cross my arms over my body.

"There are children around. Please be mindful of the conversations you're having," Ellen, one of the fifth grade teachers, says.

I roll my eyes, not hiding my reaction, and look at Andrea.

"I can't stand her," Andrea whispers.

"That makes two of us. She's stuck-up and thinks she's the best at everything."

After all of my students leave, I return to my classroom to pack up for the day and go home.

I've got plans for sushi and wine with my friends, and I can't wait for girls' night. It's what keeps me sane and acting like an adult when I spend most of my days with seven and eight-year-olds.

My students are great, but this girl needs conversations that don't revolve around unicorns, hide-and-seek, and math.

After my embarrassing situations with the Lundsten family, I need to just relax and forget about it all.

Not that I could quickly forget about Uncle Nate and his dimples.

"Please tell me again how you asked him if he was going to arrest you?" Dani snorts with laughter, and Avery joins her.

"Shush!" I lean forward and slap her arm, causing her salmon roll to drop from her chopsticks.

"Hey, I was gonna eat that."

"You still can." I point to the messy roll on her plate.

"How do I eat this mess with chopsticks?" She widens her eyes.

"Use your fork."

"I hate eating sushi with a fork."

"I know." I smirk.

"People at the bakery were saying you're looking for a rebound and chose the deputy." Avery bites back her laughter.

"Ugh. I knew people would spin this around. Anyway..." My words trail off when something catches my eye. "You've got to be kidding me."

"What?" Dani's brows furrow.

Avery looks around the restaurant.

"Nothing." I shake my head.

I'd rather them not know who just walked in, but I'm not as inconspicuous as I thought because Dani turns around to look behind her.

GUARDED DEPUTY

"Who is that? Ohhhh...wait! Is that him? No wonder you asked if he was a stripper. His ass is definitely a stripper ass." Her laughter booms, earning us the attention from the entire restaurant, including Mr. Hot Deputy himself.

I slide down in my chair, hiding as much as I can of myself. I kick Dani under the table, and she laughs louder. It doesn't even faze her.

"I think I need a new best friend."

"Don't you dare replace me." She points at me with her lips pressed together.

"I'm never going to live this down." I bow my head.

"You will," Avery says.

"Yeah, eventually, you will. Seriously, who accidentally calls 911?" Dani asks.

"Your best friend," I say emotionless.

"I love you for it. Maybe it's fate. I wonder if he's single. You should ask him. Oh! Ask him to the spring festival at the school."

"What are we, thirteen? I'm not asking him anything. Besides, I'm pretty sure he thinks I'm an idiot."

"You're not an idiot, and if he *does* think that, then good riddance." Dani rolls her eyes, nostrils flaring in my defense.

"Yeah, he isn't worth your time if he's a judgmental ass," Avery adds.

"This is why I love you both." I smile at them.

Dani is my soul sister, always ready to back me up or defend me. Avery became our friend as soon as she moved here years ago with her now ex-husband, but her divorce didn't threaten our friendship.

I sit back in my seat, unable to take my eyes off Nate as I watch him leave with a bag full of containers. He doesn't seem very friendly, and I can imagine it's hard being new in a small town.

We are a tight-knit community, and it's in our nature to be curious about the newcomers. His family definitely spikes our curiosity because we don't know much about them. His sister has been nice enough, and Walker is a sweetheart, but they're still strangers.

I know from being Walker's teacher that his mom is a widow, so maybe Nate wanted to be close to his family and moved down here.

Whatever the reason, it's sweet that he'd want to help his sister so much that he'd be willing to move to a different state.

He seems hard on the outside, but I wonder if there's a soft center hidden under the intimidating uniform and badge.

chapter 3
NATE

MY EYES BLINK FOR a beat too long as the letters on my paperwork blur. How much coffee is too much? It seems that the four cups I've already had today aren't enough to keep me focused on this task.

It's boring as hell.

A lot about this job is boring in comparison to my fast-paced life in Dallas.

It's for a greater good.

My priority is supporting Brooke in this new phase of her life and being there for Walker. I stand and stretch my arms and back.

I could be bagging groceries at the store and not regret it if it means I'm here for my family.

I sit back down with a sigh and finish filling out the report just in time to start another training. My mind wanders to the teacher with the pajama shorts that show off her legs as I listen to the speaker drone on through my computer. Although, when I saw her yesterday at the school, she looked the picture of professional.

GUARDED DEPUTY

These workshops are more boring than the paperwork I'm required to fill out, but I have to be trained in Florida's regulations. It's the curse of being the new guy from out-of-state.

Thankfully, everyone's been welcoming, but I'm definitely the odd man out. Brooke and Walker have had more time to adjust to Emerald Bay, although my sister is still too reserved. I wish she would interact with people in town more and start remaking her life.

Try as I might, I can't put myself in her shoes and understand how she must feel with the way her life was turned upside down, but it'll do her good to immerse herself into this new life since she made the decision to do so.

"Moore!" a gruff voice calls.

I look up and find Sheriff McCall standing a few feet away from me.

"Yes, sir." I stand, pausing the workshop.

"Come into my office, please."

I follow behind him and take a seat at his desk, looking at him expectantly. He steeples his hands and leans back in his chair, leveling his gaze.

"I've been working with our county to implement a school resource deputy program called Keeping Our Children Safe, acronym K.O.C.S."

I cough to hide my chuckle and look at the Sheriff. "I don't think that's a great nickname, sir."

He pauses and says, "KOCS." Then, he chuckles, and nods. "You're right. I hadn't realized it until I said it out loud. Well, we can still change the name. The point of the program is to have one of our members as a safety point on campus while leading a program about safety, anti-bullying, drug education, etcetera."

19

I nod, wondering what he's getting at, although I have a sinking feeling.

"It will be offered as a pilot program in our elementary, middle, and high schools. With your experience in Dallas working as a mentor, I thought you'd be the perfect candidate. However, you'd have to take a four-day course to learn about the school system and working with youth. It'd be a ten-week program, so you'll be at the school for the rest of the school year as the security officer as well." He looks at me with raised eyebrows, gaging my reaction.

"How will it work? Will I be on campus every day?"

"Yes. You'll alternate between the kindergarten through eighth grade campus and the high school. I'll have a schedule set with clear days you'll be at each school. I know your experience is with adolescents, but it's important to work with the younger children as well as a preventative measure."

"I understand. How about the name, *Training Our Students Against Crime?*"

"That's good." He nods, jotting it down on a piece of paper.

In Dallas, I helped with a group of kids that would end up in jail if it weren't for us. It's something I was passionate about, and I often find myself wishing I didn't have to leave that behind. This is different, though. If the kids are anything like Walker, they aren't on the path to destruction.

"The training course will begin in two weeks, and you'll be introduced to the staff the Friday before," he explains. I guess I'm stuck with more workshops.

"Sounds good."

"This pilot program has to go off without a hitch. If it's successful, we'll be able to implement it throughout the county." Sheriff McCall gives me a stern look.

"Noted." Basically, don't screw this up.

I move to stand, thanking the sheriff, though I'm not sure if I'm grateful right now. I guess this beats getting called down to someone's house because their neighbor is planting petunias on the edge of their property and the person has a petunia allergy.

At least these kids will act their age instead of adults bickering like ten-year-old children.

"Honey, I'm home!" I call out as I walk into the house and toe off my shoes.

Walker's racing footsteps echo through the house. I love that kid as if he were my own.

"Uncle Nate! Guess what!" He slides to a stop in front of me.

"What's up, bud?"

"Mom said we can eat at a restaurant."

"Really?" I lift my brows. "I brought stuff to make a pizza." I hold up the bag in my hand.

"We can do that tomorrow." He jumps around.

"Hey." Brooke smiles as she walks into the kitchen. It's good to see a grin on her face.

"I hear we're going out?" I arch a brow.

"Yeah." She nods, grabbing a glass and filling it with water.

Putting the stuff I bought away in the fridge, I turn to her and cross my arms. She seems happy, and I hope it's permanent. My sister deserves all the happiness in the world.

"We've been cooped up in here all day doing chores, so I thought we could reward ourselves with not cooking. Besides, I spent two hours cleaning the kitchen, and I refuse to dirty it." She shrugs, drinking her water.

"Sounds good." I slide my hands into my pockets and smile. "By the way, I got transferred to a different department at work, so I'll be working at the school," I tell Brooke.

"Like the security guard?" Her brows pull together.

I chuckle and shake my head. "I will be doing security, but I'll also be leading a ten-week program for some grade levels to train them in safety, anti-bullying, and drug education."

That's cool." Brooke nods. "Will it be in the high school?"

"I'll be in both schools."

"Right up your alley." She pats my shoulder.

"We'll see. It's not quite what I did in Dallas, but it'll be okay. I'm not sure how this small beach town could have kids that need help like the ones in the city did." I sigh, rubbing my stubbled cheek.

"I know the job here is different than back home, but this gives you a chance to make a big difference like Mr. Braden did for you." She gives me a pointed look that speaks volumes.

If it weren't for Mr. Braden, I wouldn't be wearing this uniform. I'd be staring at someone else with it on while in prison somewhere.

Maybe.

Who knows?

Thankfully the future panned out differently, and I didn't have to find out.

"Yeah, yeah." I shake my head. "I'm gonna shower."

GUARDED DEPUTY

I head to my bathroom, starting to unbutton my uniform shirt as I go. Once in the bathroom, I take a quick shower. It's not like I built up a sweat studying state statutes. Before I know it, I'm back in the kitchen with Brooke.

"Tell me what's really going on? You seem...different." I tilt my head and stare at her.

"I'm in a good mood. I'm allowed to have those, right?" she snaps.

"Of course you are." I hug her. "I'm so happy to see you happy."

"Redundant much?" She snorts.

"Let me have this one," I joke. "I'm not one to get wordy."

"Except when you're drunk and want to spend all night talking." She snorts in a failed attempt to hold back her laughter.

"I get needy one time and it stalks me for life." I playfully shove her away.

"More than once, but I love it so you're forgiven. It makes me feel like I get a real glimpse inside your brain." She taps my forehead.

"You always know what's going on in my head," I argue.

If anyone knows me, it's my sister. I may not let many people get close, but she's my best friend. We've been through so much together, our lives not exactly being easy, but we've had each other's support.

"Sometimes I wonder," she mumbles and gives me the fakest smile.

"I can taste the saccharine from that smile."

"It's my special," she jokes.

"Lucky me!" I uncharacteristically feign over-the-top excitement, teasing her.

23

"You're lucky to have an amazing sister like me." She jabs her finger into my chest.

"That I am." I wrap my arm around her shoulder and kiss the top of her head. "It's good to see you like this, Booky." I call her by the nickname I used when I was little.

"I moved here to embrace a new life, right?"

"Exactly. It's about time you actually embrace it."

"What're we gonna eat?" Walker walks into the kitchen.

"I think we should go to Jim's," I say.

"Yeah!" Walker nods like a bobble head.

"Sounds good to me."

"Great, I'll drive."

Once Walker has his shoes on and Brooke has her purse, I grab my car keys and head out to the driveway. My family may be small, but they mean the world to me.

I head out to the part of town that is near the beach. The scent of the salty ocean hits my senses, reminding me that I now live in an area where most people vacation. It's different than the stagnant smell from a landlocked city, and it makes me feel like I'm on a permanent holiday.

People in Florida have a right to say they live in paradise because while Emerald Bay is a small town with nosy bodies, it's beautiful with the white sandy beach.

I park the car, and we head into the packed restaurant. I spot a table and rush to claim it before someone else does. Brooke and Walker follow me, and my sister high-fives me.

"Good job, bro."

The burgers here are amazing, so I don't have to think much about what I'm going to eat. While Brooke argues with Walker

GUARDED DEPUTY

that it's too late for him to have a milkshake with dinner, I look around the restaurant.

I've become familiar with a lot of people in town already. It's part of the job being a deputy sheriff and dealing directly with citizens. One thing I've learned is that people in small towns will call 911 over a neighbor stealing their flowers, or hooking up their hose to the other person's water supply.

Or accidentally call emergency and then accuse me of being a stripper.

Some call it small-town charm. I'm still warming up to the idea. Culture shock is real in your own country.

I continue my scan, and when my eyes lock with a pair of wide blue ones, my heart lurches.

Ms. Andrews.

The woman with a messy room who's been on my mind. She looked professional at work yesterday, but I much prefer seeing her in her pajamas. Not that I'd act on anything. The last thing I need is to complicate my life, and she's a major complication.

I may not know everyone in town yet, but I am smart enough to understand that people will gossip. Besides, dating Walker's teacher is a recipe for disaster.

And if I've learned anything from my family, it's that the men in it tend to leave. I refuse to carry on that torch down the family line.

She's sitting with an older couple I assume are her parents. The woman leans forward, but her eyes remain on mine.

I nod once and look away, blowing out a breath and focusing back on the conversation between Brooke and Walker. He's spewing off all the reasons he could have a milkshake, negotiating like a professional.

25

The kid could sell a lifetime supply of candy to a dentist.

His biggest rival is my sister, who doesn't buy just anything off anyone.

I chuckle at his excuse that tomorrow's Sunday and he can stay up a bit later today. I don't want to deal with him when he's on a sugar rush, so I hope like crazy that Brooke doesn't give in.

"Hey, that's Ms. Andrews." Walker points in her direction, distracted from the milkshake.

"No pointing, Walker," Brooke hisses, shoving his arm down.

"It is her! What's she doing here? Shouldn't she be at school?" His eyebrows furrow in confusion.

I bark out a laugh and shake my head.

"Teachers have lives outside of school," I tell him.

"Weird." He shakes his head.

"She sent me a text message the other night," Brooke leans in and whispers.

"Is everything okay with Walker?" My back straightens.

"Yeah. It was an accident. Apparently, she meant to send it to her friend." Brooke laughs, pulling her phone out.

I grab it and read over the message.

Ms. Andrews sent an entire message about how men are assholes and dating sucks. Checking the date, I note this was the same night I went to her apartment. I guess she was having a rough night.

"She apologized profusely as you can see, but it made me laugh."

"That is funny."

"Ms. Andrews *is* funny. She makes a weird sound when she laughs, like a pig, but we made ice cream in science the other day

GUARDED DEPUTY

and it was good. It didn't taste like the ice cream from Cones that I loved in Dallas, but it was pretty good for making it in a plastic bag," Walker rambles.

He must've been listening to our conversation.

"Ice cream in a bag?" I lift my eyebrows incredulously. "That doesn't sound good."

"It was an experiment," Brooke explains. "Turning liquid into a solid. He loved it."

"Yeah! We got to eat it and not do so much work, so that was cool." He leans back in his chair, hands clasped together over the table.

This kid could be my twin when it comes to personalities. I've never known a nephew and uncle to be so alike, but he's almost my carbon copy. I hope he makes better choices than me, though. I'll make sure of it.

My eyes wander back to Ms. Andrews. She's eating a taco, her hands messy from the sauce. There's no filter when it comes to observing her, and it's kind of refreshing. A pile of crumpled napkins sits by her plate, some tucked under the rim of it.

"You're staring," Brooke says.

"At what?" I snap my head toward her.

"Not what, *who*." She waggles her eyebrows.

"You're ridiculous.

"You also have to make a life for yourself. Do you think I don't know what you're doing? Putting your life on hold for Walker and me? It isn't your responsibility." She shakes her head.

"You know how I feel about relationships. They're not for me." I shake my head.

"You aren't Dad. We've discussed this before."

My jaw clenches. I hate thinking about my father, but his ghost haunts me no matter how different I want to be from him.

"Let's enjoy dinner." I divert the conversation and look at Walker. "Let's do this word search." I point to his kids' menu.

"My son won't always bail you out of difficult conversations," Brooke mumbles.

She may be right, but he bailed me out of this one. I'm not in the mood to discuss the ways I'd rather focus on my family than let someone into my life.

chapter 4
LIZZY

"Shit balls!" I jump around on one foot after stubbing my toe against the corner of the wall in the opening of my kitchen.

"Goodness, gracious, shit balls of fire." I stop myself and then laugh at my stupidity.

Who the hell sings out the song and swaps the words *great* balls for *shit* balls? I've lost my mind.

Grabbing ice from the freezer, I wrap it in paper towel and place it on my throbbing toe. This is what I get for daydreaming instead of paying attention to where I'm walking. My mind has been preoccupied by a sexy deputy lately.

When I saw him at Jim's last night, it felt like his gaze was piercing me. My heart sputtered like a fish out of water. Damn hazel eyes with layers of gold, green, and brown.

I've never had a thing for men in uniform, but if he wanted to handcuff me, I'd willingly give him my wrists.

You shouldn't think about him that way.

My conscience is right. He's related to one of my students, and that could be *messy*. Despite the disaster he saw in my room, I'd rather have things neat and tidy, especially when it comes to my career.

30

GUARDED DEPUTY

"Crap." I look at the time and throw the ice in the sink before putting my shoes on and grabbing my purse. Then, I race out of my apartment.

I promised Dani I'd help her run some errands, and I'm late. Grabbing my phone, I press down the microphone icon to send her a voice message.

"I'll be there soon, sorry! I stubbed my toe and lost track of time. I'm okay just distracted. I'll meet you at Home Made." I send the message and drive to Main Street.

I speed down the street, ignoring the speed limit for once. Nothing annoys me more than lack of punctuality. I'm usually early everywhere I go, so my stress levels rise like the Nile River in ancient summers when I'm running late, even if Dani won't care.

I get to a four-way stop, and seeing as no one is coming, I roll through the stop sign and continue on. When I hear sirens, I look everywhere for the ambulance. Instead, I find a patrol car behind me.

"You've gotta be kidding me." *Please don't let it be Mr. Hot Deputy. Please be someone else.*

I pull over to the side, and my leg bounces in my seat as I wait for the deputy to come to my vehicle. I'd start looking for my documentation, but I don't want him to think that I'm grabbing a weapon or anything. Not that I own one, but people always store them in the glove compartment in movies and TV shows.

A tap on my window tears me away from my Hollywood trivia. My eyes widen when I see Mr. Hot Deputy himself on the other side of the glass, and I curse.

Of course it's him.

31

His eyes are assessing as his jaw ticks.

Just my luck. Murphy's Law never fails me.

Rolling down the window, I put on my best smile as proof of bravery when in reality I'm dying a little on the inside.

"License, registration, and proof of insurance." His voice is stoic.

"Okay," I squeak.

I reach for my license and hand it to him before searching for my registration and insurance in the glove compartment. If the earth could swallow me up right now, that'd be great. I have State Farm. Where's my agent appearing out of nowhere to get me out of a dangerous situation? I'm sure this is dangerous. For my pride, but whatever.

I hand over my documentation and his eyes scan over them.

"Do you know why I pulled you over?"

"Aren't you supposed to tell me?"

His eyes lift while his head maintains bowed.

"Are you being smart?"

"No." I shake my head. "It's the first time I've ever gotten pulled over."

"Right." He rolls his eyes. "I'll be right back."

"I'm not kidding!" I stick my head out of the window. "I've never gotten a ticket in my life."

Deputy Hot Pants—that should really be his name because, *wow he perfectly fills in his trousers*—ignores me and sits in his car. I look at him through my rearview mirror as he taps on a keyboard. While I impatiently wait, I send Dani a message letting her know I'm going to be late.

GUARDED DEPUTY

"You weren't kidding." I shoot up in my chair, dropping my phone on the passenger seat like it's on fire, my hand flying to my chest as his voice startles me.

"I wasn't."

"There's a first time for everything." He presses his lips into a straight line.

"I'm pretty sure deputies aren't supposed to be sarcastic."

"I'm not being sarcastic. You ran a stop sign and were speeding."

I bite my lip and grimace.

"Don't I get a warning?"

"This isn't school, Ms. Andrews. Warnings are for children. You"—he pauses, his eyes scanning my face—"are an adult."

A shiver runs down my spine, and I nod. "There goes my perfect record."

"Next time, don't speed, and stop when you're supposed to. Obeying the law would prevent this from happening."

"Yeah, yeah. Rules and consequences. I know all about that. I'm a teacher, remember?" I shake my head, blowing out a deep breath.

"By the way, your registration is expired. You might want to renew it. Someone else may not let you off so easily." He arches an eyebrow.

"Was that a warning?" I tease, biting back my smile.

"I wouldn't want you taking out my harsh punishment on Walker."

"I'd never do that." I shake my head, furrowing my eyebrows. What kind of person does he think I am?

"I'm not vindictive or resentful, nor would I put a student in that position—"

33

"It was a joke, Ms. Andrews," he cuts me off.

"What?" I shake my head. "It was a really bad joke. Take some comedian lessons or something." I roll my eyes.

"Comedy isn't my strong suit."

"No shit," I murmur.

"You'll have to pay the fine by the date on the ticket. Renew your registration and drive safely." He nods, walking back to his car.

What in the world? He is...odd. Hot, but odd. Or, I should say, his sense of humor is strange.

I'm equally offended and relieved. My first fine. I stare at the paper as if it'll bite me. I'm going to have to pay this as soon as I get home. And there goes my squeaky clean record.

As if you're suddenly a criminal. Get a grip, Lizzy.

Driving like an old lady who can barely see over the wheel, I finally park on Main Street and find Dani standing outside of Home Made.

"What happened?" Her eyebrows lift.

Shaking my head, I pout. "I got a ticket."

"No way!" She slaps her thigh. "How'd that feel?"

"Horrible! And guess *who* stopped me." My mouth presses into a tight line.

"The hot deputy?"

"My luck is impeccable."

"Maybe you should play the lottery." She opens the door to the shop, and I walk in.

"Should I play lucky number thirteen?" I quip.

"It could work." She smiles.

"Sorry I'm late. You could've started looking around without me."

GUARDED DEPUTY

"It's okay. I need your eye for design."

Dani recently bought her first home, and she wants a whole new look than her previous decor. In her eyes, I belong on HGTV decorating houses. I'm not that great of a decorator, but it's so much fun to mix and match different styles to create a unique one that fits someone's personality. If I made more money, I'd be like those women I see on social media videos that redo their decor every few months to match the season. All my savings is going to grad school though.

"So, how was Mr. Hot Deputy? Hot as ever?" Dani asks as we browse, breaking me from my thoughts. She chuckles when I side-eye her.

"Unfortunately, yes. Fortunately for me, I didn't look like a hot mess this time." I wave a hand in front of me.

The first time we met, I was in scrappy pajamas and a bruise on my leg with my bun falling off the side of my head.

"You do look cute today. Maybe you were the bright part of his workday. You getting a ticket is all a sacrifice to make his day better." She holds up a vase.

"You're ridiculous." I grab the vase and hold it out in front of me. It's a matte white cylinder with a narrow neck that would look great with pampas grass.

"I like this." I nod in approval.

"I can put it on my bookshelf. It'd even be pretty without flowers."

"I agree. I love the boho feel of it," I tell her.

We continue to shop, adding an eclectic combination of home decor into the shopping cart. I'm distracted by the memory of Nate attempting to joke. His lips didn't even quirk to give away that it was laced with humor. The man needs a lesson in joke-telling. Not that I'm any good at it. My idea of jokes is at a seven-year-old level.

My students think I'm funny. Adults do not.

"Earth to Lizzy?" Dani is looking at me expectantly. Her eyebrows have climbed into her hairline.

"Huh?" I look at her with wide eyes.

"You look like you've left our planet and are traveling in a different universe."

"Sorry. I was thinking." I shake my head and look at what she's holding.

"What do you think about this for the living room?"

I look at the abstract flower painting and scrunch up my nose.

"I don't like it." I purse my lips apologetically.

"Too colorful?"

"Too abstract yet not abstract enough, and the colors are all wrong. They're too primary." I look around and smile.

"Now this, I *love*." I reach for the macrame wall tapestry. The intricate design is feminine and unique.

"I do like that. Why don't you come to my apartment when we finish here and help me put everything up, and I'll pay you with pizza?" Her smile is cheesy and hopeful.

"Ugh, only because you mentioned pizza." I roll my eyes playfully.

"I know the way to your heart."

"I think you're the only one," I joke.

"I don't know... I'm feeling some competition coming on." She winks.

"Right." My eyebrows pull together as if she's lost her mind.

She's definitely crazy. There is no competition for my heart in the horizon. It's so far out there, that I think we'll be living on the moon before that happens.

I don't trust myself to choose a good guy. Considering my past relationships, who seemed like safe and nice candidates, I wouldn't know how to distinguish a rotten apple even if I took a bite out of it.

It's like I'm a magnet for jerks, and after one too many, I give up. The headache isn't worth it, not to mention the heartache. At what point can a woman say she's done with dating and not be judged for not wanting a man by her side?

Besides, my career is first, and getting my degree in school counseling is my priority. It's been my dream for as long as I can remember. Helping children overcome struggles and challenges, have someone they can talk to, work through emotions.

"How about we have some coffee? I see that you're zoning out again." Dani's words break through the fog in my mind.

"Yeah, coffee is good. Coffee knows the way to my heart."

She laughs and pays for her things. After she puts them away in her trunk, we head to the coffee shop.

"Now that we're relaxing, let's circle back to your deputy." Dani leans back in her chair with her latte in hand.

"He's not my deputy, and there's nothing to say," I respond. "I was speeding, ran a stop sign, and got pulled over."

"He didn't say anything? Flirt a bit? Did you?"

"Of course not! It's my first ticket, I was freaking out."

"Flirting could've gotten you out of it." She shrugs.

I scoff at her words. "I wouldn't flirt or use any excuse to get out of a ticket. If I broke the law, then I have to deal with the consequences."

"You are a rule-follower. It's why I think you became a teacher. It's also why I'm your best friend. I can shake you up sometimes." She waggles her eyebrows and shimmies in her seat.

I giggle and shake my head. "You're ridiculous, but you're right."

"I know." She swipes her shoulder arrogantly.

My laughter gets caught in my throat when I notice a patrol car driving down the street. I wonder if that's Nate or one of his colleagues. My belly flips at the thought of him coming in here during a break and getting another glimpse of him.

Do I seriously have a crush on the new guy in town who is also my student's uncle?

Crushes are so seventh grade.

chapter 5
LIZZY

I CLUTCH THE PAPER in my hand and take a deep breath before pulling open the door to the station. I hope to all that's holy that I find another deputy that is *not* Nate. I know for a fact that more people work here.

"What are you doing here?"

"Just my luck," I mumble, walking up to the counter where Nate is standing on the other side.

"I'm here to pay my fine." I hold up the piece of paper.

"Here?" His eyebrows pull together like a tightrope.

"I can do that, right?"

"You're serious." His hands grip the counter, and my eyes roam to his arms. The muscles are defined like the lines in an ant farm.

What? An ant farm, Lizzy?

I roll my eyes.

"No need to get sassy."

"Huh?" My eyes snap to his. "I wasn't...not sassy. I was thinking...rolling eyes at myself." I stammer and fall over my words. "I am serious. I can't get the website to work. I've tried a million times, and it doesn't take me to the right page." I sigh in exasperation.

GUARDED DEPUTY

I've tried paying this fine all day in between classes, and nothing worked. I forgot last night after getting home from Dani's house and saw the ticket in my purse this morning.

I scratch the side of my head, my bun hanging off the side, my signature look recently.

Nate's eyebrows slowly lift, his eyes stuck on the top of my head.

"Messy buns are the new updos," I spit out.

"What?" His face scrunches up.

"Nothing." I shake my head. "Bad joke. Anyway, who do I make the check out to?" I slam the paper on the counter in an attempt to seem cool, which is actually the total opposite.

I bet he's one of those people who makes his bed first thing in the morning. Me? I make coffee first. Then, I figure out the rest. And to be honest, most days my bed remains unmade.

"Right. You actually can't write a check. You have to pay online."

"Is everything about technology nowadays?"

I'm tech savvy. Well, to a point. I can't build you some computer system, but I know how to use one well. The county website is not working properly.

"It's easier and more direct," Nate says.

"Well, something's not working on the site. I don't want to get a fee on top of this fine." I shake my head.

He sighs, tapping the keyboard on the computer.

"Did you go here?" He turns the screen over so I can see it.

"Yes."

"And then you click this link." He talks slowly, as if teaching a child how to use scissors for the first time.

"Yeah…" I lift my brows.

"Here's the payment area."

"What? No. I didn't get that option. This is like taking your car to the mechanic because it's sputtering and when you arrive the devious thing purrs like a well-loved cat."

Nate looks at me out of the corner of his eyes with a small smile. "I knew you were a cat person."

"I'm not! I prefer dogs, but cat purrs are more satisfying than a dog snoring."

He chuckles and turns the keyboard my way.

"Wait, what was that supposed to mean? Do I look like a spinster living with a million cats?"

"Go on and enter your information. I'll give you a moment." He walks away with a smirk.

"I'm no spinster!" I call out.

"Lizzy." Uncle Roy walks into the lobby with a smile.

"Oh, hey, Sheriff." I salute him, which he hates. "Sorry about that." I grimace and look at the screen.

"Is everything okay? And knock-off the Sheriff talk. I'm going to retire from Sheriff, and you're still going to be saluting me."

My uncle is like a second father to me. The way my mom can be tense and nervous about little things, he's the calming sibling, talking her off the ledge. Their younger brother, my Uncle Mark, is the laid-back, brush-things-off guy.

I giggle and shake my head. "It's too fun. Everything's okay. I, uh, needed to pay a ticket. How's Aunt Natalie?" I switch topics so he doesn't linger on the ticket.

"She's great."

"I'm happy to hear that."

"What'd you get a ticket for?" Uncle Roy arches a brow, clearly not distracted by my change in topics.

GUARDED DEPUTY

"Did you say cricket? I didn't catch any." I smile sweetly.

"Wise-crack." He shakes his head. "Pay that ticket, or I'll have to charge you for internet use."

"Oh, please." I scoff playfully. "The county pays for it, not you, and it's unlimited. I could play hours of Solitaire on it and not rack up costs."

"Get to it." He tilts his chin toward the computer as Nate comes back out.

"Aye, aye, Captain. I mean, Sheriff." I salute him.

"Watch it, Scout, you're in my territory." He arches a brow and smiles as he goes back toward his office.

"Scout? Do you know him well?" Nate widens his stance, standing in front of me with his arms crossed.

Curiosity swims in his eyes, and I really shouldn't notice how cute his confused face is. This big and intimidating man seeming doubtful is not good for my heart health.

"You could say that." I shrug. Everyone in town knows I'm the sheriff's niece, but it's kind of nice for someone to be unaware of that connection.

"You seemed like you knew each other well." His eyebrows climb on his forehead.

"Were you spying on us?" I smile knowingly.

"Of course not." His jaw ticks.

"Aw, you're a closet nosy-body. It's okay. Your secret's safe with me." I wink and turn to the screen.

Who am I? Did I just flirt with him? I was clear when I told myself I don't have time for dating.

Nate clears his throat, shifting on his feet.

"He's not your father, right?" Nate's eyebrows furrow.

"Worse. He's my godfather," I say in what's supposed to be an intimidating deep voice, but Nate misses it because he shakes his head.

"This really is a small town." He blows out a breath.

"You have no idea, buddy." I pat his arm. His muscles flex, giving me sensorial overload of the kind of guns he's hiding under that uniform.

Guns? Really? With that lingo, I should be teaching high school. Unless "guns" isn't cool anymore. Is it?

Stop talking to yourself in your head.

I look at the screen and mumble a curse.

Your session has timed out.

Wonderful. Now I have to go back and restart the process.

"You do know how to input your information, right?" Nate says when I stare at the screen.

"No. Is that what this is for?" I lift the mouse, sarcasm dripping from my words.

"I was joking."

"Another terrible joke," I deadpan.

His sense of humor is not well-defined. He could tell me a clown is bouncing around in a tutu, and his face would remain impassive.

"So I've been told."

"I got sidetracked, so I got kicked out of my session. I'll be a few more minutes." I begin inputting my information.

He nods, walking behind me. He pauses, leaning into my ear.

"Don't forget your driver's license number." His breath tickles my skin, and his arm pops up from behind me and taps the spot on the screen I accidentally left in blank.

GUARDED DEPUTY

I jolt and turn to look at him. His eyes are on the screen, and I can't help but scan the side of his face at his perfect jaw peppered with scruff. A hint of mint hits my senses.

"Uh, huh." I shake my head and tug my license out of my wallet.

Having him this close is like having alcohol shot straight to my veins for instant drunkenness. What is it about this man that affects me? It's more than being hot.

When he steps back and walks around the counter, I audibly sigh and then widen my eyes. Darn. I did not want him aware of the effect he has on me. I've been able to maintain a distinct line between work and my personal life, but Nate is a walking temptation. Distance is the best option. He can stand far away on the other side of the room.

And you'd still sense him.

I ignore my conscience and focus on my task, finishing my payment.

"I'm done." I turn the screen over, and Nate takes a look at it from his side of the counter.

"Looks good." He submits my payment, and I sigh in relief. "I can't believe you have never gotten a ticket." His eyes widen as if I were some kind of alien.

"Not once in my life." I lift my chin proudly.

"Wow, so you're a goody two shoes?" The way he says this holds a hint of judgment that makes my nostrils flare.

"No." I scoff. "I'm a rule follower, a law-abiding citizen, a good Samaritan. I like to save money for other things, like coffee."

"Coffee?" He narrows his eyes, once again looking at me like a weirdo. I don't blame him.

45

I'm rambling like I have a few loose screws in my brain that refrain me from working properly. Those loose screws can all be labeled, Mr. Hot Deputy. He causes loss of brain function with his minty breath in the middle of the afternoon and stubbled face and piercing eyes that I can't tell should be attractive or intimidating. Maybe both.

"Coffee is my love language." I shrug. "Anyway, thanks for your help. I promise the computer at work wasn't showing me all that info." The last thing I want is for him to think I'm incompetent when I teach his nephew.

"It might be some type of firewall or block that the school has set up."

"You know, you may be onto something. If this gig doesn't work out, you can get a job with computers."

"This gig?" He stares at me with furrowed brows.

"I guess I also need to brush up on my joke-telling skills." I grin.

"That would be a good idea." He nods.

"Well, I gotta go. These tests aren't gonna grade themselves. See ya, Deputy Nate."

"Yup, I'll be working at the school for the rest of the school year to run a program to train children on safety, so I'll see you then."

"Whaa-?" My eyes bug out as I stare at him.

Does this mean I'll have more chances to make a fool of myself?

"Didn't they tell you?" He tilts his head.

"No." I cross my arms.

"I'll be working with your class. I double checked because of Walker."

GUARDED DEPUTY

"Right." I nod, heart stammering.

Just when I think I may not have as many interactions with him after this ticket fiasco, and *bam!* He'll be at school.

"Anyway, I gotta go for real this time." I wave at him over my shoulder as I walk out of the station.

Once I'm outside, I take a deep breath and close my eyes. Why in the hell did I act like a fool in front of him? It's like being in his presence makes me say stupid things that make no sense. Even when I repeat them in my head they sound dumb.

And now the odds of not seeing him for a while are slim with his new position. Not that it's possible to really avoid someone when you live in a small town.

I just pray that the next time I run into him I'm less mesmerized by his good looks and more attentive to the words coming out of my mouth.

I've never been one to get captivated by only the physical aspect of a person. I'm deeper than that. There's more to someone than the way they look, and I'll remind myself of that the next time he crosses my path again.

Good looks fade, but a kind heart is forever.

Heading home, I make sure to stay within the speed limit and turn up the music. There's nothing a little George Strait can't cure. All my exes don't live in Texas, but a certain hottie is from there.

I shouldn't be thinking about him at all. My priority should be my career, the new chapter I hope to open this fall when I go back to school, not some guy I know nothing about who strolled into town. My heart is closed for business. It's seen enough heartache that it's gone bankrupt.

chapter 6
NATE

"Uncle Nate, my teacher told me today that you're gonna be in my class." Walker hops on one foot in the living room, back to counting how many hops he can do without stopping.

"Not just your class, but a few others." I don't want him to think I'll be present all day every day.

From the meetings I've had and the training program, I'll visit each class once a week for an hour, two days in the high school and three in the elementary and middle school. The times I'm not in the classrooms, I'll be security and offering safety support to the staff.

"Yeah, whatever, but you'll go to mine." He shrugs and pauses, keeping his left foot lifted in the air. "Aw man, I lost count. Oh well, thirty..." He continues counting on from thirty when I'm pretty sure he was on twelve.

Brooke laughs at her son and aims her eyes at me.

"So you'll be working with Ms. Andrews." She's trying to hold back a smile, but I see the ghost of it tipping the corner of her lips upward.

"Yes." I nod.

"Interesting..." She nods slowly.

GUARDED DEPUTY

"It's not that interesting. She's a teacher at the school, and I now have some kind of mentoring role," I shrug like it's no big deal.

It shouldn't be a big deal. Ms. Andrews is kind of like a co-worker at this point. All the teachers will be, not just her. She isn't the only one my attention should be focused on. I can ignore the way her round green eyes stare at me expectantly or the way her bottom lip is puffier than her top one, making me wonder what it'd be like to bite it.

"But—"

"No buts," I cut my sister off. "Ms. Andrews isn't the kind of woman for me."

"What does that mean?" Brooke's eyebrows pull tight.

"She seems like a nice woman. Innocent, a bit naive. I'm rough around the edges and don't have the best track record."

"That's because you don't give yourself a chance to open up." She shakes her head. "You're a great guy."

She's always telling me the same thing, but I don't listen. There's no way to know that I won't be just like my father, leaving the woman I promised to commit to. Or worse, open up to someone just for them to leave me. I've always heard history repeats itself, and I'm not up for that part of my family history to do so.

"I'm gonna go work out." I stand from the couch.

"Now? I was going to make dinner."

"I'll eat after." I ruffle my sister's hair and laugh as her complaints trail behind me.

Changing into a pair of shorts and a T-shirt, I head out of the house and start to jog down the street. Each breath melts away the memory of my father and of Ms. Andrews's awkwardness

FABIOLA FRANCISCO

and cute smile. The way she teases Sheriff McCall gives me a sense of family I haven't felt in a long time.

I love my sister and nephew, but ever since my mom died, I've felt like that family camaraderie has been missing.

It's actually been missing much longer than that. I think the last time I felt a glimpse of that feeling was when I was ten and my dad still lived with us. When he abandoned us, so did the joy that filled our home.

Shake it off, Nate. He doesn't deserve your attention.

I breathe evenly, inhaling the lingering scent of saltwater and hear seagulls wailing in the distance. I make a right, running down a street that will lead me to the beach. I've become addicted to running along the boardwalk so I can take in the ocean as I do so.

As soon as I hear the waves crashing, I exhale deeply and release the memories that haunt and soothe me like the world's greatest contradiction. It belongs in the Guinness World Record book for contradictions.

Ms. Andrews probably has the best family, like so many other people in this town seem to. I understand why Brooke moved here. Besides starting a new chapter in her life, Walker's grandparents live near here.

When David passed away, she needed the support more than ever. Being Walker's only living grandparents, it was the logical choice. I also suspect that she feels guilty and wants them to have a piece of David closer to home.

My feet pound the ground as I clear my mind. Too many memories of the dead are filling my thoughts.

I wanted to stop thinking about Ms. Andrews, but that doesn't mean I want to focus on the people who are no longer with us. Ms. Andrews is a much better topic to pour my attention into, even if it's dangerous territory.

When I spot the park in town a block away from the beach, I slow my pace and walk toward the pull-up bars. Gripping the handle, I start to pull my body up and silently count backward from ten.

As I'm reaching one, I hear a voice behind me. Turning, I see the woman who's conquered my thoughts talking into her phone. She's wearing leggings that accentuate the curves in her hips and a T-shirt that falls off the shoulder.

"Can you believe that *he* is who will be working at the school *in my classroom*? This is karma, or dharma. Which of the two is supposed to be the punishment? Whatever, Mr. Hot Deputy is going to run this program, and I don't stop acting like an idiot. How do I channel cool, calm, and collected?" Her words run together as she rambles, and I can't help but choke at the nickname.

Her head snaps up, and her eyes bug out when she sees me standing a few feet away.

"Either a mirage of him is in front of me or the man just heard me talking about him. Where's that magic wand to make me disappear?" she says into her phone before pocketing it.

"Uhh..." Her cheeks are covered in a flush.

"Ms. Andrews." I arch an eyebrow. This woman is a walking Murphy's Law.

"Lizzy. At this point, formalities are null and void." She shakes her head, shifting on her feet. "Anyway, nice, uh, workout."

"Mr. Hot Deputy?" I can't help but tease her.

"What? I didn't say that. I said...Mr. Howdy Putty."

"Nice try." I laugh, unable to hold it back.

"Pretend you didn't hear that?" She gives me her best smile.

Shaking my head, I inch toward her, ignoring the inner voice in my brain yelling, *ABORT.* "I appreciate the compliment, *Ms. Andrews.*" I emphasize her name just to make her shift on her feet.

I should step back, move along and forget I heard her, but something about this woman draws me in. She's like a lighthouse, shimmering her light every so often so I know I'm not too far from the shore.

"Lizzy." She's quick to correct me.

Her eyes bounce between mine and then to my arms before returning to my face.

"We're gonna work together, and I don't need any more awkwardness sitting between us. I'm already oh-for-three with you between the call, my traffic ticket, and this. How about we start over and pretend that I'm a different person?"

"Not gonna work." I tilt my head. "I kinda like this person."

What are you doing, man? Stop flirting.

"Really?" Her nose scrunches up.

That makes me pause. Why would she doubt that? She's a beautiful woman, and she seems like a good person. Laundry spewed around her bedroom aside, but that doesn't make you better or worse.

"Don't question that."

"It's a flaw. I can't help it." She shrugs. "Anyway, I was talking about Howard Putty, soooo we're good."

I toss my head back and laugh, then shake my head. "Nice try."

"It was worth a shot. I didn't mean it in a demeaning way." Her lips purse, and she avoids my eyes.

"No worries. I'm gonna get back to my work out." I finally snap out of the flirting trance. Flirting with women isn't something new for me, but it usually has an end goal attached—slipping into bed together. Lizzy isn't the type of woman to fit that bill.

"Right. That's a good idea, great. Not that you need it. Um...never mind. I'm gonna go disappear in those bushes now." She points to the row of bushes beside us.

I chuckle and let her off the hook. She seems embarrassed enough without me ragging on her any more than I already have. Besides, we need to work together, and I don't want anything blurring those lines.

I step out of my car and walk toward dismissal to pick up Walker. I know I can't avoid Lizzy since she's his teacher, and after last night's encounter, I don't know if I want to. She's funny and quirky.

I normally don't think twice about quirky women because they could be annoying. Or maybe that's just been my experience. I can't box all people together for having a common trait.

You're the problem, not them.

Right. Got it, brain. Thanks for the vote of confidence.

Sighing, I run a hand down my face and look for Walker. I'd rather be surrounded by children than be stuck with my own thoughts—even though twenty seven-year-olds isn't my idea of fun.

"Uncle Nate!" Walker waves at me before grabbing his backpack that's thrown haphazardly on the floor.

I look to the left and see Ms. Andrews turning her head toward me. She's talking to another teacher, and a part of me fills with pride that she stops her conversation to look at me. I smirk and nod as a way of greeting.

Her smile is forced when she aims it in my direction, but it transforms to pure adoration when she looks at Walker and listens to what he's telling her. That smile punches me in the gut. The way she looks at him makes me feel an unfamiliar sensation.

Walker may be my nephew, but I love him like my own child. He's probably the only one I'll ever have. Seeing her care about him begins to claw away at the debris I've piled up around my heart. It's a dangerous thing.

"Ms. Andrews," I say when I reach them. "I trust you didn't fight any bushes last night."

Her eyes widen like saucers. "Erm...uh. Bushes?" She squeaks. "Nope. No bushes. No idea what you're talking about."

Her friend laughs and bumps her shoulder. "Chill out, Liz."

"Or was it Howard Putty?" I tilt my head.

Lizzy coughs as her face brightens with a blush. I chuckle and smile at Walker. "Ready to go, buddy?"

"I thought Mom was coming today." His eyebrows furrow.

"She has to work late so it's you and me." Brooke works at the doctor clinic as the office manager, and they had an issue to resolve.

"I need help with homework. Right, Ms. Andrews?" He looks over at her. "She said I need to practice my subtraction."

GUARDED DEPUTY

"Is that right?" I look at the woman before me with raised eyebrows.

"He'd benefit from some extra help." She nods, crossing her arms over her chest.

"In real-life, people use calculators."

"Mr. Moore, we teach children the proper skills to defend themselves. When they're older, they can use one but it's necessary to know how to solve a problem. Imagine that calculators evaporate." She arches an eyebrow, looking really fucking cute fired up like this.

Noted, make Ms. Andrews mad but not too mad or she'll bury my body in her backyard.

"Evaporate? Can you elaborate on that?" I fight my smirk.

"You never know when dinosaurs will return and eat all of technology."

Her friend snorts beside her, and Lizzy glares in her direction.

"I hadn't realized *Jurassic Park* was an alternate reality waiting to merge with ours."

"You never know." She shakes her head, not letting up.

"Dinosaurs are dead. They can't come back, Ms. Andrews," a little girl tells her.

"I know, Dana. It was a joke." Lizzy sighs, looking back at me.

"I guess you thought I needed some company on the bad sense of humor side." I grin and wink.

"That's it. Solidarity, man." She holds up her clenched fist in the universal symbol of solidarity, and I laugh.

"We'll see you tomorrow." I grab Walker's hand and head toward my vehicle.

"Solidarity, man?" The other teacher questions, and I hear Lizzy quietly cursing.

"I keep making a fool of myself," she says.

Lucky for her, I've got a craving for *fool* and can't seem to get enough of it. Lizzy may be embarrassed, but her awkwardness and untimely events are charming. She could ignore me the next time she sees me, but it's not how she rolls. She faces me, humiliated and all, and it makes her that much more interesting.

Not that I can or will act on it. My focus is on Brooke and Walker. Besides, things will become messy, and I can't let my attraction to her get in the way of Walker's education and stability or my own job.

Not only will I be working at the school now, she's related to the sheriff. I don't need to have any issues with my boss.

chapter 7
LIZZY

HAVE I SPENT ALL day mentally preparing for Nate to come into my class? Yes. Because after the whole Howard Putty incident in the park, I'm certain that I'm destined to make a fool out of myself in front of this man for eternity.

The door opens, and Walker yells, "Uncle Nate! Told you guys." He looks at his friends with the proudest grin. He's been telling his friends all day that Nate would be in our class today.

"Walker," I warn softly with a smile.

He sits tall in his chair, waving at Nate, who nods and winks at him. Goodness gracious.

Be still my heart.

When his eyes meet mine, his smile drops. Taken aback, my head jerks as my eyebrows dip.

"Ms. Andrews," he says coolly.

"Deputy Moore." I narrow my eyes.

Is it just me, or is his lack of enthusiasm offensive? It's a contrast to our recent encounters. He should be happy to enter my classroom. I'm a joy to work with. I've got teachers lining up wanting to be my work wife. I make cookies and bring them to school, help plan their classes, and decorate for each season.

I'm a peach.

58

GUARDED DEPUTY

I'm better than a peach. I'm the entire orchard.

Sitting at my desk, I grab a red pen and the stack of tests I've procrastinated grading. I hold back my laughter as I glance out of the corner of my eye and watch him squat down and sit. He looks like a giant in a regular person's world.

When my eyes scan the length of him, pausing on the way his trousers stretch over his thighs, the bubbling laughter catches and turns into a fiery flame inside of me. The man knows how to fill in a deputy uniform in a way that should only be legal in romance novels.

The fabric does nothing to hide the hard and defined muscles. After seeing him at the park, I have true confirmation that Nate Moore works hard for his muscles.

The children giggle when Nate shifts in the chair. To be fair, I fit just fine on it, but then again, I'm five-foot-two where he must be about six feet. I didn't imagine he'd look this big on it.

"Hello all, I'm Deputy Moore."

"My uncle!" Walker calls out.

"Walker," Nate warns. "Manners, buddy." He looks at the class and continues. "I'll be coming to your class on Wednesdays to teach you all about safety rules."

His eyes move to mine, and he silently lifts his eyebrows. If he's trying to communicate telepathically, I'm not catching what he's saying. He clears his throat and focuses back on the students, bringing out a picture book titled: *Safety Steve Fights Danger David*.

I bite down my smile and keep my eyes on the tests while my ears are completely focused on the story Nate reads to the kids. I hadn't realized how sexy it was to watch a man read a book to a bunch of children, but the way he deepens his voice and makes it rise in certain parts as if he were the character is enough to make me want to get down on my knees and propose.

Kidding. Not happening. It's a metaphor.

Don't forget your single-not-ready-to-mingle status, Lizzy.

Regardless, I risk peeking up to get a glimpse of the man when one of my students blurts out a comment about the story. He's smiling at the kids with a boyish grin that would be found in the dictionary next to the word Heartbreaker.

After he finishes the story, Nate looks at the class and begins discussing the story with them.

"What do you think Safety Steve did that helped keep Danger David away?"

Walker's hand shoots up, and Nate calls on him.

"He didn't talk to David and ran to his friends."

"That's right, and what else did he do after that?" Nate prompts.

"He told his mom," Walker adds.

I smile as I listen, enjoying seeing my class get involved in the story. Teaching children about safety is so important, and I think it's great that the county is taking steps to improve that aspect of education.

"Exactly. It's super important to tell your parents everything. If someone talks to you, make sure they know. What other things did Steve do?"

"He didn't take the drink David gave him," Stephanie calls out.

"Exactly. We never take food, drinks, or toys from a stranger. The best thing to do is walk away and find an adult you do know to keep you safe."

GUARDED DEPUTY

"Yeah, and if a stranger asks you to help them do something, say no and yell Stranger Danger," Parker says.

"That's right." Nate smiles at the children. "Sometimes people aren't very nice, so we need to know how to act so we're safe. A person might tell you that they know your mom or dad, might even guess their real name so that you trust them. If you've never seen the person before and your parents haven't told you someone is picking you up, don't go with them," he says softly.

The conversation turns more serious, and I'm impressed with the way Nate keeps the language simple and easy for the kids to understand.

"What if our mom and dad didn't tell us, but we know the person?" Danny asks.

"Then, you should make sure with your teacher and have her call your parents to ask them. Although we know the person, that doesn't always mean we're supposed to go with them. It can scare your parents if they come pick you up, and you already left without them knowing."

"Okay." Danny nods.

"Yeah, when Uncle Nate came to pick me up the first time, Ms. Andrews asked for his information even if I live with him," Walker explains.

I smile at him. Sometimes we don't realize how much kids are actually paying attention.

"That's right, Walker." Nate glances at me. "Ms. Andrews was making sure I was safe for you to go home with."

The hour passes quickly between trying to focus on my work and reminding myself that the man in the center of the room is not someone I should crush on. I gratefully don't make a fool of myself.

61

Thank you, humiliation gods for giving me a break.

"All right, kids, I'll see you next week." Nate stands.

"Thank you, Deputy Moore." I stand from my seat and walk around my desk. "What do you say, boys and girls?"

"Thank you," the class sings out.

"You're welcome." He looks at me and nods before grabbing his book and heading out. He pauses with his hand on the knob and looks at me. "Ms. Andrews, next time you're welcome to take a break."

"Right. Well, it was your first day, and you're a stranger to most of the students," I say and instantly regret it. "I don't mean it in a bad way. They just don't know you." I try to fix my mistake.

"Understood." He walks out of the class, and I lean against my desk, exhaling loudly.

"Ms. Andrews, why's your face red like Danny's when he runs for a long time?" one of my students asks.

My hand presses to my cheek, and I look away from my students to take a deep breath and will my blush to disappear.

"I think she's blushing. That's what my mom tells my big sister when she talks about her crush," Stephanie says.

Kids nowadays know too much about crushes at a young age.

"Why would your big sister crush anyone?" A boy asks, and I giggle. That was the break I needed to gain my thoughts and refocus.

"Okay, class, let's get ready for science."

GUARDED DEPUTY

"If his nephew was in my class, I'd request a meeting every week just to get some one-on-one time with him." The fourth grade teacher sighs as I walk by, no doubt talking about Nate.

"Wouldn't that be with his mom?" Andrea asks, rolling her eyes when she sees me.

I bite back my laugh and try to ignore the comments I've been hearing all day. It's getting old when teachers who barely talk to you are suddenly telling you how lucky you are to teach that "piece of arm candy's nephew." Their words not mine. I'm ashamed enough about calling him Mr. Hot Deputy.

Ready to head home, I grab my things and walk toward my car, rummaging through my purse for my car keys. I wish I had a car with the keyless lock so I wouldn't have to go on a deep search every time I need my keys. It's that or clean out my purse. A keyless car sounds easier.

"Watch it." Hands hold my biceps, and I step back, snapping my head up.

"Uh, sorry." I press my lips together.

"No worries." Nate releases my arms and steps back, crossing his arms. "Figured I'd stop you before you crashed into me."

"Yeah, definitely. No need to smack myself on the wall that is your body."

Oh, my God. Shut. Up.

"Wall?" He tilts his head and smirks just enough that one side of his lips rises.

"I mean... Oh hell, you know you're fit. Your muscles"—I wave a hand in front of him—"are hard. I give up on trying to fix my outbursts."

Nate laughs, tossing his head back, and I'm caught by surprise at his reaction. Based on his stoic mood when he was in my class, I'd expect something different than this.

"Uncle Nate, I'm hungry." I see Walker's head sticking out the window of his car and laugh.

"Duty calls." I step away from him, still no key found.

"Right. Have a good evening, Ms. Andrews."

"Lizzy." I correct him with a small smile.

"Lizzy." He repeats my name as if testing the way it feels coming from his mouth. A very nice mouth with full lips and slightly crooked teeth that make him imperfect and yet so perfect.

So much for not crushing on him.

At this point, I think that's hopeless.

I stop by my car, placing my bag on the hood, and start moving things around in my purse until I finally find my keys in the bottom corner.

"About time," I mumble to myself.

Getting in my car, I drive off, not wanting to go home. For once, all my papers are graded and my classes are prepped.

I make a right, driving toward the boardwalk. The weather is nice and having a coffee with the sound of waves crashing from the beach nearby is exactly what I need. Finding a spot not too far from Bay Brew, I park and step out of my car.

As I walk to the coffee shop, the ocean breeze feels like home. As long as I can remember, my senses have been invaded with the salty smell of the ocean and the gentle breeze cooling my skin.

Living in a beach town has major perks, and I can't imagine living somewhere that's landlocked. I need the ocean the way a lumberjack needs a forest full of trees.

GUARDED DEPUTY

I order a Frappuccino to go and wander the boardwalk, saying hi to people I pass. The great thing about small towns is that everyone feels like family. The bad thing is that everyone knows your business. Although, I wouldn't trade my community for the world. When something happens to someone, we all come together in support, like when a hurricane took out a lot of the beach houses and we all gave our friends a place to sleep while they rebuilt. You never feel alone in Emerald Bay.

Spotting an empty bench near the shore, I sit down and stare at the crashing waves. If I had a towel or blanket with me, I'd sit on the sand and dig my toes into it.

People pass by as they laugh, some carrying shopping bags. When I see a young couple holding hands and the guy spinning the girl around, a pang of envy hits me square in the chest. I shake it off, slurping on my straw as I try to grab as much of the whipped cream in my frap.

"Ms. Andrews." A student I had last year waves at me with a bright smile.

"Hi." I smile at her as she walks by with her parents.

Having Ava in my class was the push I needed to consider going back to school for my school counseling degree when I had given up on the idea. When I taught her, she was going through a rough time at home, and she confided in me throughout the year. The spark to help kids in a different environment grew stronger than ever before, reminding me why this was my life-long dream.

Running into her cements the idea that I've made the right choice in prioritizing my career, even if it means putting my love life on hold for a bit especially with the terrible dates I've been on in recent months. Helping children overcome any struggles or challenges beyond the academic field is what's important right now.

The sound of the waves and the laughing sounds the seagulls make lull me back into a daze.

"Hi." An unfamiliar voice interrupts my daydreaming.

I really should've chosen a less busy area to disconnect at.

"Oh, hi." My eyes widen when I see Walker's mom standing in front of me.

"How are you?" She smiles, but I'm still not over the text message fiasco from a few weeks ago.

Is it ever okay to face a parent after venting why you hate men?

"I'm good, and you?" I place my cup on the seat beside me, unsure if I should stand to talk to her or remain seated but too many seconds have ticked by that if I get up now it'll be awkward.

"I'm good, doing some shopping." She lifts the bag in her hand.

"That's nice." I nod, feeling so weirded out by this encounter.

It's probably all in my head. I'm a pro at making situations much worse in my mind than they are in real life and that in turn makes it weird because I react how I think it is in my head. It's twisted.

"How's Walker doing? He talks about his class all the time, telling us about the fun activities you've done. Thank you for making his transition so easy for all of us."

"It's my pleasure. He's adapted so well that it seems he's been with us since the beginning of the school year. He was so excited Nate was in class today. I mean, Deputy Moore." I bite my

GUARDED DEPUTY

tongue and grimace at the pain, but it's better than the awkward smile Mrs. Lundsten is giving me.

"He was really excited to show off his uncle to his friends." She laughs.

"He did." I nod and smile at the memory of Walker's beaming smile when Nate walked into the class. "He was a proud nephew."

"That's great, and I'm glad he's doing well. I'm sure having Nate there will be good for him, although at times I wonder if those two teaming up is for anyone's best interest." She laughs as if I have insider information on her son's relationship with his uncle.

"I'm sure," I tell her because I really don't know what else to say.

"I'm going to go. Thanks for the unofficial update on my son's progress."

"No problem." I watch her walk away and sigh deeply.

I'm much better at interacting with kids than adults.

chapter 8
LIZZY

My EYES STARE AT my phone screen as I take a blind bite of pasta, engrossed in the story I'm reading. For some reason, no one's in the lunchroom today, which means I get to read in silence for thirty minutes. It's a rare occurrence that I'm taking full advantage of.

When the door swings open, I groan and look at the intruder with my fork-full of food in my mouth. My eyes widen when I see Nate standing there holding a brown paper bag. Something about the view makes my heart clench and race at the same time like muscles tightening during a sprint.

"Hey." He nods and walks around the table, sitting across from me.

Can't he sit like on the side so I don't have to stare at his gorgeous face? I mean, it's pure torture.

"Hi," I say when I've swallowed my food, thankful I remembered my manners.

Nate takes out a sandwich and bag of chips, placing them on his flattened paper bag, creating a makeshift placemat. I keep my attention on my phone, but the words on the screen are a blur. I'm attuned to the man across from me silently eating his lunch.

GUARDED DEPUTY

I should make conversation, but my voice is gone. I'm suddenly the Little Mermaid and he's Ursula, who stole my voice. If Ursula were a man and wicked handsome.

When I glance up, I notice he's looking at me. Shifting in my seat to sit straighter so I'm not slouched over like a slob, I smile tightly.

"How's your first week going?" I finally ask.

"It's good." He shrugs.

"Ah, a man of few words," I joke.

"Something like that."

"Right." I awkwardly draw out, trying to figure out why sometimes he's more talkative than others. Is it because we're at work? Whatever the reason, this hot and cold mood is confusing.

I go back to my book, focusing on my current book boyfriend, who can do no wrong even when he's flawed, and ignore the man before me. I don't have time to waste when it comes to reading romance novels, and the clock is ticking away toward the end of my lunch break. Time is of the essence.

"Are the kids always talkative?" Nate interrupts me mid-paragraph, and I clench my teeth before looking up at him.

"Yes. Until they get used to you, but right now you're a free pass from learning in their eyes."

"I swear those fifth graders wouldn't shut up," he says.

"Ah, yeah, that group of kids is definitely special. They've always been that way. Just be firm with them and show them that what you have to say is important. They're at that age where they think they know it all when in reality they don't know shi—crap."

Nate chuckles at my almost-curse and nods. "I can see that. Thanks for the advice."

"No prob." I finish my lunch and rinse my container before placing it in my lunchbox. Since I have a few more minutes, I get back to the story, but the rustling of paper distracts me.

"Walker's okay?" he asks when he sees I'm looking at him.

"Yeah," I say slowly, as if it's a ridiculous question.

"Good, good. He loves school." Nate balls up the aluminum foil that held his sandwich.

"I'm glad he does. He's a great kid." I smile.

Walker has done such an amazing job of incorporating himself in the classroom. It's not always easy being the new kid when most of these children have known each other since preschool, but he fits in.

"He is." Nate grins with pride, showing off his dimples, and it jostles something inside of me begging for attention. This mostly serious man has a smile that could light up an entire universe. The fact that his smile is so wide due to his nephew is a punch to my gut.

Down, heart, no need to overreact.

I think it's safe to admit that I like Nate, however, confessing that to myself means I will now be even more awkward around him because I don't know how to act around guys I like. I revert to a thirteen-year-old that waves at the guy she likes when in reality he's looking at someone behind her so he doesn't even acknowledge her greeting.

I've always been that girl, and the guys I do settle for aren't exactly the best catches. I'm tired of reeling in rotten fish.

"Anyway, I gotta go." I stand, grabbing my lunch bag.

GUARDED DEPUTY

As I walk out, Ellen, the fifth grade teacher I can't stand, enters.

"Oh, Deputy Moore, I'm so glad I caught you..." she says in an almost sultry voice that makes my eyes roll.

Most of us have dated the guys in town, are related to them, or are just friends. Small town living equals small dating pool, which means putting a man like Nate in a place primarily filled with women is like the *Hunger Games*. All of the teachers will volunteer as tribute to show him around and help him adapt. The poor man doesn't stand a chance against these single ladies, who are more like vultures.

Except for me because I've had enough encounters with the man, and I'd probably lock us in a closet—*by accident*—and then have everyone talking about how I wanted to shag him at work.

No thanks.

Ellen can have him.

My jaw clenches at the thought. I don't actually want Ellen to have any piece of him whatsoever. I'm not usually territorial, especially about a man that is nothing to me, but the idea of her winning him over makes my stomach turn with acid. It has nothing to do with him and everything to do with Ellen's idea that she's better than everyone. He could find someone more down-to-earth. If he wanted to date someone else like Andrea, I'd be happy for them.

Liar, liar.

"Ugh!" I toss my head back.

"Are you okay, Ms. Andrews?" an older student asks.

"Oh, yeah, I'm fine." I wave him off with a smile and continue toward the cafeteria to pick up my class.

71

FABIOLA FRANCISCO

Teaching math to twenty sleepy first graders will be better than thinking about an imaginary situation where someone I can't stand ends up dating the man I can't stop thinking about.

Honestly, Lizzy, get a grip.

I scrub a hand down my face and call for my class to line up. They're loud today, probably due to the weekend approaching, and I'm not sure I have the energy to deal with them. Some days I wish teaching including playing a movie and sitting at my desk.

As we start math class, Walker raises his hand to do one of the problems on the board. I smile as he works through it with ease, praising him for his hard work.

"Great job. I can see you've been practicing," I tell him as he takes a seat.

"Yeah, I've done lots of problems at home."

"And no calculator." I smirk at the comment his uncle said.

"No way, Ms. A. I told Uncle Nate I gotta learn it by myself."

"Ms. A?" I chuckle at his nickname.

"Yeah, that's what my uncle calls you at home."

My laughter catches, turning into a choke that has me sputtering. Nate calls me Ms. A at home with his nephew? I smile at the idea that he has a nickname for me.

The vision of him sitting beside Walker, helping with his homework makes that flutter in my belly grow wilder. I've read single dad romance books and those are always swoon worthy, but a hot uncle seems to be my cup of coffee—tall, dark, and steaming.

"Ms. Andrews?" one of my students says.

"Huh? Yes?" I shake my head and look at her.

GUARDED DEPUTY

"Can I do number three?" Her bright eyes shine with excitement.

Stephanie loves math the way I love coffee. The girl could volunteer to do all the problems and she'd be happy. Just don't ask her to play kickball during recess.

"Of course." I hand her the marker and focus my attention back on the class.

I can't wait for the day to be over so I can go home to take a long bath.

***

"Roy told me that one of his deputies is working at the school." My mom's eyebrows lift as she looks at me.

My long bath got axed when my mom called me to have dinner at her house. My stepdad is traveling for work, and supposedly she made more food than necessary. I know that it was her plan all along to get me to go over, using an abundance of food as an excuse.

"Yes." I nod slowly and exaggeratedly.

"I'm glad you'll have someone on campus to keep you safe."

I sigh, shaking my head. I love my mom, but she's definitely one to worry about every little thing. I can understand where part of her concern comes from, but at some point she needs to let go and enjoy life a little more.

My dad passed away when I was a little girl. I don't remember much about him except for the pictures my mom has saved. I wish I did, but the mind of a five-year-old is limited in the memories she keeps.

My mom, on the other hand, has memories imprinted in her soul. I sometimes wonder how she got remarried, but Gary is great for her. He's patient and kind and understands her, and I'm grateful she has someone like him in her life.

"I know you worry about me, Mom, but my workplace is safe. This entire town is safe." I smile softly, reaching for her hand. "Life happens and it sucks sometimes, but we need to celebrate what we're given."

She sniffs, looking away and reaching for the bottle of wine. "Want some more?" She holds it up.

"Sure."

She fills my glass.

"What are you doing this weekend?" She smiles at me over the lip of her glass.

"I'm going to the country music festival at the beach with Dani. As much as I love concerts, I'd rather sleep in and lay low this weekend." Dani's family owns the local country music radio station, and they work with a ton of artists to put together concerts and festivals. The entire town has been buzzing about this one with Mason Hall and Sutton Wright.

"You say you'll sleep till late, but you'll get up early anyway. You've always been that way."

"Eh, one day I'll surprise you," I joke.

"I birthed you, I know you too well," she teases.

"Oh, whatever." I roll my eyes and take a bite of lasagna.

She's right, though, she does know me well. Sometimes I hate it because it doesn't give me time to process when I'm feeling upset since she picks up on my mood.

If I'm not careful, she'll pick up on my crush on Nate and tell the whole town her daughter and the new deputy are getting married. She exaggerates things like that, and I'm usually the victim of her elaborate misunderstandings.

"That new deputy is quite handsome." Her eyes gleam as if she was reading my mind. I look around the dining room in case there's a tap to my brain that feeds information to my mom.

"What?" My eyes widen.

"Don't tell me you haven't noticed. I was at the market the other day talking to Shelly, and we saw him walk in wearing his uniform. Oh, boy, what a hunk." My mom fans herself, and I don't know if to laugh or be horrified by this conversation.

"Ew, mom, he's like thirty years younger than you and you're married to Gary!"

"Not for me, for you! You need a man like that who can protect you."

"Here we go..." I mumble.

"It's true."

"You overdo it in your mind, Mom."

"Look at what happened to your father." She frowns.

"Mom, what happened to Dad was an unfortunate accident. He was at the wrong place at the wrong time. No one expected that criminal to be loose and with a weapon." I shake my head, hoping she finally gets it.

My dad's death is a terrible case of the justice system gone wrong when a criminal was given time off for good behavior and then committed murder.

Taking a deep breath, I scoot my chair back and clear the plates.

"I brought brownies from Sprinkles of Joy. I'll go grab them."

I head into the kitchen, breathing evenly as I rinse the plates and place them in the dishwasher. I may not remember my dad, but his death is something that has haunted me my whole life.

Shaking those thoughts away, I grab the box of brownies and smile as I return to the dining room with the delicious dark and gooey chocolate treat. Avery makes the best desserts.

"Brownies and wine?" I smirk as I hold up the box.

"My favorite combination," she says, and I see a glimpse of the sadness lift. "I still think dating that new deputy would be good." She winks.

"Mom, I just broke up with Sean a few months ago. I am taking a break from relationships."

"Sean was never good enough for you." She scoffs. "But a man like that deputy would be."

Just when I thought I'd stop thinking about Nathan Moore so I can do my job without making it more complicated than it already is, my mom pokes the sleepy bear of attraction trying to hibernate.

chapter 9
NATE

"I MAY BE WORKING with kids now, but I sure don't miss the calls about neighbors bickering and complaining about one another over stupid things," I tell Luke, my co-worker, as we walk toward the boardwalk.

He was telling me about a call he got yesterday from the two infamous feuding neighbors.

According to Luke, they're well-known rivals, and one of them is always hooking up her hose to the other's water supply.

When Margie's water turned ice cold while she was in the shower, she called the station to put in a formal complaint.

While he questioned her neighbor, she smiled innocently and offered fresh-squeezed orange juice. It's drama all around for those two. From what Luke said, the pettiness stems from when they were younger and Margie dated her neighbor's crush in high school.

I couldn't make this shit up if I tried. Who moves in next door to the person they can't stand and then goes on to taunt them for years?

He laughs, clapping my back. "It's small town America."

We walk down the boardwalk, and I take in a deep breath of the salt and sea air that creates a unique mix. Living in Dallas

GUARDED DEPUTY

didn't offer the opportunity to visit the beach often. Emerald Bay is right on the water, and the change in atmosphere is nice. There are worse places to live.

People are usually around enjoying the water or the shops and outdoor areas. The town always feels like it's full of pumping energy. If I had all the time in the world, I'd also sit on that white sand and let the waves steal my worries.

I sound like a Kenny Chesney song.

"Ready for some live music?" he asks with a wide smile.

I look out at the beach area and take in the view in front of me. Hundreds of people crowd the space in front of a stage. When he asked if I wanted to come to the beach concert, I hesitated for a beat before Brooke practically pushed me out of the house.

She should be here enjoying this, but she promised she wanted ed a day to relax at home and do nothing.

We show our tickets at the entrance—courtesy of the station—and join the rest of the people ready for a show. The energy buzzes with anticipation as everyone waits for the first band to come on stage. It's a new artist making a name for himself, but that doesn't diminish the excitement. From what I hear, he's local to the area, so a huge crowd is out here supporting him.

"There's Erik." Luke points ahead of us to another co-worker. We move through the crowd to meet up with him and a few others, making my steps falter when I realize who's with him.

Lizzy's eyes widen as she notices me before snapping her gaze away. Of course my co-workers would know her. They're all about the same age, so they probably went to school together.

"Ladies," Luke says to Lizzy and the other women she's with. One of them is another teacher at the school, but the third woman is unfamiliar. "You know Nate, right?"

79

"Yeah," Lizzy and the teacher say.

"I haven't had the pleasure of meeting you yet," the stranger says with a knowing smile as she glances at Lizzy.

"D," Lizzy warns quietly, but her friend keeps going.

"I'm Dani, Lizzy's best friend."

"Nice to meet you." I nod.

"Be nice, D," Luke tells her, wrapping his arm around her shoulder.

"I'm always nice," she complains, pushing him off. "Shouldn't this shindig be starting already? I'm ready for some music and a beer."

"Shouldn't you know since you work at the station?" Luke raises his brows.

"I'm off the clock today." She grins.

"I can help with the beer," Erik tells her with a wink.

"Stop flirting and get me a beer." She laughs, handing him some cash.

"Coming right up." He bows.

Watching them, it's clear they're a tight group of friends who have known each other for years. I never had a group of friends like this. When I was in high school, I didn't hang out with the best company. I have a couple friends back in Dallas, but nothing that would make me miss spending nights out with them.

"How many beers?" Erik looks at us, but I shake my head while Luke and the other teacher raise their hands. "Lizzy?" He lifts his eyebrows in question.

"Not for me. I think I need coffee first." Lizzy suppresses a yawn, and I chuckle.

GUARDED DEPUTY

"I could actually go for some coffee." I had a rough night of sleep since I kept hearing Brooke in the living room watching TV instead of going to bed. I wanted to make sure I was awake in case she needed someone to talk to. Ever since David passed away, she's struggled with sleep.

"Really?" Lizzy scrunches up her face.

"Coffee at a concert? These events were made for day drinking," Erik says, and Lizzy shrugs.

"I'll let this pass for now." Dani points at her. "Beer makes you frisky and the day is too young to handle that."

Lizzy's eyes widen and she hisses Dani's name, but she's already walking away with Erik.

"It doesn't make me frisky!" she argues.

Luke laughs beside me, and I stare at Lizzy, the idea of her being frisky shouldn't seep into my brain. Her cheeks are pink as she looks away.

"That's why you got drunk and tried to kiss my cousin when he was visiting." Luke cackles, but my eyebrows furrow. I didn't take her for the kind of girl to corner guys and kiss them. It doesn't matter if she is, but something in me stirs uncomfortably.

"Luke! I was seventeen and hadn't been kissed. I wasn't about to have my first—or any—kiss with you guys." She throws her hands up in the air, face flaming as they laugh. "I'm gonna go grab a frap." She walks away while mumbling, "And crawl into a hole to hide."

Seventeen... So she was a late bloomer when it comes to kissing. I smile at that because for some reason it doesn't surprise me after the interactions we've had. There's an innocent sweetness to Lizzy that is so different from the life I had growing up.

81

"I'm joking, Lizzy," Luke calls out.

"I'll be back," I say, following her in the direction of the coffee shop. I have a feeling this is going to be a long day, and I need caffeine before I sit on a bench and fall asleep like an old man.

"Coffee is your love language, right?" I stand in line beside Lizzy.

She jumps and looks at me with her hand on her chest. "You scared the crap out of me. Coffee is a must. I woke up way too early, and if I start day drinking, I won't be awake to watch the closing song."

"I get that." I nod, stepping along with her as the line moves.

Silence stretches between us while I try to think of what to talk to her about without using Walker as a conversation crutch.

"Walker told me you helped him practice his subtraction," Lizzy says, using my nephew as her own crutch. I smile at the idea and nod.

"I figured he's too smart to rely on a calculator. You know, in case the dinosaurs return," I tease her.

"I say the stupidest stuff." She shakes her head and looks straight ahead.

"Creative stuff," I correct her.

"Right. Creative, silly, ridiculous. Take your pick on the adjectives, but I'm queen of making a fool of myself." She rolls her eyes.

"We don't need to take ourselves too seriously."

"Says the man with a terrible sense of humor and short responses." She arches an eyebrow, staring at me shamelessly now.

"Sense of humor is relative." I shrug.

"That's true. Some people think comedians are hilarious, but a lot of them just make me cringe. Now, there's this video on

GUARDED DEPUTY

social media about a goat always stealing the phone from its owner, and that cracks me up." She giggles, and the sound of it hits like a sip of whiskey after a long day of work. It's warming and soothing.

"A goat?" I lift my eyebrows.

"Yeah, he thinks he's super sly, but we're all watching him attempt to steal it. It's comedy gold, though, because it just shows the personality. Who knew goats were so mischievous?"

"Not me," I say.

"What can I get you?" The barista interrupts our conversation.

"I'll have a caramel frap," Lizzy orders.

"Make that two, please." I reach for my wallet.

"Oh, no, you don't have to." She shakes her head, arguing, but I ignore her.

The barista smiles between us, unsure of who to listen to.

"I've got it."

"Nate." She warns when I hand the barista my card. "Honestly, I can pay for my own."

"I'm sure you can, Liz." I drop some change in the tip jar and smirk.

"You're stubborn. Now people in town are going to say we're on a date." She shakes her head, taking a deep breath.

"There are worse rumors they could start." I wink before I can catch myself, and I don't miss the way her jaw drops.

A small part of me swells with pride that I caught her by surprise and left her speechless. And when she bows her head and smiles sweetly, I want to pull her to me and wipe that smile away with my lips.

Fuck, I need to get under control. She's a co-worker now, and I've got enough baggage to make sweet Lizzy unpack it all. She'd probably run until the ocean has swallowed any sign of her.

With our drinks, we head back to the entrance.

"Hi, Bill," Lizzy says, reaching into her pocket for her ticket stub.

I grab mine from my back pocket and show it to him. I turn to look at her, ready to go, and find her brows furrowed.

"Hold on to this, please." She shoves her Frappuccino in my hand and pats her pockets, shoving her hands into them again.

"What's going on?" I ask.

"My ticket stub. I can't find it. I know I have it." Her voice rises with agitation as she digs into her pockets as if they'd magically grow in size and her ticket stub would be there.

Her chest rises with a deep breath, and she looks at Bill. "I must've dropped it somewhere, but you know me, Bill, and you know I wouldn't try to sneak in. Heck, you saw me come out to go to the coffee shop," she tells the man.

"You know the rules, Lizzy."

"Oh, come on." She throws her hand in the air and rips her cup from my hand, taking a gulp of her Frappuccino.

"She's with me." I hold my badge and ticket. Bill arches an eyebrow and looks between us with a sly smile.

"Well, I'll be... You shoulda said that from the beginning." He steps to the side so we can enter.

"Not like that, Bill!" Lizzy hollers.

"Your momma know yet?" he responds.

"Ugh!" She throws her head back. "When my mom comes knocking on my door, I'm sending her your way. You can deal with her." She shakes her head, stepping ahead of me. I laugh

GUARDED DEPUTY

at her attempt to be upset, but someone's mom isn't going to intimidate me.

"I was just being nice."

"That kind of nice in a small town is always misinterpreted," she says over her shoulder.

We reach our friends, and they're all laughing with beer cups in hand.

"Come on." Luke claps my shoulder. "Concert's gonna start."

We all follow him as close to the stage as we can. When a young guy walks on stage with a cowboy hat, faded jeans, and...flip flops, everyone starts cheering. My eyes narrow with uncertainty when I see his footwear. This guy could be the definition of beach cowboy.

I shrug and wait to make my judgments until he starts singing, but being from Texas, this seems like a contradiction to me. After all, I'm from the land that brought us George Strait.

As the strums of his guitar echo around us, the noise quiets and a smooth voice hums the opening beats of the first song. When his deep and gravelly voice begins singing, he proves me wrong. He may be wearing flip flops, but he sings great.

The song picks up rhythm and everyone starts dancing. My eyes move to Lizzy to see what she's doing, and I smirk watching her dance with her friends. She laughs as she sings along, messing up some of the words.

"Let loose," Luke says before taking a chug of his beer.

"I am loose," I argue.

He stares at me with a furrowed brow that slowly lifts. "Right, and you letting loose looks like you're constipated? Is that why you opted for coffee?" He chuckles, shaking his head.

I glare at him and finish my Frappuccino, searching for a garbage to throw it out. When I head back to the group that's adopted me, I find Lizzy's eyes on me. I arch an eyebrow, a slow smile tilting my lips. She looks away, knowing she's caught, but I stalk toward her.

"People are going to get the wrong idea if you keep staring at me," I whisper, grabbing her hand and spinning her around as an excuse to talk to her.

"Absolutely not. I was staring off, and it so happened to be in your direction."

I toss my head back and laugh. "Were you looking for Howard Putty?" I tease her some more.

"No." She lifts her chin in defiance, and it takes everything in me to keep control as her blue eyes stare into mine with a twinkling challenge that makes her look less schoolteacher and more vixen.

I spin her around again before my hand lands on her waist, moving to the fast beat of the song.

I lean down to whisper in her ear, "What will people say about this?"

"Oh, you're in dangerous territory." Her voice is shaky with laughter. "They'll be saying you're going to take my last name."

I laugh at the ridiculousness before my breath catches when I realize people are staring at us with deep curiosity. We're sure to be the gossip in town this weekend. As much as I enjoy Lizzy's company, I don't want to be part of Emerald Bay's gossip mill. Everyone is already curious about my family and me, and I don't need them now digging into my love life.

Besides, I don't deserve a woman like Lizzy, who's sweet and kind, when I carry my father's DNA.

GUARDED DEPUTY

When the song ends, I release her and step back in an attempt to douse those rumors a bit. And the doubt stirring in the pit of my stomach.

chapter 10

LIZZY

I GRAB A BEER from the stand and hum along to the song Sutton is singing. After Mason finished his set, Sutton Wright started hers. I absolutely love her music and have followed her since the beginning of her career.

I love a good music festival. The drinks, the camaraderie with music lovers, the live music. It's all unbeatable. But it can be such a tiring day, too. My calves are burning from dancing on the sand.

After our dance earlier, Nate abruptly stepped back and has kept a distance from me for the rest of the day. Maybe it's for the best, but we were having fun dancing.

He did the same thing at work the other day when he practically ignored me and then spoke to me openly in the parking lot as we were leaving. He runs hot and cold, giving me whiplash. I hate it. When I think he might be opening up to me, he closes right back up.

I shouldn't care. Come fall, my time will be tied to work and studying my butt off to get my master's degree. The fast-track program I got into will be intense without adding a new relationship so I don't know why my mind keeps going back to him.

GUARDED DEPUTY

And yet it bothers me. Mostly because I can't get a read on him when he's moody.

Either he's concerned about our work situation, or he's undecided about me.

Or he's playing games.

If that's the case, then I'm the wrong player to engage.

I chug my beer as I head back to my friends. Nate stands feet away from me, staring at the stage.

First fact I've learned about Nate: He's an avoider.

Second fact: He can dance like the best of them.

"I love this song," Dani calls out, using her cup like a microphone.

I laugh and sing along, ignoring everything else. It's not my problem if Nate has issues dancing with someone while we joke about small town rumors. That's all it was, a joke. It's not like I actually think about marrying the guy. I barely know him.

"I'm hungry," Andrea whines.

"Me too." I nod. "Let's grab something to eat after."

"Yes, please. Before my stomach eats itself. I'm gonna go find some chips or something to hold me over." She stumbles a bit on her feet and giggles.

"Maybe you need some greasy pizza."

"Oh, yeaaaaahh..." She nods eagerly.

"We'll get some food," I assure her.

"Fine." She pouts.

When she stumbles again, Luke wraps his arm around her and steadies her feet. Andrea blinks up at him in a daze, and I swear she blushes. That's interesting. I've never noticed her react like that to him. I'm going to have to ask her about that when she's sober.

89

I look at Avery and Gabriel, who joined us after closing the bakery a little earlier, and ask, "You guys want to get pizza after?"

"We're going to pass. I'm exhausted and need to sleep." She covers her mouth when she yawns. "It's like the word sleep triggers my yawns," she says after.

"You wake up too early for the bakery."

"Yeah. We're closed tomorrow, but I can barely keep my eyes open now. I'm glad we were able to make it here for a bit, though."

"Me too." I bump my shoulder with hers.

Erik grabs Dani's hand and spins her around, making me step away and look around. I refuse to glance at Nate or he'll think I'm begging for a dance partner. I'm capable of enjoying this without anyone, namely a sexy yet moody deputy.

After all, I'm one of those people who actually likes to go to dinner alone. It's refreshing to be comfortable with your own presence. If I can't stand myself, then no one else will be able to either.

When the song ends, Sutton speaks into the microphone.

"Y'all are an amazing crowd!"

We all erupt in cheers, making her wait to talk again.

"I'm having a blast and loved watching Mason perform. Now, I have a surprise for you." Her smile widens, and everyone questions what it could be.

"Help me welcome Knox Bentley!" she hollers, waving one of her arms out to the side. "He's a good friend of mine, and I begged him to come perform our duet live."

"What?" I stare at Dani. "Did you know about this?"

GUARDED DEPUTY

She shakes her head, seeming as shocked as I am. "I had no idea. My dad didn't mention anything."

Knox Bentley is a huge country artist, so having him here is a huge deal. He's one of my favorite artists. He walks out on stage to a cacophony of applause, whistles, and cheers.

"Good evening, Emerald Bay." His deep voice echoes around us through the speakers. "I'm so happy to be here. This Florida weather sure beats the cold Wyoming spring," he jokes, and we all laugh.

"Stop stealing my show," Sutton teases him.

"Right, I guess I need to share the spotlight with her, guys. Get ready to dance." They both laugh, and Knox gives her a side hug. I love seeing the dynamic between artists, and a situation like this gives us a glimpse into the friendships between them.

Music begins to play as Sutton and Knox take their position on stage. I smile as I watch them perform, listening to the way their voices mesh so perfectly.

I sway to the beat, getting lost in the music. After they finish, we all clap some more.

"How about a few more songs?" Knox asks. As if any of us are going to turn down a performance by him.

Thinking he came just to sing a song with Sutton is one thing but knowing he's going to give us his own show is one a whole different level of excitement.

I walk toward the beer stand and grab a fresh one as Knox talks to the band before starting. The cold liquid is heaven as I take a refreshing drink. When I return, Nate arches an eyebrow.

"Are you sure you should drink another?"

My face scrunches up as I shake my head. "I'm fine. Don't worry, I won't be asking you to kiss me by the end of the night."

I roll my eyes, mentioning what happened with Luke's cousin because I was *seventeen*.

It's one story I'll never live down. It'll be my wedding day and one of my friends will be sharing it with my family and friends, all of them laughing and stealing my drinks but by then I'll only be asking my husband to kiss me—sober or drunk.

"That's not... Never mind." Nate breaks my off-rail thoughts by speaking.

"Right." I wave him off and join Dani, wrapping my arm around her shoulder and swaying to the music.

"What's going on?" she asks as quietly as possible.

"Just having fun." I smile.

"And with the hunky deputy?" Her eyebrow lifts in a perfect arch, imitating a Southern accent. She thinks she's good at it, but usually it comes out as a cross between a terrible Southern and British accent.

I chuckle and shake my head. "Nothing."

"Right, I saw you dancing."

"So you saw how he stepped away and has ignored me the rest of the afternoon?" I pinch my lips together and glare at her.

"What was that about?" She shifts on her feet, turning to face me completely.

"No idea." I shrug. "I'm here to have fun." I throw my hand up and whoop.

Dani laughs and joins me, both of us having our own party.

She reaches for my beer cup and takes a drink.

"Hey!" I complain. "Grab your own drink."

She laughs and chugs my beer. "I'm too lazy to go. Besides, it's like you don't know me at all. It's not the first time I steal it."

GUARDED DEPUTY

I roll my eyes and reach for the cup, but she's quicker than me and holds it over her head. She loves to steal my drinks, and I usually let her because by that time I have too many drinks in me.

She has a much higher tolerance than me and has never once begged a guy to kiss her, drunk or otherwise.

"I'm back, but I need tacos or pizza when we're done," Andrea says, chowing on chips.

"Deal." I nod and high-five her.

The concert comes to a close soon after with Knox, Sutton, and Mason on stage. They all thank us once again for being such a great audience. Everyone is still in shock that Knox showed up, commenting at the surprise.

I link my arm with Andrea's, and we walk away from the stage. That's when I notice Nate isn't around anymore.

"Where'd the deputy go?" Dani asks.

"Nate had to go." Luke shrugs.

"Aw, shucks. I was hoping to get to know him better." She smiles mischievously.

"Thank goodness," I mumble, guiding Andrea toward the exit. "Let's go grab pizza," I tell her.

"Yesss," she hisses.

"I'm down for pizza," Luke says and looks at Erik, who agrees.

We say goodbye to Avery and Gabriel and walk down the boardwalk to House of Pies, running in to grab a table before the rest of the concertgoers have the same idea.

"Got one." Andrea giggles, dropping on the chair.

I sit beside her while Dani takes the chair across from me.

"Luke and Erik were talking to some friends, and they'll be right in. Now, tell me what in the hell happened." She looks at me.

"With what?" Andrea's voice rings with concern.

"Our friend here was dancing with Hot Deputy and suddenly they were like two strangers."

"Oh yeah." Andrea sits up, scooting her seat closer to the table. "I saw that, and you guys looked cute."

"We didn't," I argue weakly.

"They were flirting, for sure." Dani nods, looking at Andrea. I roll my eyes and shake my head.

"I think she likes him," Andrea whispers, giggling on a hiccup.

"I don't, but we've had some really awkward encounters before I even knew he was Walker's uncle. Apparently, I can't keep my mouth shut around him. I accused the man of being a stripper and telling him he was in the wrong house for goodness sake." I throw my hands in the air, letting them slam hard against the wooden table on the way down.

"Usually awkward encounters mean you like the guy," Andrea informs.

I don't bring up her reaction to Luke because I don't want to embarrass her in front of Dani if it's a secret crush, but I plan to bring it up another day because she says that with too much certainty.

"It's complicated with him being Walker's uncle and now working at the school. Sure he's hot, but it has drama written all over it, especially with how quickly he pushes me away."

"You're right." Dani nods. "You deserve better than that, especially after your last couple of relationships."

GUARDED DEPUTY

"Exactly!" I say too loud, but inside I'm dying a little at the thought that my best friend thinks I'm better off without Nate. A part of me sinks at the idea of moving on from someone I didn't even start anything with.

Just because he's handsome doesn't mean he's the right person for me.

"Anyway, nothing is even going on between us to have to spend a whole conversation on it. What'd you think about the concert?" I look at my friends with a smile.

"It was amazing." Andrea takes a sip of water the waiter dropped off. "I can't believe Knox freaking Bentley showed up!"

"I know." Dani nods with wide eyes.

"Me either." I spin my cup around and around, making a flower pattern of water rings on the table. "I'm glad concert season is back. We should try to go see Rebel Desire at the amphitheater this summer."

"I'm down," Andrea says.

"I'll see if we get any tickets at the radio station," Dani offers, taking a drink of water and scanning the crowded restaurant.

"By the way, did you talk to your dad about DJing at the spring festival at the school?" I ask Dani. "I'm on the planning committee, and Ellen asked me who was finally going to be the DJ."

"Yeah, he's gonna make a decision this week about who will go, but I'm pushing to be the one to do it." She smiles.

"The kids are so excited about it," Andrea says.

"I know. My class keeps begging to make their crafts, but I'm keeping it for closer to the festival."

Erik and Luke saunter over to our table with wide smiles.

"We're back ladies," Erik says, taking one of the empty seats while Luke chuckles and sits near Andrea.

When the waiter comes by, we order pizza and breadsticks, and I take in the camaraderie in the restaurant. I love Emerald Bay for this very reason. There are always people out and about thanks to our mostly good weather year-round.

We'll get chilly weather in the winter, but it's nothing like some other states up north. And while our summers are scorching, it's just more reason to go to the beach and spend time with friends in a laid-back atmosphere.

"I'm so tired," I say.

"Me too. Concerts are exhausting." Dani yawns.

"Day drinking is what's exhausting," I challenge on a laugh.

"You're just a weakling," Erik teases me.

"Whatever." I stick my tongue out at him.

"I'm sleeping in tomorrow." Andrea rubs her eyes.

"I wish. I have to go to the station," Dani rolls her eyes.

"At least you got to enjoy today instead of working it," I tell her.

"Yup, I'd hate to miss you and Nate firing things up." She winks.

I widen my eyes and kick her under the table.

"What?" Luke sits up with a smirk. "You and Nate?" He arches a brow as his grin widens.

"No." My heart races. The last thing I need is for my guy friends to rag me about this, especially since they work with Nate. "We danced, and you know how Dani is. She's already making things up in that head of hers." I press my lips together. My leg bounces under the table to burn off my nerves.

GUARDED DEPUTY

I don't need more people thinking anything is going on between Nate and me. Nate is someone I should keep as an acquaintance. If the nice guys I've gone out with have turned out to be toads, I can just imagine what the handsome devil would become in my life.

chapter 11

NATE

"Like stranger danger we talked about the other day?" a little girl asks.

"Exactly, but sometimes people aren't quite strangers. You should always wait for the adult in charge of you to tell you if you're leaving with someone else," I explain, following up on our last lesson.

"But if I know them, they're no stranger," a boy argues.

Sometimes it's hard explaining these things to children because they're still innocent, and I don't want to steal that from them or traumatize them. Unfortunately, in my line of work, I've witnessed how sometimes the people who do the most damage are people close to the victim.

I take a deep breath, staring at the wide and confused eyes as I shift in this tiny ass chair without falling. My knees are up by my chest because this chair is so close to the ground.

I look at Lizzy, but her attention is on a stack of papers with a pen in one hand and the fingers on her other hand twirling her ponytail. She's engrossed in whatever she's working on, and likely ignoring me after the way I behaved on Saturday.

"Yes, it's why I said sometimes the people may be familiar, but unfortunately, not everyone we know is nice. It's important to

GUARDED DEPUTY

put your trust on the adult in charge of you, even if someone is telling you to leave with them when it's not a normal occurrence."

"Occurrence?" Another girl scrunches up her nose. I can't keep all their names straight.

"Thing," I say, trying to clarify my words. "When it's not a normal thing to happen."

It's so much easier to talk to older kids where you can be straight with them. The high school students I'm working with on Tuesdays and Thursdays are easier in that sense. Looking at this group of first graders, I wonder when my life went down this path. I had a great job in Dallas. One where I was able to help at-risk teens and dealt with adults instead of defining the words I use so small children can understand me.

But Brooke needed you.

"Uncle Nate is a cop. He knows who the bad guys are," Walker says, coming to my rescue.

Gotta love the unconditional love of a child. I chuckle and focus on the conversation again, asking the students what they should do if someone who isn't direct family comes to pick them up from school as a way to assess that they remember what we've already discussed in the workshop.

As they get into the conversation, my eyes move to Lizzy again. She's bent over grabbing something from a drawer so I only see the curve of her back and shoulder, and yet that's intriguing. Everything about her is alluring, even the most unattractive part of a body.

A back or shoulder could be sexy. Naked soft skin that I can skim my lips on until she's shivering and breaking out in goosebumps.

"Deputy?"

I clear my throat and look back at the kids, unsure who called for me. My heart's racing at the vision in my mind, and it's what I've been avoiding all this time. Lizzy Andrews has the sweet innocent look to her with those blue eyes and shy smile that drives me fucking crazy because I know I'm not good enough for her and yet I want to be.

Not to mention my boss is her godfather, and Sheriff will likely have my balls if I do anything to her.

It's why I put distance between us on Saturday. We were getting too close, too familiar, and it's a safer bet to admire her from afar. It may have seemed like I was watching the concert after we danced, but my attention was completely on her, the way she danced and laughed and sang along.

I wanted nothing more than to stalk back to her, wrap my arms around her curves, and spin her around until she was so dizzy that I was all she saw clearly.

"Deputy Moore, are you okay?" Lizzy's voice beckons me.

"Yes, of course." I nod and look at the students again who are staring at me as if I've lost my mind.

I know, kids, I totally have.

I finish off the lesson distracted and pack up my things to go on to the next group of students. Lizzy doesn't even acknowledge me as I leave. She's been avoiding me all week, and I know it's intentional because she's unsure of how to act. I can read it in her body language. I don't blame her though.

"Deputy Moore." The principal stops me in the hall.

"Hi, Mrs. Sanders." I nod.

"I'm glad I saw you. We're preparing the spring festival that will take place the following weekend, and I'm hoping you might be able to work the event," she informs me.

"Okay. I'll just need the times of the event and anything specific you'll need from me," I tell her.

"The planning committee will help you with that. You can talk to Ms. Revilla or Ms. Andrews since they're in charge of the committee."

At the mention of her name, I already know who I'm going to talk to. It'll be the perfect opening without having to make things awkward. Not only that, but Ms. Revilla is clingy as hell every time I go into her class or run into her. I have no desire to be in that position with her. Somehow, her hands always find their way to my biceps.

"Thank you, I will," I tell Mrs. Sanders and head toward my next class, thinking how I can get Ms. Andrews alone.

For work...nothing else. Definitely not to see how smooth the skin on her shoulder is or the way my stubble might scrape it possessively.

When I finish working, I head to Lizzy's classroom.

"Uncle Nate, you're here! Ms. A said you'd probably come get me when you finished so she brought me back to the class," Walker says excitedly.

I close my eyes when he uses the nickname I came up with when we were doing homework.

"Yeah, I need to talk to your teacher a sec. Wait for me here?" He's sitting at a desk, looking at a book.

"Okay."

Lizzy's narrowed eyes are aimed in my direction as I approach her. She crosses her arms and tilts her head.

"What can I do for you, Deputy?"

"Mrs. Sanders told me to talk to you about the spring festival since I'll be the deputy working it." I widen my stance and place my hands in my pockets.

"Right. The festival is on the fifteenth. It's on campus, and we'll be setting up early in the morning. We would need you to be here at seven and stay until everyone is done cleaning up, likely six. It's a long day, and we'll need to make sure no one comes in that shouldn't. We'll have someone running the ticket booth, and there shouldn't be any strangers since Emerald Bay is safe, but you can never be too careful. The high school is also involved and sometimes teens like to get into trouble." She's talking fast yet her face is impassive.

"I agree."

She nods, dropping her arms and taking a step back, placing her hand on the edge of her desk.

I'm not sure what else to say. She pretty much summed up everything I needed to know in a minute, but I was hoping we'd have to talk longer.

"Walker is doing okay?" I tilt my head in his direction.

"He's doing great."

"Good, good. I'll make sure to tell Brooke." I look around the class, trying to come up with anything else to talk about, but the silence stretches beyond the point of making conversation.

It shouldn't bother me that she's not giving me much attention. I've already decided it's for the best to keep my distance, but she does something to me. Like opens a piece of me that's been locked up. A part that's always made me feel inferior to the rest of the world.

"I'm hungry," Walker announces, and I turn to look at him.

GUARDED DEPUTY

"We'll go home now." I look at Lizzy again, staring into her eyes trying to read whatever she's not saying, but she's fenced in and keeping me shut out.

I deserve it, but it doesn't mean I like it. This is complicated, though. I don't even know if the school has a no fraternization rule, but regardless, I don't like to shit where I eat. History has proven that it's a terrible idea to get involved with someone you work with. Even though this position could be temporary depending on what the county decides, for the next few months, Lizzy and I are essentially co-workers.

But she's tempting enough to make me want to test that theory to see if it'd be different for us.

"Are y'all gonna kiss?" Walker's voice sounds disgusted, and I snap out of the trance not realizing I'm standing close to Lizzy.

"What?" I spin around to glare at him.

"Of course not!" Lizzy says tightly and glares at me.

"It looked like it." He shrugs, putting the book back on the shelf and grabbing his backpack. "I wanna leave. Bye, Ms. A."

I groan and look over at her.

A small smirk ghosts on her lips, and I'm tempted to kiss her and prove Walker right.

"See you tomorrow, Ms. Andrews." I place my hand on Walker's shoulder and guide him out of the school.

"You sure you weren't gonna kiss her?" He looks up at me with furrowed eyebrows.

"Positive," I deadpan.

"Ookay." He shrugs. "Can we get ice cream?" His smile beams.

"Maybe on Friday, kiddo." I squeeze his shoulder and open the car door for him as he frowns.

"Friday's too far away."

"It's in two days. I'm sure you can hold out 'til then." I hand him the seatbelt and make sure he buckles it before closing the door.

My mind wanders as I get into my own seat and turn the ignition. I'm distracted as I drive thinking about Lizzy and her blue eyes and the way it felt to hold her for a little while as we danced.

Ignoring the way she makes me feel is going to be more difficult than I thought, but I need to be sure to keep a straight line dividing my professional and personal life. It seems as if that's an impossible task in a small town.

chapter 12
LIZZY

I'M WALKING DOWN THE hallway after using the restroom, glad I have a short break while my students are in Spanish class. It's been a long week, and I'm ready for the weekend. At least it's already Friday and my afternoon will be pretty easy.

"Lizzy." A deep voice I've become all too familiar with calls out behind me.

I turn around and see Nate waving me down as his steps hastily swallow the space between us. I could dive into the bushes and ignore him, but five days of avoiding him are enough. I should act like an adult and face the man as if we're two regular co-workers.

Who ever said dancing and a little flirting meant anything anyway? Erik flirts with us all the time, and we're only friends.

"Do you know where the supply closet is? The secretary told me it's on the second floor but I'm not seeing it." He runs a hand through his hair, his biceps flexing with the movement in a way that makes the fabric tighten and stretch.

"Liz?" he asks.

"Huh?" I blink away from his arm and look at his face to catch him smirking. "Right, I'll show you."

106

GUARDED DEPUTY

He smartly doesn't comment on my lack of attention and follows beside me in silence.

"I take it you don't have the key?" I look over at him as we turn the corner toward the hall where the supply closet is.

"Uh, no, she just told me to come up here. Now that I think about it, she was looking at her phone and it seemed like she was playing a game." He scratches the side of his head and frowns.

"She loves playing Tetris." I roll my eyes. "It might be open." I pull the door and smile when it swings open. "You got lucky."

His eyes lock with mine for a moment before nodding. "Thanks," he says.

"You're welcome." I shift so he can enter.

"This place is tiny," he comments, squeezing into the walk-in closet. "Any chance you can help me?" His head moves around the crowded space. "I have about twenty minutes to look for some old social studies books Mrs. Sanders told me might be helpful for some of my groups."

"Sure." I walk into the small room. Maybe this could be the opportunity to make things less awkward between us. It's not like I'm holding a grudge against him, I'm more so embarrassed.

"Do you know which books they are?"

"No idea. She said the cover had a group of kids on it with a globe."

"Right, well, let's get to it." I clap my hands.

"I also need some construction paper. Any chance there's some in here?" He lifts his brows.

"Yeah. We're lucky to have some great parents who donate supplies every semester, and we store the extras here." I reach for the construction paper and hand it to him.

"Thanks."

"No problem."

I help him find the books, both of us moving around the tight space as we search through the stacks of old editions.

"Sorry." I move to my right and he moves to his left, and then we both move to the other side. "Looks like we're dancing." I laugh and instantly regret it because it reminds me of Saturday.

"Yeah." He chuckles and stops moving. "You go on first."

I move around him, my front brushing against his side, and Nate tenses. Not the reaction you want from a man, but since this man has different professional connections in my life, it could be a good idea, even if my pride is scuffed up because of it.

I move through another stack of books, making small talk.

"Do you like working with the kids?" I ask, looking over at Nate.

"It's nice." He shrugs.

"Not convincing at all."

"It's interesting and different than what I'm used to." He turns to face me.

"Do you prefer the high school students? You worked with children before, right? That's what my uncle mentioned to me." I furrow my brows, wondering if I misunderstood.

"Your uncle?"

"Yeah, Uncle Roy. The sheriff," I clarify.

"Oh, I thought he was your godfather." Nate shuffles beside me.

"Godfather and uncle. He's my mom's brother." I'm so used to people knowing this connection.

"Cool. Well, yeah. I worked with troubled teens. Kinda different than this." He chuckles, holding up the construction

GUARDED DEPUTY

paper to emphasize his point. "But I can be more candid with the high school classes so that's good."

"It makes sense. My students like it when you come in if that helps, and I hear them talking about what you've taught them so far."

"That's good to know." His brows lift and his mouth scrunches as if he didn't think it was possible.

"Smile." I shove his shoulder playfully. "It's a good thing. You may not be fighting crime, but you're making a difference."

"Is that why you became a teacher?" His eyes hold mine captive.

"Yeah." I shrug. "It's silly, but I like that I can help kids learn in more ways than one. Sure, I teach them to read and how to do math, but I can also foster other types of teachings like self-esteem, forgiveness, and acceptance."

"That's important," he says. "I bet you're great at it."

I smile as his compliment. "Thanks," I whisper, returning my eyes to the books on the top shelf. I reach up on my tiptoes and pull one down.

"Hey, is this it?" I practically shove the book in Nate's face.

"Yeah. I remember her now mentioning it had a symbol of a compass on it as well. Thanks."

"You're welcome."

"Anyway, should we go?" He straightens, masking his emotions once again.

"Yup."

He turns the knob but the door doesn't open. "Uhhh...this isn't opening."

"What do you mean?" My eyes widen, and my hands clench at my sides.

Nate pulls the knob tightly and stares at me. "It's stuck."

"Let me try." I push forward, crushing my body to his as I turn the knob and pull so hard I crash into him but the door doesn't open. "Great," I mumble, my heart racing.

I turn to face him, and we're toe to toe. Suddenly, the space is tiny and hot. Why is it so hot in here? Sweat builds on the back of my neck, and I lift my hands to tie my hair up until I realize I don't have a hair tie.

"Shit." I move back and lean against the door.

"Are you okay?" Nate bends down to look into my eyes.

"I'm fine," I breathe out, drying my palms on my skirt. "It's all good. We aren't going to die in here."

"You're claustrophobic," he states, not asks.

"I'm not." I shake my head. "I go in elevators just fine."

"Yeah, but you've never been stuck in one."

"True." I gulp a deep breath. "It's hot in here, right?" I fan my face with my hand.

Nate steps back, probably regretting asking me to help him because I'm crazy and shakes his head. He reaches for a construction paper and bends it until it's a fan.

"Here, use this." I look at the device and nod, fanning myself.

"Thanks," I whisper.

My heart is hammering as he looks around the supplies we have stored here. He grabs a pair of scissors and looks at me.

"Let me see if I can open it."

I step aside and watch him fail at fitting the kid scissors in the thin space between the door and the frame. My heartbeat echoes in my ears as he frowns at me. I fan myself faster, but the paper is too thin to keep intact with the speed I'm using.

GUARDED DEPUTY

"Lizzy, it's okay. Take a deep breath. Just one." His hands land on my shoulders as he lowers himself again to look into my eyes. I follow his instruction, taking a deep breath.

"Good," he praises me. "Now another breath." He guides me, trying to talk me off the ledge. I close my eyes to avoid looking around the small space and tense when I feel his arms around me. "Keep going," he whispers in my ear as his hand soothingly brushes the back of my head.

"We'll be okay. Someone will come by soon," he says quietly.

"Yeah," I respond weakly.

"You're safe, okay? The room is the same size it was before. I won't let anything happen to you." His words are a comforting blanket that help to calm my racing heart and shaky nerves.

"Thanks," I whisper.

"Better?" He leans his head back, but we're still so close that his breath tickles the tip of my nose. I nod silently, enraptured by the layers of gold and brown in his eyes.

"Good." He swallows thickly.

One of his hands moves to cradle my cheek, and I lean into the rough touch of his calloused hands and close my eyes. When I blink them open again, I swear he's closer to me. My breath hitches for a different reason now. He tilts his head, every movement slow and deliberate.

The door swings open, and I jump back.

"Uhhh..." The art teacher stares at us with raised eyebrows.

"Oh my God, thank goodness!" I leap around Nate and into the hallway, gasping for air. "Freedom!" I call out before looking at them. "We got locked in," I explain.

"Oh," she says, not quite believing me.

I don't know if I'm more shaken up about the panic of being locked in or the fact that it seemed like Nate was about to kiss me. Either way, I don't have time to think it through because I hear my name over the loudspeaker paging me to get to my class and I curse.

"Need to go, sorry!" I breathlessly race down the stairs and toward my classroom.

My mind is reeling from what happened in the supply closet and my reaction to being stuck in there. Who knew I'd be such a mess in a situation like that?

"I'm here, sorry!" I tell the Spanish teacher, who looks annoyed as hell. "I got locked in the supply closet and couldn't get out until someone opened the door." No need to specify that I got stuck in there with Nate.

"Are you okay, Ms. Andrews?" A student asks with fearful eyes.

"I'm okay." Thanks to Nate, but I keep that to myself. "All right, well, let's, uh...get your science books."

"I'm sorry again," I tell the Spanish teacher who nods and leaves.

"Ms. A, we don't have science now, we have social studies," another student calls out on a giggle.

"Oh, yeah, that's what I meant." I'm a wreck as I walk around the classroom without really knowing what I'm doing because my body is somehow over in the supply room with Nate still embracing me as he stares into my eyes as if his life depended on it.

"Are you sick?" Stephanie calls out.

"No," I shriek so loud and high-pitched that I'm surprised the windows don't crack. "I'm fine, all fine." I wave my hands

GUARDED DEPUTY

in the air and search for the social studies plans to see what the hell I'm doing.

I might as well call it a day and let the kids color a town map and label the different parts so I can sit and catch my breath.

Nate *was* going to kiss me. I wasn't imagining that, right? Would I have let him? I'm not sure I had much of a choice since I was pulled in, head leaning back so his lips would have easy access to mine.

Would I have let him? It'd definitely not be aligned with my determination to focus on my career.

"Ms. A?" Great, all my students are calling me that nickname now, and it only makes me think more about Nate.

"Yes." I blink and look at my class.

"Are we gonna start?"

"Of course." I am scatterbrained and need to get myself leveled.

I've always been focused and on top of my job, and now this man is making me into a mess in the one place I always had things under control. I may not make my bed every morning, but my lesson plans are always done a week or two in advance and my classroom is impeccable.

One man isn't going to interfere with my career. I need to get it together, keep that line between Nate and me clearly defined, and not stare at his biceps because they are the cause of distraction.

So are his eyes, and jaw, and scruff, and the dimples he hides but every so often aims your way.

Yeah, I'm screwed.

113

chapter 13

NATE

WALKING AROUND THE SPRING festival, I don't have much to do but keep an eye out to make sure everything is okay, which it is because this is Emerald Bay where people help each other up when they fall not bring out their smart phones to record.

"Deputy Moore, hi!" A girl waves at me. Her parents smile and thank me for the work I've been doing in the classroom. Apparently, the girl goes home and tells her parents everything she's learned.

I guess my work here is actually serving for something.

"Deputy! Come 'ere!"

"Yeah! Cooooome." A group of children cheer, and I look around hoping no one is watching but it's useless. Everyone is smiling as the kids wave me over, jumping up and down.

I walk over to them, arching my eyebrow. They're standing by the face painting stand, one of them getting a Batman face painted.

"Deputy, you gotta get your face painted!" one of Walker's friends says.

"Yeah, you should do Spiderman," Stephanie comments. "Right, Ms. A?"

GUARDED DEPUTY

I turn my head and see Lizzy standing a few feet away. Somehow I had missed her, but now I can't keep my eyes off her. She's wearing form-fitting jeans and a school T-shirt with the Shark logo on it.

All of the students in her class are calling her Ms. A now, and I wonder if Walker spilled that it was me who came up with it. Regardless, I like the smile that lifts her lips when she hears it.

"Yup, I think Deputy Moore should support our school this way," she says.

"Really? And what about you, Ms. *A*?" I arch an eyebrow, challenging her.

"You should get Elsa!" Stephanie says, clapping.

"Elsa would be fun," Lizzy says, looking at the woman who's in charge of face painting. "Can you do Elsa?"

"Of course." The woman smiles, pointing to the empty chair. "Sit down."

It's my cue to step away and stop teasing her. Instead of leaving, I stay and watch the way she giggles when the blue paint touches her skin.

I should go away and continue working, but her mood is infectious and has me smiling. Lizzy is the type of person that shines happiness. She's like a rainbow, whenever you look at her, you can't help but smile. It makes her even less attainable—something you admire from a distance but know you'll never catch.

Her eyes blink up to mine, holding me captive and cementing me in place so I can't walk away and do the job I was hired for. As the woman adds finishing touches on what seems like a blue crown on Lizzy's forehead, she smiles and looks down at her hands on her lap. The color brings out her eyes, and I don't want her to hide them from me.

"All done. Deputy, you're next." The woman looks over at me.

"Ms. A, that's so pretty. You're just like Elsa," Stephanie says. I almost forgot the students were standing here with us.

"No, that's okay. I need to get back to work." I point over my shoulder.

"Oh, no you don't. I'll make it quick." She smiles, and I know I'm going to lose this battle when the kids push me forward.

"Fine," I grumble. "But I don't want a whole face thing. Something small...for the children." I drop on the chair, hiding my embarrassment with a scowl.

"Aw, come on, Deputy, be a team player." Lizzy laughs.

"I am," I deadpan. "See?" I stretch my arms out, almost knocking down some paint from the table.

"Do Thor!" one kids calls out.

"No, Spiderman," another says.

"A football!" a third one says. I lose sight of who's talking.

"A football works." I nod.

Something simple and not as attention-calling.

"What do you think, Ms. A?" The woman looks at her. "What best suits our deputy here?"

I swallow thickly, looking at Lizzy with pleading eyes.

"Hmmm...how about a dragon?" She taps her lips, avoiding my eyes, but I see the way she's holding her laughter.

"Ohhhhh, yeah!" The kids all say in unison.

I curse under my breath and glare at the woman who's bound to make me crazy. She's biting her lips, but she snorts.

"It's for the children," she reminds me.

GUARDED DEPUTY

"Right." I look at her, unamused, and hold my breath. I did not move to Emerald Bay to get my face painted at an elementary school event.

"Uncle Nate, cool!"

Brooke guffaws when she sees me on the seat, green paint starting to streak my face.

"Not a word." I lift a finger to my sister.

She lifts her hands, unable to stop laughing. Then, she looks at Lizzy, and they both start cackling louder. I want to shut them both up, but I'm stuck in this chair with green paint on my face and a group of students and parents, so I need to keep myself together.

For a moment, I can see these two women teaming up against me, and I like the sight of that as much as I shouldn't. Lizzy and Brooke would get along great, and in a different life, it could happen.

"All done," the woman says, patting my shoulder. "Don't worry, you won't be scaring children with this." She hands me a mirror, and I see a small dragon that goes from my cheek to my jaw.

It looks like something from the *Dragon Tales* cartoon. I couldn't even get something respectable like a dragon from *Game of Thrones*.

"Thanks." I attempt politeness, but knowing I have to walk around with this all day is not something I'm excited about. "I need to get back to work." I stand, glaring at Lizzy and then at Brooke.

"Looks...intense," my sister says with a chuckle.

"Thanks for the sibling support, sis," I tell her.

"Aw, come on."

"I want a dragon like my uncle," Walker says.

"Me too," another boy exclaims.

"You see, you're a trendsetter." Brooke smiles, giving me a side hug.

I shake my head, wishing I could hide this side of my face.

"Chin up, buttercup," Lizzy calls out, and I glare at her.

I'd like to shut her up another way, but I'm restricted from doing so. So I head off to check the perimeters of the campus to make sure nothing is off, and then walk around the festival, keeping everything safe.

Some of the teen students say hi to me as I cross them, and others are too engrossed in their conversations to even notice me.

I definitely enjoy going to the high school more, but even these students are great compared to the teens I used to work with.

Throughout the festival, children laugh and scream as they jump in a bounce house, others run around. Some are eating cotton candy and hot dogs. It's the definition of happiness and camaraderie. Adults and children alike are laughing and enjoying themselves as they come together to support the school. I've never experienced something like this.

"Deputy Moore." Sheriff McCall stops me. A woman, who I assume is his wife, stands beside him.

"Hi, Sheriff."

"How are things going here?" His eyes linger on my face, and his lips quirk.

"Good, great. I don't have much to do, to be honest. Everyone behaves." I shrug.

GUARDED DEPUTY

"I see you're enjoying the activities yourself." He points to my cheek, holding back a chuckle.

"Uh, yeah." I reach up to scratch my cheek and then think better of it. "The kids wanted me to paint my face." I look around awkwardly.

"That's good. Better you than me." He laughs.

"Yup." I press my lips together.

"That's precious. So sweet of you to do that for the kids," the woman says.

"Oh, this is my wife, Natalie. Natalie, this is Deputy Moore, our newest employee." He introduces us.

"It's nice to meet you. I've heard so much about you." She smiles kindly, but I bet she's heard all the gossip people in town like to speak.

"Nice to meet you as well."

"Roy!" A woman calls out behind me, but in a split second she's standing near him and staring at me. "You must be the new deputy." She extends her hand and smirks.

"Sarah," Sheriff warns.

"Let me meet him. After all, he's been spending time with my daughter." The woman arches her eyebrow, keeping her gaze on mine.

"Excuse me?" My eyebrows drip as I look at her, and then realization hits. This isn't good. My eyes cut to Sheriff, but he's glaring at the woman.

"With my daughter, Lizzy. From what I've heard, you two danced at the concert and had coffee together. She refuses to tell me what's going on, so I'm taking over."

"Sarah!" Sheriff growls this time.

"We're just friends," I say. "We work together, and she teaches my nephew," I explain, hoping to talk myself out of this situation.

"Friends," she says, giving me a knowing stare. "She's friends with Luke. You are not friend material."

"That's it. I apologize for my meddling sister. Natalie, take Sarah to...anywhere," Sheriff demands.

It looks like he wants to kill his sister, and I don't blame him. He's probably trying to be professional, and she's making that impossible.

"I apologize," he tells me. "My sister means well, but she's...overwhelming at times. She wants what's best for Lizzy, as we all do." He holds my gaze steady.

"I understand. Like I said, Lizzy and I are friends."

"Good." He nods without expanding on his thoughts. "Glad to hear everything's going okay here. Keep up the good work. We can never be too careful."

"Absolutely, sir." My jaw ticks as I walk away.

Just as I imagined, Sheriff McCall wouldn't be on board with the idea of me dating his niece. I can't blame him. It wouldn't be hard to dig up my past and see I had a few misdemeanors when I was a teen. What good man would want someone like that with his niece?

Bored out of my mind, I walk around the area, pretending I'm doing intense security work when in reality I just want to go home, drink a beer, and forget that conversation. Forget about Lizzy Andrews and her blue eyes and the way she shines. I don't know if moving to Emerald Bay was the best decision. I had a life and job that didn't require me to work with young children instead of acting like a true law enforcement officer.

GUARDED DEPUTY

But my sister was here, and she needed me. Maybe I needed her just as much.

"Hey." I look up and see Brooke walking toward me.

"Hi." I lift my chin in form of greeting.

"I see you still have the dragon." She giggles.

"Yup. What are the odds that I can wash it off and tell the kids the dragon flew away?" I glance at her.

"Slim." She smiles. "How's work going?"

"Boring." I shrug.

"At least it's more relaxing." She pats my arm.

"Yeah."

"What's wrong?" Brooke crosses her arms and narrows her eyes.

"Nothing."

"Does this have to do with Ms. Andrews?" Her eyebrow lifts into a perfect arch.

"What? Why would you say that?"

"I'm not stupid. I saw the way you two looked at each other while you were getting your face painted." Brooke rolls her eyes as if I were the stupid one.

"We weren't looking at each other in any way. Ms. Andrews isn't the kind of woman for me."

"Why? She's sweet, caring, and super nice." Brooke throws her hands in the air.

"And I'd likely end up hurting her. Commitment isn't for me, Brooke." My jaw clenches, thinking about my parents' disastrous relationship. Just the thought of my father makes anger race through me.

"Nate." Brooke places her hand on my arm. "It's okay to open up. You can't live your life alone or taking care of Walker and

me. I want you to find what I had with David. Love is worth it."
She sniffs, and I hug her.

"I come from a man who abandoned his family. I'd rather not go through that. Either hurt someone or get hurt the way Mom did."

"You're nothing like Dad. What happened between Mom and Dad is on them. I also hate that he left us, but if we live life based on fear, we lose so many opportunities life throws our way." She squeezes me before releasing the hug and smiling sadly.

I nod silently, not wanting to continue this conversation here.

"I'm going to check on Walker." Her smile brightens and she walks away.

I continue wandering around, taking in the happy families. At one point in life, my family had that. I have no idea where it went wrong. I was too young to fully comprehend relationships back then.

"Tell me it isn't true." Lizzy stands in front of me with wide eyes.

"What?" I can't take her seriously with that paint on her face.

"Did my mom corner you? I swear I didn't tell her anything." Her eyes are wide as she shakes her head.

"It's fine." I wave her off.

"It is *not* fine. You're a man of the law. How hard is it to hide a body?" She drops her face in her hands.

"Lizzy, that's not a joke." Losing a mother should never be joked about, even if you're frustrated and being sarcastic.

"Sorry, but sometimes she drives me crazy. I am sorry. She gets these ideas in her head, and it's hard to reel her in."

GUARDED DEPUTY

"It's fine, honestly. You said it, we live in a small town and people would get the wrong impression." I shrug.

"Right." She nods, her back straight and face emotionless. "Okay." She scratches her forehead and then curses. "The paint, damn it." Her fingertips are blue.

Using the heel of her hand, she rubs it as carefully as she can without ruining the paint, but it's already got streaks from where her nails scratched.

"Are you okay?"

"Yeah, just itchy from sweat."

I step closer, and she steps back.

"Let me see," I argue, grabbing her hand.

"No." She looks away.

"I think you have a rash." I grab her chin with my other hand and lift it so I can get a better view. Sure enough, she has small dots under the paint. "Are you allergic to face paint?"

"No...I don't know. Beside what you might think, I don't make this a regular occurrence." She rolls her eyes, and I fight a smile. I love it when she gets sassy.

"I thought this was a hobby of yours," I tease her.

"Funny," she deadpans, scratching her forehead again.

"You should clean it off and put some cream. Come on." I tug her by the hand I'm holding, but she digs her heels in the ground.

"Where? I don't need your help. I can get to the bathroom on my own."

"Don't be stubborn, I have some cream in my desk that will help." I drag her along, grateful we're near the building and away from lots of people.

"Do you get rashes often?" I hear laughter in her voice.

"No."

"You sure? Quite odd to have rash cream at your desk," she teases.

"You can never be too careful. Besides, I wanted to have some in case Walker ever needs it."

"Oh," she pauses. "Well, that's sweet."

"I know. Now, let me help you."

"Nate, I'm fine," she says exasperatedly.

"Stop being stubborn." I pull her toward me, and she stumbles into my chest.

"I'm stubborn?" she seethes. "You...you're maddening!" She throws her hands in the air before pointing her finger at my chest.

"What did I do? I'm trying to help." I lift my hands.

"Ugh." She stalks away from me and toward the school.

I follow behind her, needing to make sure she gets that face situation under control. When she walks into the teacher's bathroom, I stop by the entrance and cross my arms. Lizzy cups water in the hands and washes her face, rubbing to remove the paint.

"My forehead burns," she complains.

"Can I help you?" I ask softer now.

She looks at me through the mirror and nods, so I grab paper, wet it, and turn her so she's facing me. Carefully, I wipe the paint off her face, noting the way her rash is red.

"Careful," she flinches and whispers.

"Sorry." I continue to wet the paper and clean off the paint with smooth strokes so not to hurt her. Lizzy closes her eyes and breathes deeply.

"Almost done," I whisper.

GUARDED DEPUTY

"It stings," she says, squeezing the wrist on the hand that's holding her chin.

"A little more, and I'll give you some ointment."

"How bad is it?" Her voice is full of concern.

"It'll be okay."

"You're a terrible liar," she challenges.

I finish and step back, nodding to the mirror. When she sees her face, her eyes widen and a gasp echoes in the small space.

"Oh, my goodness. This is *bad.*" She turns her glaring gaze to me.

"I'll grab the ointment." I head to my desk and grab my First Aid Kit.

Lizzy is leaning close to the mirror, fingers gently brushing her skin when I return. Her face is fire red and bumps cover her forehead and temples. I notice the way her fist clenches, and I assume it's an attempt to stop herself from scratching it.

"Here." I hand her the ointment.

"Thanks."

She puts it on, covering every inch that's bumpy with the rash.

"This is so embarrassing. How am I going to go back out there like this? The sun probably won't help."

"You can say my dragon burned you," I joke, and she actually laughs.

"That sounds...dirty." She shakes her head, looking in the mirror.

I clear my throat because the idea of my other dragon doing things to her, I can guarantee it wouldn't burn. It'd be pure pleasure.

"Right, well, I hope the cream helps." I shift on my feet.

"I should go home." She looks at me with round eyes. "It's bad, right?"

I can't lie to her. Not when I already made it seem like I don't feel anything for her.

"I've seen better." I press my lips together.

"I knew it. I look like some ogre."

"Ogres are green."

"Well, then... I don't know. What monster is red?" Her eyes are wild with worry.

"Take a deep breath, Lizzy." I grab her shoulders, remembering the way she freaked out when we got locked in the supply closet.

Suddenly, I want to hug her again, hold her to me, kiss the worry off her face and swallow it so she can go back to being a bright and colorful rainbow full of hope.

"I'm trying."

"It'll be healed before you know it," I whisper, holding the side of her face before I can stop myself. My thumb brushes her cheek as I soothe her.

"I hope so." She croaks.

I may have told Lizzy's mom that her daughter and I are just friends, but everything I feel about her bypasses friendly territory into heady and needy. What I'd give to lift her up until her legs are wrapped around me and take her lips in mine to see if they taste sweet like the cotton candy I saw her eating earlier. I want to see if we fit together the way I fantasize about.

"Nate," she whispers.

"Yeah?" I look into her eyes, getting a read on what she's thinking but I can't figure it out, too consumed by lust.

GUARDED DEPUTY

"You're not Mr. Hot Deputy anymore, you're Mr. *Packing* Deputy."

"What?" I look down between us, dumbfounded. At some point, I pressed us together, and she's clearly feeling the effects of what my mind is imagining.

"Shit." I step back. "I'm sorry."

Lizzy laughs, but her cheeks flame and it's nothing to do with the rash. Something comes over me, and I stalk toward her, grab her face with both hands, and I smash my lips to hers.

I have to see if kissing her would be as good as I imagined.

No more pretending.

I need to taste her, and it's heaven on earth when she kisses me back, gripping the front of my shirt.

"Finally," she whispers against my lips before flushing her body to mine.

Every rule I've written for myself flies out the window as we devour each other in this tiny bathroom. A sense of belonging enters me, and I wonder how I ever lived without this. Up until now, I've met women, but I've maintained a very clear line about where I stand. Relationships only hurt people.

Lizzy has done something to me. Or maybe it's Emerald Bay in general that has captivated me.

Whatever it is, I wonder if Brooke has a point. I shouldn't imprison myself and lose out on actually living.

With her hands still on my shirt, she leans her head back and stares into my eyes.

"Was that a bad idea?" She chews on her bottom lip.

"It was horrible, but I like trouble every now and then." I smirk and stroke my fingers over her skin.

"It'd be more romantic if I didn't look like I was transforming into a reptile," she adds.

I laugh and shake my head. "I think romance left the room when I kissed you in a bathroom."

"That is true." She nods, pensive. "I guess you're going to have to get a redo some other time and make up for it." She winks and releases my shirt, smoothing the fabric as if that will undo what we did. My body is coiled from that kiss. Fixing my shirt isn't going to make me forget.

"Fuck, Lizzy." I step back, running a hand through my hair and down my face.

"Thanks for taking care of me, Deputy."

"You know what they say, kiss it to make it feel better," I toss out, and she giggles.

"I can now attest to the truth behind those words." She steps out of the bathroom and looks at me. "Are you coming?"

Oh, I'm coming in more ways than one, but I have self-control.

"I'll be right out."

She nods and walks away, giving me space, and I stare at myself in the mirror.

"Nate, you don't know how to do this. Your dad left your mom with two kids. How the hell are you going to be able to be with someone like Lizzy and be sure you're not going to take after your father?" I talk to myself in the mirror, but instead of the pep talk I need, my inner-self takes the chance to put me down.

Wonderful.

Now, not only did I kiss the girl, I'm risking breaking her heart.

chapter 14
LIZZY

I TAKE DEEP, EVEN breaths as I walk out of the building wishing I had a cap to cover the rash on my face. Surely, the sun won't be good for it. With all the extra things I keep in my classroom, how is a hat not one of them?

You're focusing on the wrong thing.

Right, brain, thanks for reminding me that I just kissed Nate at work, in a bathroom. A smile breaks free on my face before I can control it, and I squeal quietly.

We. Kissed.

We freaking kissed, and it felt amazing. Dangerous, but exhilarating. It may have been a bad idea, but I don't regret it.

"Hey!"

I leap back and blink. Andrea stands in front of me with raised eyebrows and her mouth drops.

"What happened to you? Are you okay?" She leans in to look at my face.

"I'm fine." I wave her off. "I got an allergic reaction to the face paint, but I cleaned it off and put some ointment. Any chance you have a hat somewhere?" I plead, hoping she's better prepared than I am.

GUARDED DEPUTY

"I don't, sorry." She frowns and shakes her head. "It'd be a good idea to have one in the classroom, although it's probably best to not cover the rash." She grimaces.

"I know, but I can't walk around like this." I wave a finger around my face.

She fixes her ponytail and pauses halfway. Her eyes widen with a spark. "Shelly probably has some in her class. I mean, they'll be kids size since it's for her student's dress-up station, but your head isn't very big." She analyzes my head from different angles.

"I don't think that would work." Worse than showing off this rash is wearing a kid costume. Shelly teaches Pre-K 4, and she has a ton of costumes for her students to play with, but they're not exactly ideal for this situation.

"Maybe she has a cowboy hat or something that won't be too obvious. Let's go ask her." She grabs my hand and drags me toward wherever Shelly is.

"Lizzy, are you okay?" Aunt Natalie stops me.

"I'm fine, just allergies." I wave her off and continue walking with Andrea.

A parent stops me to ask what happened, and I have to explain that I had an allergic reaction, which caused her stress in case her daughter is also allergic.

Great, now I'm making parents worry.

"It's just my sensitive skin," I assure her, staring at Andrea for an escape plan, all the while scratching the parts of my face that aren't covered in the rash in hopes that helps alleviate the itchiness where I wish I could scratch.

"Oh, we need to go to...help at a game," Andrea says, pulling my arm.

131

On our way, at least five more people stop me, and I'm so over having to explain the situation.

"I can't blame them, your face is an angry red." Andrea cringes apologetically.

"Wonderful. Let's find Shelly. I'm desperate." I shake my head and sigh.

As we walk, I can't help but look around the area in case I spot Nate, but I haven't seen him since I left the bathroom. Doubt creeps in as I question if he regrets the kiss, but I don't have time to consider this because someone gasps.

I snap my head toward the sound and find Shelly with her hands over her mouth. "What in the world happened to you?"

"Funny story," I begin sarcastically and explain what happened. "Any chance you have a hat in your classroom?"

"I have the ones the kids use for dress-up. Some of them are bigger since parents donated some of the siblings' costumes. Let's go." She leads the way.

I have a feeling I'm going to wish I didn't accept their help and just grab the megaphone and tell everyone what happened so I don't have to explain it five-hundred-and-thirty times. Actually, Dani would probably lend me the microphone she has at the DJ booth.

Shelly unlocks her classroom door and goes straight to where she has the costumes. She rummages through the items until she holds up a few things.

"I have this hard hat, this fireman hat, although these are both plastic and I don't think it'd be comfortable." She tosses them to a side and continues looking. "Oh! This could work." She throws me something, and I don't catch it in time.

GUARDED DEPUTY

Looking down at the floor, I stare at the dark blue hat. It isn't plastic, so that's a plus, but it's a cop hat, and well, that could be awkward. Andrea snorts beside me, and I glare at her.

"You don't have a cowboy hat? One of those straw ones?"

"It broke, sorry. I only have these."

I look at the hat on the floor as if picking it up would electrocute me.

"Maybe I'll grab the microphone and announce to everyone what happened so they stop asking," I say.

"The sun will irritate it more, though. Wearing something to cover it would help."

I grab a shirt and place it on my head. "Head scarves are in style, so this could work." I tie it in an attempt to make the shirt look like a scarf and by the laughter coming from the two, I'd guess it isn't my best look.

"Maybe not." I scratch my forehead, and Andrea slaps my hand away.

"Don't scratch it. Wear the hat, who cares?" Andrea picks it up from the floor and hands it to me. "It could look cute."

"I can't." My voice is tight.

The last thing I need is for Nate to take this the wrong way, as if it were a way of claiming stake on him. The way a dog pees on something to mark its territory.

"Wait..." Andrea tilts her head and looks at me. "Is this because of Nate?" Her eyes widen.

"Who?" Shelly asks.

"No one," I say quickly.

"Deputy Moore," Andrea says at the same time.

"Ohhhh..." Shelly's eyes widen in understanding.

"Who cares, Lizzy? It's not like you're wearing his hat, you need something to protect you," Andrea argues.

"It's this or risk the rash spreading more." Shelly shrugs.

"Fine," I huff out, placing the hat on my head. It doesn't even have a form to it. It's flat and tight, but the bill does cover my forehead. "I can't believe this," I mumble, walking out of the classroom as I hear them announcing players for freeze dance.

"Don't be embarrassed," Andrea says.

"Right," I say flatly.

They don't know that Nate and I kissed, and this could be a super strange headwear option.

As soon as people see me, their eyebrows lift and look at me as if I've lost my mind. I haven't yet, but I'm about to. Embarrassing myself isn't a new feeling, but this crosses the line into *kill me now* territory.

My eyes remain on the ground as I walk toward the basketball court where the DJ stand is and pray no one makes a big deal about this, but that's like praying for snow in South Florida. I can't blame them. Why in the world would I be wearing a kids cop hat?

Sweat rolls down the back of my neck as I feel eyes on me. For all I know, people think I'm going to break out in dance while imitating one of the Village People. It's the only logical explanation for me wearing the hat unless you know that I'm hiding my face.

"Are you ready, kiddos? You know the rules, once the music stops, so do you or you take a seat." Dani talks into the microphone, totally in her element.

The kids cheer and urge her to begin while I stand back and watch with a smile. The festival has been a huge success, and

GUARDED DEPUTY

while I'm not sure how much money we've raised, it's going to be a huge help to the school fund.

"Lizzy?" Ellen says beside me.

"Huh? Yeah?" I turn to look at her.

"What are you wearing?" Her narrowed eyes judge me. "Never mind." She shakes her head as if it's too much trouble to deal with me. "It's your turn to monitor the art center."

"Oh, darn, right. Sorry about that, I had a...situation." Nothing is worse than giving Ellen the opportunity to signal that I'm not doing my job—not even a rash on my face. I race to the table where kids are painting so that the teacher there can take a break.

"Hey, sorry about being late. You're free to go and enjoy the festival," I tell the teacher and take her place, looking at what the students are painting on canvases.

"That looks wonderful," I tell an older student, who is painting a detailed mermaid. "Impressive."

"Thanks, Ms. Andrews." The girl smiles over her shoulder. "I want to take art classes."

"You should."

I move on to another student but hear a snicker and look toward the person who's laughing. My eyebrow arches, and I cross my arms in my best attempt to seem intimidating.

"I've had women tell me they like me, but none has ever gone to the extent of showing me by dressing up in uniform." A crooked smile appears on Nate's face.

My arms drop, and I fight the urge to cover my face from the blush that creeps up my cheeks.

"Funny." I shake my head, using an unimpressed tone to hide my embarrassment.

135

"Here you are." My mom walks up to us, eyeing Nate. "Why are you wearing that?" She points to my head.

"I got a rash from the face paint, so I'm using the hat to shield from the sun."

"Did you put anything on it?" Her brows furrow with concern.

"Yeah, Nate, uh, had some ointment that I applied." I cut my eyes to him, who's watching us with an amused grin.

"That's so nice of you." My mom smiles at him, and I'm ready to shove her away because I know that look. And she already mentioned the rumors to Nate so there's no telling how far she'll go now.

"Just helping a friend out." Nate smiles, his dimples making an appearance.

"A friend." My mom scoffs. "Not from what I've heard."

"Mom." I grab her arm and drag her away. "Watch the kids for me a sec?" I look over my shoulder, and Nate nods with a chuckle.

"Please don't make this a big deal, Mom," I whisper as I stand with her a few feet away.

"A big deal about what?" she asks innocently, batting her eyelashes.

I glare at her with pinched lips.

"Oh, fine." She lifts her hands. "I don't understand why you're being so secretive."

"I'm not. There is nothing going on between Nate and me. You know I'm focusing on my career at the moment." It's a white lie because we did kiss, but she'd hire a cheer team to congratulate us.

GUARDED DEPUTY

"Yes, I know." She sighs. "And I'm proud of you for going after your dreams and all, but it doesn't mean you can't date a nice guy."

"How do you even know if he's a nice guy? You just met him today." I look at her incredulously.

"I am good at reading people. Something about him reminds me of your father."

"Really?" I stare at her with furrowed brows.

"Not sure what it is, but he does."

"Maybe it's the uniform," I say softly.

"Could be." She shakes her head. "Anyway, are you sure you're okay?" She signals to my forehead with her hand.

"I am. Once I'm home, I'll wash my face again and add some more cream."

"I think you should do that now. It's spread to your cheeks."

"Really?" I touch my face, and sure enough, I feel some bumps on my cheeks. "I'll be back." I speed-walk to the building and go into the teacher's bathroom and remove the hat, looking at myself in the mirror.

I groan when I see my mom was right.

I splash my face with cold water in hopes that it alleviates the burning sensation and go to Nate's desk in search of ointment he gave me earlier. I know he had that First Aid Kit here somewhere.

"What are you doing?"

I leap back, guilt written on my face. The school secretary looks at me, her head tilted.

"I was looking for Deputy Moore's First Aid Kit." My chest rises and falls with each breath, knowing this looks bad.

"Why would you look there?" She arches a brow.

"He lent me some ointment earlier, so I was hoping to borrow it again since my face has a rash." I point to the obvious.

"Oh, my." She gasps. "I have some." She rushes to her desk and opens a drawer, handing it to me. "Keep it."

"Thanks." I press my lips together and head back to the bathroom, adding a thick layer in hopes that it kills the itching. I could use some Benadryl, but I'd fall asleep in the middle of the field and get trampled. Or worse, get drowsy enough to confess how hot Nate is, telling everyone that he gave me a damn good kiss.

I'll pass on the account that I like my job and have already embarrassed myself enough to last me a lifetime.

When I head back to the art station, without the toy hat, Nate lifts his eyebrows.

"Not a word about her comment." I point a finger at him. "She doesn't know when to stop talking."

"She's being a mom." He shrugs, thankfully cool about the situation.

"Right, but my mom loves to give her opinion about everything and everyone, inserting herself into my life as she sees fit."

"She cares about you. Don't take her for granted. It must be nice to have someone that loves you that much."

I look at him, and he offers a forced smile before he walks away. What in the world does that mean? Does he not have a good relationship with his mom?

Nate has reverted back into the mystery I admire from afar. It seems there are layers to him left to discover, and it doesn't all have to do with his good looks and kissable lips.

chapter 15
LIZZY

On Sunday I got together with Dani and spilled about the kiss between Nate and me, and she squealed like crazy before congratulating me like I won a state championship. We spent hours talking about him, my hesitation because of grad school, and how the entire town is gossiping about us.

I also spent the rest of the weekend dodging questions about Nate from my mom and thinking about what Nate said before he walked away at the festival. I didn't see him again afterward since things got pretty busy with the kids and talking to parents.

He is an enigma. An enigma that kisses amazingly. But I want to know more about him.

I walk into my classroom, stashing my purse in the bottom drawer of my desk, and plop down on my chair.

"Whoa!" My arms fly out and grip the desk as the wheels slide and almost throw me off this thing.

This is not a good start to my Monday. I need coffee, even if it's the watered down version in the teacher's lounge. I should've stopped there first so I could hide out here the rest of the day. I don't want to hear anyone gossiping about the rash.

Thankfully, it's mostly gone now, and some concealer covers up the remnants of what I now call, Attack of the Face Paint.

Good times in the life of Lizzy.

As soon as I enter the teacher's lounge, I stop in my tracks and my heart jackhammers. Nate turns his head to see who the newcomer is and lifts his brows when our eyes collide.

Wonderful. I was hoping to avoid him for a bit until I could *not* be embarrassed about this weekend or prove I'm no longer daydreaming about our kiss. A kiss we never discussed, so I don't know what it means.

Maybe it was ignited by pity because I was at a weak point. Or he goes around helping girls and then locks lips with them.

You're standing in the doorway looking like a deer in head-lights. Move, Lizzy.

"Good morning," Nate says.

"Morning." My tone is flat and bored.

"How are you feeling? You look better."

"Yup, almost like new. Thankfully." I press my lips together and head to the coffee maker, grabbing my mug. We all have our mugs in the cupboard here for easy access.

"I brought my hat in case you needed to borrow it." His tone is teasing, and I cut my eyes his way in an attempt to glare, but when I see his smile, I shake my head and giggle.

"Thanks, but I'm good now." I point to my forehead as if he didn't know exactly where the rash was.

"Glad to hear it, though I'll miss the reptile metamorphosis." He smiles, stepping back from the coffee maker.

"Thankfully I left my reptile ways behind me." I serve myself coffee before glancing his way.

"Shame, I like reptiles."

My eyes widen and face twists in disgust.

"Eeewww. No!" I shiver.

"Oh, come on. Cute little lizards. They eat bugs." His fingers pinch together to show a tiny size when in reality some of the lizard families are like dragons.

"I rather the bugs than those devil creatures." I almost gag just thinking about it. At some point in my life I grew a phobia of anything lizard-family related.

"Devil creatures?" He laughs incredulously. "Snakes are devil creatures. Lizards are... I don't know what, but not a danger to humanity."

"Except that one time I went to the Dominican Republic on vacation and there were these Hispaniolan curly-tailed lizards that sting with their tail."

"Are you sure that wasn't a scorpion?" He bites back his smile.

"I'm positive. It was a lizard. Lizards, actually. Plural. The locals warned us to be careful, proving my theory that lizards are out to kill humanity."

At this he laughs boastfully, tossing his head back. "I don't think that's the case, but it's adorable that you do." He catches his breath and looks at me with sparkling eyes.

"Adorable?" I ask.

"Yeah, it's cute." He shrugs as if it's no big deal, but after the kiss we shared, I have questions. Mainly, what in the world is going on between us? And how can I sign up for more kisses?

I open my mouth to speak, but the door to the lounge opens, cutting my words off. Nate nods and steps away, masking his emotions into the perfect professional.

"Morning, ladies," he says as he exits the teacher's lounge and leaves me with giggling teachers that probably fantasize about his lips, too.

GUARDED DEPUTY

Except I know what it feels like to have his stubble scratching my face and his demanding mouth moving with mine.

I shiver and suppress the desire to touch my lips. Leaving the teacher's lounge with my head a mess, I sit at my desk and stare at the dry-erase board until I hear chatter outside my classroom and snap out of it.

Right now, I have work to do that does not involve daydreaming about Nate's body pressed against mine. That will have to wait until the day is over.

By the time lunch break comes around, I'm starving and in dire need of a conversation that doesn't revolve around the joke about why six is afraid of seven or making whale sounds after I showed them a video about ocean animals last week.

I respond to a text Dani sent me asking if I've snuck away into a closet and made out with Mr. Hot Deputy.

I burst her bubble telling her we haven't even talked about the kiss as I head to the lounge to eat.

"Watch it." Nate's teasing voice makes my head snap up.

"Hey." I pocket my phone on the outside pouch of my lunchbox and smile at him.

"How has your morning been?" He steps up to me.

"Long." I groan. "I wish my lunch break was an hour."

"Ah, perks of being a contract employee. I have an hour break." He winks.

"Now you're just being mean rubbing it in my face." I playfully shove his arm, and he doesn't even budge.

"I'd never be mean to you."

"I still need to decide on that." I smile coyly.

Nate bends his head and leans in until he's close to my ear. "From what I remember, you thought I was very nice on Saturday."

His breath tickles the shell of my ear, and I shiver before I'm able to control my body. Nate stands tall again with a cocky smile while I fail to keep my cool.

"About that," I begin.

"I'm sorry if I crossed a line," he says before I can get my thoughts in order.

"You didn't."

"Are you sure? I never want you to feel uncomfortable." His expression is full of honesty and gentleness that I want to get wrapped up in.

"I'm positive." A smile brushes my lips as we stand in the middle of the hallway staring at each other.

"Good, good." He rubs his hands together, but nothing like a cheesy cartoon villain. Nate's actions are as if he's contemplating what to do with me, and my body perks up at the options.

I'd bet my collection of coffee mugs that he'd know exactly how to make me feel good.

Nate clears his throat and I shake those thoughts out of my mind. A burning path creeps up my neck to my cheeks, and I have no doubt that my face is the color of a fire ant.

"I should go."

"Yeah, I need to have lunch." I lift my lunchbox.

We both step to the right and then the left in an attempt to move around each other. Laughing, I snort and cover my face.

"If you wanted to dance, you just had to tell me," he teases.

"Ditto." I stand still. "Go ahead first."

GUARDED DEPUTY

"Ladies first." He winks, and I get the sense that he lives by that philosophy in all aspects of life—in and out of the bedroom.

We may not have had an open conversation, but his attitude tells me he's clearly not thinking the kiss was a one-time thing.

"Thank you." I curtsy and freeze halfway.

Why did I do that? Who curtsies to the guy they like? As if I were in some royal movie.

Nate chuckles and heads in the opposite direction while I wonder if I can hide from him for the rest of the day. I take one step forward and three backward with him. It seems I'm destined to make a fool out of myself with this man.

Lunch is uneventful with school gossip. Because of my run-in with Nate, I have to eat faster than usual. I don't regret it, though. Those few minutes in the hallway with him were fulfilling.

Checking my mailbox before rushing to pick up my students from the cafeteria, I find a folded piece of paper. Curious about what it could be, I unfold it and read the small handwriting as I make my way to the cafeteria.

Lizzy,

I've kissed many women in the past. Wait, that came out wrong. I don't mean that the way it sounds. You're something different. Since the moment you called me a stripper, I knew you were trouble. That kiss was amazing, and I don't regret

FABIOLA FRANCISCO

*it in case you were thinking that, but I don't want
your work life to be a mess because of me.*

—Hot and Packing Deputy

I snort at his sign-off name and shake my head, a blinding grin
on my face. As soon as we're back in the classroom, I tell my
students to read a page from their science book and grab a paper
and pen.

A haiku for you

You didn't start the right way

But you are still cute

*This is the worst thing I've written, but I promised
myself I'd give you whatever I wrote on this paper.
I'm glad you don't regret it. It's not every day I go
kissing guys, even if they did take care of me when
I had a rash.*

GUARDED DEPUTY

—Lizzy

I fold the paper and look around my classroom, wondering how I can get this to him. Walker sits at his desk, focused on the page of his book. I should wait until the end of the school day and not use Nate's nephew as messenger.

That's what the responsible teacher would do. And that's what I am—Ms. Responsibility.

I stare out my classroom window on a sigh and smile to myself. Who knew accidentally calling 911 would lead me to meeting Nate. A meet-awkward for the books, and yet it's somehow turning out to be unexpectedly wonderful.

"Ms. A? Ms. Andrews? I'm done."

"Huh?" I look away from the window and stare at my students. They look at me as if I'm crazy.

I know, kids, I've lost my mind. We can all blame one tall, handsome deputy.

"Are you thinking about your boyfriend?"

"She doesn't have a boyfriend," one student argues.

"How do you know?" the other asks.

"Look at her hands. She doesn't have a ring like my mom does."

My students go off on a mortifying debate about my love life, arguing about whether or not I have a boyfriend, children, or am married. I clap my hands three times to settle them down.

"We're here for class, not to discuss my personal life." I stand, getting myself together.

147

Nate working at the school is not good for my heart or my job. That man is a distraction even when he isn't standing in front of me all six-foot-one glory with defined muscles and full lips.

chapter 16

Ms. A,

I can't stop thinking about you. I like that you stay in class during my lessons, but it's sweet torture watching you focus on work instead of on me. Tell me, do you also think about our kiss like I do? Because it's all I've thought about since Saturday. I shouldn't confess this, but I'm weak when it comes to you. All my truths tumble out of me.

Mr. Hot Deputy

ell

Mr. Hot D,

You can't confess these things while I'm at work.

Ms. A

ell

Lizzy,

Mr. Hot D sounds dirty, but I'm going to keep my thoughts to myself. Do my notes distract you? If so, I'm not sorry. I want you thinking about me the way I can't stop thinking about you. What's your favorite color?

Mr. Hot D

GUARDED DEPUTY

Mr. Hot Deputy,

Are we playing 21 questions now? My favorite color is lavender. Do you prefer sweet or savory food? And I don't need your notes to think about you, but I kind of like this old school way of communication.

Ms. A

Lizzy,

If 21 questions is the way I get to know you, then sure, we can play. I want to know everything about you. Whether we're playing a game or sitting somewhere together. I prefer savory food. Are you sure you're not a cat person?

Nate

Nate,

I am offended that you question my word. I have nothing against cats except that I'm allergic, so they lose by default. Do you like living in Emerald Bay?

Lizzy

Lizzy,

Emerald Bay takes some getting used to, but someone has made the adjustment worth it. I want to see you. If we were in high school, I'd tell you to skip third period and meet me under the bleachers, but you'd probably get in trouble for missing class, huh?
Nate

———

Nate,

Sorry to burst your bubble, but we don't have bleachers. And yes, I'd get in trouble. No secret make-out session is happening. Although, I'd like to see you, too. I have class all afternoon so no time for getaways.
Lizzy

———

Lizzy,

Never underestimate me. I don't need bleachers if you want a secret make-out session. If the lady wants a kiss, then the lady will get a kiss.
Nate

———

Nate,
That sounds like a promise you may not be able to keep.
Lizzy

———

GUARDED DEPUTY

Ms. A,
I never break my promises.
Nate

chapter 17

NATE

WHEN I LIVED IN Dallas, I focused solely on work. Brooke made me promise that I'd balance life and work when I decided to move to Emerald Bay, especially after a scare that I call my battle wound.

When a bullet graced my shoulder in a domestic violence incident, Brooke was terrified that my job would kill me.

After she lost her husband, I couldn't put that worry on her, and I moved here sooner than I had planned.

There are very little risks or gun wounds in this area, but there are greater risks like a certain tempting teacher who crosses my path almost every day.

"Smile, little bro. You look like I'm torturing you." Brooke laughs as we walk into the laser tag facility.

"Coming to a seven-year-old's birthday party is practically torture. You owe me dinner afterward."

"Whatever you want, it's on me."

When Brooke begged me to come with her since she doesn't know many of the parents in Walker's class yet, I begrudgingly agreed.

Now, these kids are my students in a sense, and it's awkward.

GUARDED DEPUTY

"Deputy Moore!" A boy calls out, waving at me as we enter the party area.

"Wonderful," I mumble while Brooke giggles.

"These kids admire you." She pats my arm.

"Yeah." I sigh, walking behind her and Walker, who's already racing off toward his friends.

Watching him interact with his new classmates makes me smile. I love seeing him become a part of the school when it could've been a harder transition for him.

Brooke says hello to the birthday boy's mom while I find us some seats in the small party room. I don't miss the way some of the parents look at me while whispering to each other. I bet those who are unfamiliar with me are becoming quickly acquainted with my role in the school through parent gossip.

"Deputy Moore, are you here to play laser tag with us?" Paul, the birthday boy, asks.

"Sorry, buddy. I'm here to bring Walker," I respond.

"Aw, man."

"I told you. He's too old to play with us," another boy, whose name I can't remember, says.

"Old?" I lean back and look at him.

"Yeah."

"I bet Ms. Andrews will play," Paul says, forgetting all about me as he runs toward the entrance. "Ms. A," he calls out excitedly.

I look in his direction and see Lizzy ruffling Paul's hair with a bright smile as she wishes him a happy birthday. I sit up straighter in my chair, curiosity piqued.

155

I may have seen her yesterday, but that was at work where I couldn't really spend time with her. This may just work out in my favor.

We've been sending each other notes throughout the week, and I feel like a thirteen-year-old with a crush.

"Well, well, well..." Brooke sits beside me with a shit-eating grin.

"What?" I arch an eyebrow and lean back in my seat.

"Someone perked up instantly when they saw a certain teacher walk in."

"You're ridiculous," I say.

"If I'm ridiculous, then..." She scrunches up her nose.

"What?" I tilt my head.

"I can't think of an analogy right now but you're ridiculous for lying." She crosses her arms, annoyed with herself.

I chuckle, shaking my head. "No analogy would work. You're ridiculous, and I'm—"

"Hey." I'd recognize Lizzy's sweet voice anywhere. And those lips.

"Hey, hi." I shift in my seat to get a better look at her.

"Hi, Mrs. Lundsten."

"Hi, Ms. Andrews. It's nice to see you." Brooke is failing at hiding her smile, and I want to kick her so she stops making this weird.

"You, too. I don't normally come to students' birthday parties, but Paul is a family friend and he begged me to come. I couldn't say no." Her unprompted explanation makes me smile.

"I'm sure he appreciates it," my sister says, cutting her eyes to me.

GUARDED DEPUTY

"I'm gonna go say hi." She points toward the rest of the parents, her cheeks turning pink.

She walks away without me getting a word in.

"I don't know what you're hiding. It's obvious she likes you, too," Brooke says once Lizzy is out of earshot.

"It's complicated," I tell her, not quite ready to tell her how things have progressed.

"Why? Because you work at the school? You're not hired by them."

"I know I'm not, but she is Walker's teacher and her uncle is my boss. Besides, you know people will talk, and I don't want her to get shit from parents." I shrug, stretching my legs out in front of me.

"That shouldn't matter. You are mature adults that can act professional."

When I don't say anything, Brooke speaks up again.

"If this is about Dad again, I'm going to record myself saying you're nothing like him so you can listen to it in your sleep. Maybe that will help get through to your brain. I know it's hard to open up to people, but it's worth a shot. Take your time. No one said you need to rush into marriage, but I want you to know what it feels like to be loved." Her smile is soft, carrying a hint of sadness.

"Yeah." I lean back in my seat, ending the conversation with my one-word answer like I've done my entire life.

Ever since we kissed, I've been dying to get Lizzy alone and try for round two. I should ask her out already, but there's still that voice in my head that tells me I'm all wrong for her.

She's sweet and kind, and I'm rough and broody. Although, she makes me smile a whole lot. Every time I find a folded piece

157

of paper in my mailbox, this unknown sensation fills me. Like my team is down seconds and the winning shot depends on me.

After the way we've communicated this week, I have no doubt I want to spend time with her, though. I need to first figure out if there are rules about teachers and students' family members dating. I don't want her getting into trouble.

Not to mention, I live with my sister and her son, and going out in public may cause a stir in this small town.

"Ms. Andrews will play laser tag with us," the boy who called me old announces, getting everyone's attention.

"Uncle Nate will, too, right?" Walker looks at me with round eyes and a slight pout.

"You know what? I changed my mind. Let's play." I stand and walk toward him. I refuse for him to think I don't want to spend time with him or for his friends to rag on him because I'm a boring elder.

I still can't believe that kid called me that. I'm going to show him my old man skills in that arena.

Lizzy raises her eyebrows when I look at her and hides her smile before she looks at Paul when he pulls her hand toward the guy by the counter who's carrying vests. He steals her attention from me, but I'll have her in a dark room. I should be able to outsmart these kids and find a corner to talk to Lizzy without an audience.

And by talk I mean taste those lips again as soon as she allows me to.

The guy hands out the vests, and then looks at me.

"Don't think this one will fit. Let me grab an adult size."

"Yeah, please." I won't fit into a small vest for kids, and I now have a plan in place propelling me to go into that dark arena.

GUARDED DEPUTY

"Get ready, Deputy Moore," Lizzy says as she cracks her knuckles and adjusts her vest.

"Game on, Ms. A." I smirk, knowing damn well I'm going to get her to myself once we're in that arena.

When we're ready to start the game, we enter the dark room brightened by glow-in-the-dark designs, and I keep an eye out for the boys while I search for my main target. I have other plans besides shooting her.

Laughter and voices carry through the dim place as I take confident steps in search of Lizzy. I look to my right when I hear giggling and lift my hands.

"Don't shoot," I tell her as I crowd her personal space in a tight corner behind a stack of tires used as a barrier.

"And let my guard down so you can take me out?" She keeps her gun pointed at me.

"If you take me out of the game now, I can't spend some alone time with you. I believe I have a promise to keep, Ms. Andrews." I smirk when she lowers the gun.

"What's that?"

Stepping toe-to-toe, I hold the side of her face. Lizzy sighs and tilts her head to look at me.

"Why haven't we been able to be alone this week?" I whisper.

"Because we work at a place full of nosy teachers and dependent children."

"We need new jobs," I joke.

"I very much like my job." She shoves me playfully, and then keeps her hand on my chest, above my beating heart.

"I'm starting to like mine, too. Are there any rules for teachers dating their students' family?" I lean my face closer to hers.

"I'm not sure. I've never had to look into it."

"Then, I better be careful until we're sure." I rub my nose against hers, and Lizzy breathes deeply. "I want to kiss you," I murmur.

"I do, too." Her confession is music to my ears.

My lips press against hers in a soft kiss. As soon as they meld together, I feel like I'm home. This is new to me. I'm no stranger to the female population, but when it comes to Lizzy, I could spend weeks kissing her and it wouldn't be enough.

Her hand comes around to my back, gripping my shirt below the vest I'm wearing, and her body flushes against mine.

I angle her head, deepening the kiss as my body reacts to hers. I need more. I'm growing desperate for this woman.

Her other arm comes around me, keeping me close to her as her lips move along my cheek to my jaw, soft kisses that make my skin break out in chills. I hold back a groan and press my other hand to her lower back.

"Your mouth is torture," I tell her.

"You're torture," she retorts. "We probably shouldn't be doing this."

"But it feels so good."

"It does." She moans softly, finding my lips again with her demanding mouth. She kisses me as if she's chasing an orgasm. As much as I want to push her there, this isn't the place for it, but I'm more determined than ever to get her alone in a private place.

This attraction is a burning sensation that sparks fire in my chest that intensifies the more I get to know her.

A loud clank scares the shit out of me, and I step back, breaking the kiss.

"What was that?" she whispers.

GUARDED DEPUTY

"My gun," I say, cursing to myself. "I dropped it by mistake." I bend to grab it from the floor.

Lizzy laughs as she places a hand on her chest. "It scared me."

"There they are!" a boy says.

"Shit. We've been caught," I tease her.

"Should we let them win or give them a hard time?" Her face glows in the neon green light, and I catch her arched brow.

"One of the kids called me old, so I'm taking him out."

"Nate, he's seven. You are old to him." Her voice of reason is no match for my pride, though.

"Whatever, I've got years ahead of me and amazing stamina." My voice drops.

"Stop it." She shoves my shoulder and lifts her gun.

I see the kid who made fun of me and point my gun to him. His eyes widen before aiming at me. I press the trigger to take him out so he knows not to mess with old men, but my vest vibrates.

"Got you!" Walker shouts, and I'm left standing there in shock while Lizzy laughs.

"You're supposed to be on my side, kiddo." I can't believe my own nephew shot me, although a part of me is proud of his aim. I didn't even see him amongst the group of three boys who found us.

"It's part of the game, Uncle Nate," he shouts as he races off, likely to hide from the rest of his opponents.

Lizzy's vest vibrates, too, and she looks at me with a shrug. Reaching for her face, I stroke her cheek and wink.

"We're not done, but it's time to play this game."

"You're on," she smiles and races away from me, each of us with four more lives left.

161

After twenty more minutes of playing without more kisses, we finish the game and walk out of the arena. The boys are laughing and talking about their moves and shots while I keep my eyes on Lizzy.

She shot me once, and I can't complain by the way she cheered and danced around right before another boy got her.

"Did you have fun?" Brooke asks.

"Yeah, but Walker shot me. I don't know if to be impressed or offended by the betrayal."

"He's your nephew after all. You'd expect him to have good aim." She bumps her shoulder with mine.

"I know." My eyes scan the room until I find Lizzy again, talking to Paul's mom.

"You should just ask her out," Brooke says.

"Maybe," is all I say.

I have big plans to spend time with Lizzy. I can no longer continue talking to her through handwritten notes when I want to have a real conversation with her, see her smile, and hear her laughter. And definitely kiss her again.

chapter 18
LIZZY

INTOXICATING IS THE PERFECT word to describe Nate's kisses. I feel like I drank my weight in wine and am spinning. Except I won't wake up with a killer hangover.

As much as I've enjoyed passing notes this week, I'd much rather see him in person, even if it is at a child's birthday party, although probably not the smartest idea, but I have no self-control when it comes to him.

Fighting back my feelings due to my career isn't working anymore. I like him a lot.

I say goodbye to the people at the party and search for Paul to wish him a happy birthday again. As I'm walking out of the building, I hear heavy steps behind me. Turning, I see Nate walking toward me with a sheepish smile that's nothing like I've seen on him before.

"You forgot to say goodbye to me." His smile turns arrogant, more like the man I've gotten to know.

"Oh, did I?" I ask coyly, fighting back a smile.

"I don't know how you could forget. I'm everything you think about."

164

GUARDED DEPUTY

I shake with laughter at his comment. He's way too cocky for his own good. As I catch my breath, I see he's getting closer and looking at me like I'm his next meal.

"As much as you do cross my mind, you're not the only thing I think about," I tease, though I have a careful eye on him as he approaches.

My breath catches when his hand cups the side of my face, and he strokes his thumb along my cheek.

"I'll have to make sure to overshadow the rest of the things on your mind because you're all I think about." My lips part at the intimate touch as I succumb to the sensation he creates in my body.

"Nate," I whisper.

"I know. I'm trying really hard to keep my distance. If anyone asks, I had a question about a lesson I wanted to do with your class. Go out with me. I can't stand this anymore. I wanted to keep things professional, but I'm not good at that."

"Neither am I," I confess.

"So let's see what this thing between us could be."

"How do you propose we do that?" I shift on my feet.

"By going out with me. I promise to be the perfect gentleman." He crosses an X over his heart.

"Really?" I arch an eyebrow.

"I can behave myself. I took care of your rash."

"And kissed me afterward," I counter.

"Do you blame me?"

"No, I know I'm a catch." I shrug and flutter my lashes.

Nate laughs, scratching the back of my head with his fingers. "Tonight," he whispers, leaning forward.

"Not here," I warn. We're out on the street, and I know people are watching. It won't take long for this encounter to join the rumors about our coffee non-date and dancing at the concert.

"I know. I'll pick you up, and we'll go somewhere. No need to give me your address, I have it logged in our 911 calls," he jokes.

"Har, har." Heat creeps up my neck.

"I love when you blush. It gives me insight to your feelings." He steps back, releasing my face. "Tonight, Ms. A. I'll be by your apartment at seven."

"Make it eight."

"You've got yourself a deal, and don't worry about people in town. I've got the perfect plan to make things private." He winks and walks away, leaving me rooted in place.

Snapping out of it, I walk to my car and drive home, calling Dani.

"Hey, sugar, what can I do for you?" She puts on her best Southern accent, which is terrible.

"I can't even." I laugh.

"It's my best so far. What's going on?"

"You're not at work are you?" I focus on the road, leaving my phone on speaker.

"Nope, worked in the morning. Do you want to do something tonight? I feel like I've been locked up at home and my neighbor is driving me insane." She practically growls.

She and her neighbor have a rocky relationship at best.

"I can't go out tonight. Nate asked me out." I bite my lip waiting for her reactions.

GUARDED DEPUTY

"Whaaaaat?" Her voice deepens in the most exaggerated way, like a donkey possessed or something, and I throw my head against the headrest as I laugh, tears springing to my eyes.

"Oh, my goodness. Do that sound again."

"Shut up and don't change the subject. Tell me *everything*."

"I saw him at Paul's birthday party, and we kissed inside the laser tag arena. When I was leaving, he followed me and asked me to go out tonight. I'm freaking out in a good way but also wondering if it's a bad idea to shit where I eat. Not to mention, I should hear back from the university soon." I tell her my doubts and hope she can provide wisdom.

"First of all, kissing at a kid's party? Girl, you're brave. Secondly, what are you afraid of? He's not technically a school employee. Thirdly, many people date and go to school and work. You won't be the first or the last. You can accomplish your dreams like a badass and be happy in a relationship. No one said you could only have one or the other."

"I know you're right. I've just waited so long to chase this goal that I get tunnel vision. However, Nate and I do work together." I remind her.

"Unofficially, but it could be awkward if things don't work out."

That is not what I wanted to hear from her, but it's the exact thought I've been having since Nate and I started this whole flirting slash kissing situation.

"Or if things don't work out, maybe I won't have to see him ever again because he'll decide not to continue with this job next school year."

Dani laughs. "We live in Emerald Bay. You're going to run into him. Besides, stop thinking about the worst case scenario before even going out with the guy. You could end up getting married."

"Oh, please." I sound appalled but my face heats, and I'm glad I have no witness to that reaction. Not that I think about marrying anyone right now, but something about Nate in my future, sharing intimacy, makes me flush.

"You never know, so go out tonight, enjoy it, and leave your doubts in the trash where they belong. Do not dare recycle them for another day."

"Yes, ma'am." I park my car in my spot and turn off the ignition. "Thanks for the pep talk." I get out and walk to my apartment.

"No need to thank me, but I expect a full update tomorrow morning since I'm doing the afternoon show at the station. We can have breakfast, unless…you're busy having your hot date for breakfast."

"Dani!" I shriek.

Her resounding laughter is the only response I get before she calls out goodbye and hangs up. With that image, I head to my apartment to get ready for my date. I promised myself I was going to enjoy my single status for a while and then a sexy deputy stormed into my life, making me throw that out the window.

"Hey," Nate says when I open the door.

"Are you a stripper?" I spit out without thinking to break the ice and imitate our first encounter.

He laughs and shakes his head. "Nope, but I'm also not here on official duty." He winks.

GUARDED DEPUTY

"Shame. I was looking forward to official stripping."

Oh, my God. Shut. Up.

"Sorry, I didn't mean that. I'm just...nervous and say the worst things." I look away from Nate, who's laughing at my expense.

"I like that you're nervous. It means you care about tonight." He reaches his hand out to grab mine, giving it a comforting squeeze.

"Of course I care." I widen my eyes. "If I didn't, you would not be here and I'd be in PJs watching *Gilmore Girls* repeats and eating cookie dough. Few things come between me and cookie dough."

"I'm glad I fall under that category." The crooked smile he gives me screams danger, and I'm about to hop on the ride without a seatbelt.

Mr. Hot (and Packing) Deputy is looking at me like I'm cookie dough. And I wouldn't mind if he took a bite.

"Are you ready to go?" he asks after a moment of silence where I'm lost in fantasy-land.

"Yeah." I step out of my apartment and lock up before walking toward his car together. I pause when I see the truck and smile. "I should've known a boy from Texas drove a pick-up truck."

"I'm here to feed your Texas stereotypes." He smirks.

"That's not..." I shake my head. "I meant, you look like the guy to drive a big vehicle." We get to his truck, and I pause, looking up at it, realizing just how high it is.

"I'm just teasing you, Lizzy." He chuckles, opening the door for me.

169

"Well, teased I was." Sometimes I question the things that come out of my mouth.

"Up you go. You think you can handle it, or do you need help?" He lifts an eyebrow in challenge.

"I've got this." I lift my foot onto the step and grab a hold of the handle above the door, hoisting myself and settling in.

"Impressive." Nate nods in approval and closes the door.

I admire his confident strides as he walks to the driver's side. When he brushes his hand through his hair, I take in the defined muscles on his arms through the scrunched up sleeves of his Henley shirt. Not to mention, the shirt fits him tight in all the right places, stretching over his broad chest.

Nate is strong and masculine. Being around him makes me feel more feminine, more safe. It's weird. I don't need a man to make me feel beautiful and yet someone like Nate brings out this innate delicateness.

"Seatbelt." His words break through my thoughts.

"Right. It's always the first thing I do in a car." I snap on my seatbelt and lean back on the cushion.

"I didn't say it before, but you look beautiful."

"Thanks." I smile, running my hands down my dress. I opted for a flowy floral dress with cap sleeves that could be dressed up or down since I wasn't sure where we are going.

"The other day when I was out for a run I found this secluded area near the beach. I thought we could go there and have a picnic. I promised I'd keep nosy people out of our date."

"Quite romantic, Deputy." I look over at him.

"I can be." He nods, focusing on the road. "I ordered a pizza to pick up, so once I grab it we'll be on our way."

GUARDED DEPUTY

"Sounds good." I sigh, listening to the soft hum coming from the engine and looking at Nate's profile every so often. His nose has a slight bump, as if he got hit when he was younger and it didn't heal properly. It adds character to his features.

The man is gorgeous, but besides that, he's interesting. I've seen him working with the kids and despite his hesitation at first, he's great with them. From what I hear, the high school students are also happy to have him.

"Are you gonna keep staring at me?" His lips twitch, and I snap my head to the front and hope like hell he doesn't see my blush. "I don't mind." He reaches for my chin and tilts my head, briefly making eye contact. "Go on, look at me."

"I wasn't staring," I reply lamely.

"You don't have to be embarrassed with me." Nate chuckles arrogantly, and I roll my eyes. "If you were the one driving, I sure as hell would be staring."

My heart leaps at his words, and I look at him with a soft smile.

"Really?" I ask because he doesn't seem like that kind of guy to stare at a woman.

"Yup. In fact, I think we should switch places and you can drive so I can take you in."

I shake my head with a grin at his ridiculousness and look out the window, noticing we're almost at House of Pies.

Nate is bringing out all the big guns on this date, and I know I won't be able to resist his charms. I already feel like I know a lot about him based on our notes and yet there's still more to discover. I hope he'll give me the chance to get to know all of him.

171

chapter 19
LIZZY

AFTER QUICKLY GRABBING THE pizza, Nate drove off to this secret location. The truck rocks as he drives down a path that opens up to the ocean.

"Wow," I breathe out as I lean forward on the dash when I see the crescent moon's reflection on the water. "So you brought me to Emerald Bay's make-out spot, huh?" I glance over at him.

"What?" His eyes widen as he turns the car to park in reverse so the bed of the truck is facing the water.

Laughing, I shake my head and open the door. "People come here for a reason." I wink and try to gracefully step down from the truck, but there's no way to be graceful climbing down this monster. I end up hopping down, my skirt flowing around me. A light breeze sweeps over me and the scent of the ocean fills my senses.

"I had no idea," he defends as he comes around to my side of the pick-up.

Thankfully, no one is here, and we'll get our privacy.

"How would you know?" I smile. "I'm only half-kidding, although teens do come here to make-out."

"Is that what you want?" He grunts, wrapping his arms around my waist and tugging me toward him.

172

GUARDED DEPUTY

My breath catches at his unexpected movement, and I place my hands on his biceps. Looking up at him, I want to beg him to kiss me, but we can't base our relationship on how compatible we are in that department. I want to know his heart.

"Maybe later. I'm hungry." I smirk and squeeze his biceps before taking a step back or I'll jump him right here.

"This place is beautiful." I look out at the peaceful water.

It's not quite a beach like he described it, but the water is a few feet away with some rocks and grass separating it, and we're near the entrance to the state park.

"I'm glad you like it. Come on." He opens the back door and grabs the pizza box from the seat.

I follow him to the rear and widen my eyes when I see that the bed of the pickup truck is covered in a thick blanket.

"We can sit on the ground if you prefer," Nate says.

"This is perfect." I look in awe when I realize there are some pillows and a cooler, too.

He places the pizza on the dropped tailgate and smirks, grabbing my waist. Nate lifts me until I'm sitting on the edge, but instead of moving back, he stays rooted between my legs, staring into my eyes.

His hands flatten against my body, moving slightly to my back. It tickles, but I'm more engrossed in the way his eyes shine. Involuntarily, my legs squeeze around his hips, and he smiles. My body heats, flames licking my skin as time stands still.

"Thank you," I finally say with a smile and reach up to comb my fingers through his hair.

Nate breathes out, closing his eyes. He's unguarded in this moment, expression soft. I like seeing this side of him.

"You're welcome," he says hoarsely.

Stepping away, he moves, lifting himself until he's sitting next to me. We scoot back onto the bed, and Nate pulls out some plates.

"You've planned it all."

"Almost. I forgot dessert." He presses his lips into a tight line.

"It's okay. I care more about the company than the food." I smile at him.

He grunts and serves me a slice of pizza before grabbing one for himself.

"I agree. I brought beer and wine. Which do you prefer?" He leans against the pillow and extends his long legs. My eyes swoop down his body to his strong thighs and back to his handsome face.

"A beer would be great."

He nods, reaching into the cooler and grabbing two beer bottles, popping the cap before handing mine over.

"This is amazing." I breathe out, seeing the stars starting to pop up against the dark backdrop of the night sky. While everyone in town knows this area, I don't come here often. It's further away from the town lights, so it allows the sky to show-off its magic.

"I told you I'd plan something private. Even if I had no idea what this area meant to people in town." His hand squeezes my waist and I squeal, throwing my body away from his.

Nate laughs, reaching for me again, but I move.

"I found a tickle spot." His tone is taunting.

"Nate," I warn. "I'm going to end up throwing my food, and you don't want to see me hangry."

"Maybe I do." He waggles his eyebrows.

"I'd eat you."

GUARDED DEPUTY

"Oh?" His eyebrows slowly rise. "Please do."

I realize how bad that sounds and shake my head. "Not like that. Wonderful." I cover my face. "I meant...never mind. There's no fixing this."

His laughter rings all around me as he tugs me to his side, keeping his arm around my back and leans in.

"I'm only kidding, Lizzy." His breath is hot against my neck.

I shiver at the soft sensation, turning my head to look at him before realizing that our lips practically touch. Our eyes lock for a moment, and then his dip to my lips. I lick them, wishing I could feel his kiss again even if it's been a few hours since we last kissed.

Nate clears his throat, leaning back, and breaking the tension.

"The pizza's going to get cold." His voice is husky.

"Yeah." I grab my slice and eat in silence.

"Did you always want to be a teacher?" he asks after a stretch of silence.

"I guess so. I knew I wanted to work with kids, and while the idea of being a counselor crossed my mind, I went into teaching. Last year, I got the courage to start the process to apply for grad school, and I start in the fall." I go for a second slice, devouring the flavorful combination of tomato sauce and mozzarella.

"Counseling, really?" His brows lift. "What the fuck!" he shouts, ducking his head.

"What?" Why would he react that way? I look over at him and widen my eyes. "Oh, my goodness." I laugh when I spot the seagull trying to steal his pizza.

"Crap." The slice of pizza flies out in front of us when Nate shakes his fingers. He then swings his hand left and right, trying to fight the bird. All he's gaining is for the seagull to continue pecking his fingers.

"I dropped it already, evil thing! Go grab it over there!" Nate yells.

I clutch my stomach, unable to stop laughing enough to help him. The seagull takes the pizza and flies away.

The bird makes a noise that sounds like it's cracking up, which makes me guffaw. "Is it laughing at me?" he asks incredulously. "Not only does it steal my dinner, it makes fun of me?"

"Oh, you think that's funny?" He reaches for me, his fingers tickling my ribs without remorse.

"Stop," I beg, laughing and twitching in his arms, trying to get away.

Now two birds laugh overhead, and Nate tenses. "I do not want to get a black eye from those animals. Listen to them!" He tries to imitate the noise they make, which sounds like laughter. "*Ha ha! Ha ha!*" He calls after them. "It's like they are straight up mocking me." He tilts his head back to look at them.

"That was hilarious." I giggle.

"I'm glad you enjoyed the show. Now, I'm afraid to eat anymore."

"And here I thought you were some badass deputy. I may have to change your nickname to Mr. Beat by a Seagull Deputy."

"Har, har. I can take on a seagull if it isn't a surprise attack." He crosses his arms and looks adorable as he pouts.

"You're cute when you're defeated." I jab my finger at his ribs, and he twitches.

"Careful or you'll be defeated in a tickle fight."

GUARDED DEPUTY

I arch a brow in challenge, ready to attack, but the seagulls laugh again and Nate stares up at their silhouette in the sky.

"I hope they fly away." He shakes his head and looks at me. "So, counseling?" He changes the subject back to our previous conversation, and I chuckle.

"Yeah. Either a school counselor or a child therapist. Although my job allows me to help children with their emotions as well as educate them academically, I've felt like something is missing." I polish off the last bite of my pizza and set the plate beside me. Now I'm also afraid of eating anymore in case the seagulls come after me.

"I can understand that. How did you get into teaching?" His body is slightly turned to mine, and his eyes are on me with attentiveness.

"I started substituting while I was finishing college and got offered a job soon after graduation. It's not always that easy to get a job in a small town, but I got lucky, I guess. I took it and told myself I could go to grad school later on. Four years later, I finally applied." I lift one hand, palm up.

"That's great. So you're going to stop teaching?"

"No. The program I applied for is online, so I'll be able to keep my job and go to school. I'll figure out how it'll work out once I have to do my internship. That is if I even get into the school." I tuck my lips between my teeth.

"I'm sure you will." He smiles encouragingly.

"How about you Mr. Deputy?"

Nate tries to stealthily grab another slice of pizza, barely opening the box and sliding it out. Sitting cross-legged and glancing around for seagulls, his knee presses into my thigh.

177

"When I was eighteen I knew I needed to make a decision about my future. I had a neighbor in Dallas who helped guide me—Mr. Braden. He was in law enforcement, so that influenced me."

"I think we all have adults like that in our past."

"Yeah," he says quietly.

"Do you miss Dallas?" I tilt my head.

"In some ways I do. I miss the buzzing energy from a city, having a variety of places to go out, the anonymity. I'm not used to people knowing who I am everywhere I go, even when we haven't met." He breathes out and turns his head to look at me.

"I bet it's a hard adjustment. I've never been to Dallas. Or Texas for that matter. I studied in FSU, and Tallahassee, while being our state's capital, isn't exactly a big city."

"It's different than this." He waves his hand. "But Emerald Bay has it's positive points, like a sexy teacher with no filter."

"Smooth talker," I tease. "Did you leave a trail of broken hearts in Texas?" I arch a brow.

"Nope." He finishes off his pizza without any more attacks and moves the half-empty pizza box to the side along with our plates and tugs me closer, keeping his arm around me.

"I doubt that." I challenge with a smirk.

"Are you the one with a collection of broken hearts?"

"Highly doubtful. You've had first-hand experience on the mess I am when it comes to the opposite sex."

"It's charming." He laughs.

"Right." I shove him playfully, but that only allows him to tighten his hold on me and pull me closer until I'm cuddling into his side.

GUARDED DEPUTY

His fingers brush my hair away as his eyes search mine. "You really are stunning."

I smile at his words and rest my head on his shoulder, looking up at the sky. "The stars are so bright in this area."

"They are." His fingers comb through my hair in soft strokes, making my skin break out in goosebumps. My body grows heavy at the constant sensation as I take in the bright dots.

"Tell me more about Mr. Braden." I hope I'm not pushing the limit, but he sounds like an important person in Nate's life.

Nate's muscles tighten beneath me. When he remains silent, I think he's going to ignore my request but then surprises me.

"I wasn't the best kid. I got into trouble, did things I'm not proud of."

I reach for his hand on his chest and lace my fingers with his as I give him the time to collect his thoughts.

"I didn't have support at home. My mom did her best to raise us, but she had to work like a dog in order to keep a roof over our heads, food on the table, and clothes on our backs. I was resentful, angry, and I took it out the wrong way, mingling with people who didn't have my best interest at heart."

"I'm sorry to hear that," I whisper, looking up at him.

"It's fine." He shakes his head.

"What about your dad?" I risk asking.

Nate grunts but remains silent.

"Sorry."

"You don't have to apologize, but I don't like talking about it."

"Then don't." I sit up and smile softly, hoping he sees the sincerity in my eyes.

179

"I want to. I haven't given many people the chance to get to know me, but I want you to."

"Why me?" I tilt my head.

"Because something about you makes me feel safe." He cups my cheek, and I lean into his touch, getting lost in the roughness of his palm.

"You make me feel safe, too." I blink my eyes open to find him looking at me.

Nate leans forward, pressing his lips to mine in a chaste kiss. When he leans back, his eyes shine with deep emotions, and his thumbs brushes my cheek. Staring into my eyes, he takes a deep breath.

"My dad abandoned us when I was a kid. I haven't seen much of him since then, and it made me harbor a lot of anger, confusion, and hatred. I took it out by going out, stealing, and treating people like shit. My mom deserved a better son, and fortunately, Mr. Braden took me under his wing. She got to see me become a real man and make something out of my life before she passed."

"I'm sorry." I frown, tears trying to build in my eyes but I don't want him to think I pity him. I feel for him, for the pain he must've felt, for the pain I'm familiar with when it comes to losing a parent.

"My dad died," I blurt out.

Nate's brows furrow, and my heart snaps as I get ready to tell him about my dad.

"He was in law enforcement. He was Chief Deputy, working with Roy. A criminal was let out early due to supposed good behavior, and then once he was out, he killed my dad in a shooting."

GUARDED DEPUTY

"I'm so sorry. I had no idea." He wraps me tighter in his arms, creating a cocoon of safety. "I saw your mom with a man at the spring festival and assumed that was your dad."

"That's Gary, my stepdad. I was little when my dad passed away, so I don't remember much about him, just loose memories here and there." I sniff, trying to keep my emotions under control. I always wished I had more time with him, especially when people tell me how much I remind them of him.

"Are you okay?" Nate whispers.

"Yeah." I lean back down, wrapping my arm around his chest and taking in the quiet and emotion-packed moment.

Nate's fingers caress my arm as we both get lost in our thoughts. It's comforting when it should be awkward considering it's out first date. I've never talked about heavy topics like this with someone so soon after meeting them.

I shiver as a breeze sweeps over me, sighing contentedly.

"Are you cold?" Nate asks, rubbing my arm.

"Just a chill."

"Let's go." He scoots up, and I want to fight him and keep him like this for a little while longer.

"I'm okay," I argue weakly.

"Your skin is covered in goosebumps."

"It'll pass."

"I know you want to stay like this longer, but I don't want you getting sick." He grabs my chin and kisses me hard and fast. "Do you think the coffee shop is still open?"

"They close at eight."

"We'll grab coffee another day then." He puts our empty beer bottles in the cooler and stashes our plates in the pizza box. "Don't want the seagulls choking on plastic."

"Look at you being kind to the enemy," I tease him.

"That little shit bit my finger." He scowls at the sky as if the seagull were watching him.

"And yet you're protecting him."

"What kind of deputy would I be if I didn't?" He gives me a blinding smile that makes him seem like pure temptation.

Bravely, I lean forward and kiss him before he has a chance to hop off the bed of the truck. Nate's arms are instantly at my waist, pulling me close to him until one of my legs drapes over his lap. I don't even bother to fix my dress. I'm too lost in him and the way his scruff scratches my skin in a delicious way that makes my entire body tingle.

Heat travels up my spine and fills my belly. His tongue tangles with mine, making me moan at the way his demanding lips take me.

Able to kiss him without reservations or fear of getting caught, I get lost in him. In the dark, with the saltiness of the ocean in the air, Nate and I take our time.

His hands roam down my back slowly as if feeling every dip and curve while his lips leave mine and trail hot kisses down my neck. Arching my back into him, I fight back a moan and hold the back of his head, keeping his mouth below my ear.

"Nate," I whisper.

"Hmm..." His tongue swirls along my sensitive skin.

"So...good." I'm breathless and desperate for more. My nails scratch his scalp and tug his hair.

How can kissing be this good? This enticing? This much of a turn-on?

I yelp when he grabs me until I'm straddling his lap, his erection bulging against me. I already knew he was packing, but

GUARDED DEPUTY

hot damn, I feel him very close to where my body is pulsing for him.

His hands move further down my back until they're trailing from my hips down my thighs.

"If I don't stop, I'm going to embarrass myself." His voice is hoarse.

I giggle, pushing myself into him, and he grunts.

"I may, too," I whisper, angling his head toward me so I can kiss him softly.

Nate opens his eyes, and I see hunger swirling in his gaze. A hunger that I feel in the pit of my stomach. Heated, desired, uncontrollable.

"I really like you, Lizzy, which means that I don't want to act on impulse and ruin tonight." His hand comes up my back, stopping in the middle to push me toward him. "We need to take our time. I want to get to know everything about you. I've never done the whole serious relationship thing with someone, but I want to with you. That means, being patient, even if it pains me." His lips are a breadth away.

I brush my fingers across his face and smile when his eyes shut. His chest rises and falls rhythmically as I trace each inch. I brush my lips against his and then drop a kiss on his cheek before moving to his ear.

"Who knew you were such a gentleman." I smile as I tease him, carefully moving off his lap and fixing my dress.

Nate's eyes burn into mine with desire. "I'm not usually this well-behaved, but you deserve it."

If they paid me a million dollars to frown, I still wouldn't be able to wipe the smile off my face. I'd live poor if it meant having Nate tell me all these sweet things. The tough guy I met doesn't fit in with the gooey center I'm discovering, and I love that there are so many layers of him to explore.

It's like the old Tootsie Pop commercial—how many licks does it take to get to the chewy center?

chapter 20
NATE

I GRAB LIZZY'S ARM as she walks past me and drag her into the hidden corner where I was just talking on the phone. I have her pinned against the wall in a split second.

"Whaa..." Her eyes widen as the word gets stuck in her throat, and I throw my head back and laugh at her terrified expression.

"Nate!" she hisses. "You scared the shit out of me." She slaps my chest as laughter rumbles out of me.

I drop a hard kiss on her lips, stealing her complaints.

"Sorry, but I had to see you and say hi." I haven't had a chance to talk to her at all today. "It was necessary for my health."

"Really?" She lifts a brow. "You know, I'm not a doctor."

"No, but you can be my nurse." I waggle my eyebrows. "Besides, your kisses are all I need to be cured."

"Are you calling yourself *Sleeping Beauty*?" She fights back a smile.

"Hell, I'll be every Disney princess if it means waking up to your kiss."

"You're funny." She relaxes and beams a smile. "It was quite a hello."

"Yeah?" I press against her, trailing my nose along her cheek.

GUARDED DEPUTY

Lizzy sighs, bringing her hands around my back, and I smile. Her touch is my kryptonite. She could weaken me with a single stroke, and I wouldn't even complain.

"We shouldn't be doing this here." She drops her hands from me, and I frown, staring into her eyes. "Don't look at me like that." She laughs. "I teach kids. I'm very familiar with the puppy-dog face."

Instead of responding, I deepen my pout, which causes her smile to break free.

"You, sir, are trouble." She points at me.

I push off the wall and put some space between us. It's a feat since I want to feel each curve of hers against mine for an indefinite amount of time, but she has a point.

Footsteps echo nearby, and Lizzy tenses. I hate that she reacts that way, but I can understand that she may want to keep our relationship out of school gossip. I wink and walk away from our hiding spot with my phone in my hand.

"Oh, Deputy, I hadn't seen you there." Ellen practically purrs, and I cringe but keep my smile in place.

"I'm glad I ran into you actually. I have a question about one of your students." I make up the lie so we can turn around and Lizzy can make her escape without raising any questions.

"Of course." Ellen looks at me attentively, and I wrack my brain for anything I could possibly ask the woman.

"Are Gina's parents divorced?"

Ellen narrows her eyes slightly and then nods. "They are. Is everything okay? Is there something we need to discuss? We can get together after school to talk about it." Her hand clutches my arm, and I keep my professional smile in place while stepping back.

FABIOLA FRANCISCO

"Everything is great. I must've confused her for someone else. I want to make sure I touch up on all the home situations during my lessons. Thank you." I walk away, hoping Lizzy didn't witness that and get the wrong idea.

When it's finally lunch break, I head out of school today, needing some fresh air. I haven't seen Lizzy again, and I know keeping my distance at work is the best option. There may not be any set rules about dating, but we don't need to get rumors started or have a kid catch us making out.

I drive out of the school parking lot toward the sub shop to grab something to eat. When I see a coffee shop on this side of town, I smile, formulating a plan. I eat quickly and head to the coffee shop, grabbing a caramel Frappuccino like Lizzy ordered the day we were at the concert. If anything, I hope it gives her an afternoon pick-me-up and makes her smile.

Back at school, I sneak into Lizzy's classroom since they should be at recess. I drop the cup on her desk, then get an idea. Grabbing a permanent marker from her pencil holder, I scribble, "You're my cup of coffee" and leave before I get caught leaving love notes.

Love notes. Me. When the hell did I become this guy? I blame the hypnotizing blue eyes and full lips that taste sweeter than caramel.

I step out of the classroom and run into Andrea, who raises her eyebrows and tilts her head with an accusing grin.

"I was dropping something off for Walker," I lie.

"I'm sure." Her smile widens. "This can be our little secret." She pats my arm as she walks by, and I stare at her dumbfounded.

188

GUARDED DEPUTY

Andrea is Lizzy's friend so I doubt she'll go off spreading rumors about me being in her classroom. Normally I wouldn't care if someone talked about me, but this involves Lizzy, and I don't want her to feel uncomfortable in her place of work.

Lizzy turns me into a mess when I'm used to being in control and stoic. I was able to remain that way when we first met, but the more I saw her, the more my armor chipped away until it crumbled. She's dynamite, and I have no chance against her.

I look out the office window and see Lizzy in the playground with her class. The kids run around, playing tag and catch. Lizzy sits on the edge of the play set and laughs with some of her students. She's a natural with kids.

One of the girls grabs her arm and tries to pull her to her feet, but Lizzy shakes her head. The others cheer her on, nodding their heads. I smile, waiting to see what she does. When she stands, the girls high-five each other.

Lizzy stands on the platform she was sitting on and holds on to the monkey bar. I hide my smile with my hand and stare on. She looks around, biting her lip. What is she looking for?

Then, she tucks her dress skirt between her legs, and I chuckle. The secretary looks at me with raised eyebrows.

"Sorry, just a note a student left me. Kids. They're funny, right?"

"They are," she says.

I look back out the window and watch in time for Lizzy to move through the monkey bars with impressive endurance. When she reaches the end, she drops her hands and her skirt balloons around her as she lands on her feet. A sliver of pink shows but nothing more. Instantly, her hands cover her skirt, and she looks around with wide eyes.

I guffaw, slapping the desk.

"Are you okay?" The secretary is looking at me, her nose scrunched up.

"Yup." I press my lips together as another chuckle passes through me, and I put my head down to avoid the secretary's judgmental gaze.

When I glance up again, I don't see Lizzy's class anymore, so she must be getting back to class now, and I wish I could see her reaction when she finds the Frappuccino.

chapter 21
LIZZY

MY FACE HEATS, AND I hope I didn't flash any of my students when my skirt went up as I hopped from the monkey bars. I should really start wearing biker shorts under my dresses when I wear them for work. It would lead to less situations where I'm wondering if anyone became acquainted with the color of my underwear.

Thankfully, none of my students mentioned anything so I should be in the clear.

"Line up," I call out, standing by the wall in the playground.

"Already, Ms. A?" One of my students complains.

"Yup, you got five extra minutes. Now, we get to do science." I smile widely and clap my hands, overdoing my excitement, and he frowns.

Same, kid. I never liked science either, so I try to find fun activities to enhance my students' learning.

"Boys, let's go," I tell a small group of boys that are still running around the playground. "Now," I say firmly, and they look at me and race to the line.

"Hey!" A girl yells when one of the boys accidentally pushes her in his attempt to win the race.

GUARDED DEPUTY

I need patience today. It's the *Monday-est* Monday that ever *Monday-ed*, and I'm over it.

We walk back to the class and the children get settled in their desks, some already taking out their science workbook before I even have to ask. At least they're cooperating in small ways. Nothing pricks my patience more than having to repeat something a million times when it's clear they hear me and choose to ignore me.

My steps falter as I get to my desk, finding a Frappuccino I definitely didn't buy. I grab the cup, condensation cooling my hand, and see words scribbled on the plastic.

You're my cup of coffee.

I can't fight the smile that covers my face. Happiness swirls inside of me, and I hold back a squeal because that would be more embarrassing than my underwear flashing if my students were to ask what I'm so happy about.

I take a satisfying sip and place the cup back on my desk, getting ready for class.

"Ms. A, who gave you that?" Dana, a student, points to my cup.

"Oh, just a friend." I wave her off, focusing on the lesson about the different habitats.

"Was it Ms. Church?" another student calls out. "She's your best friend."

"Maybe it was her boyfriend," another calls out.

My eyes widen, and I shake my head. "It doesn't matter. Let's focus on the class." I clap my hands.

I go over the five main habitats, explaining the characteristics of the first when another student interrupts me.

193

"Ms. A, shouldn't it say, *I'm your cup of coffee* and not *you are* since it's written on the cup?"

I sigh, rolling my head back. Goodness, who knew a Frappuccino would create such an upheaval in class?

"That looks like Uncle Nate's handwriting," Walker speaks up, and I almost throw my marker at him. I wouldn't really hit him with it, but why did he have to say that?

"What?" I squeak. "No." I shake my head.

"He scribbles like that and my mom always calls it kitchen scratch," Walker adds, willing to demonstrate his point.

I chuckle and correct him. "Chicken scratch."

"Yeah, that." He shrugs.

"Is Deputy Moore your boyfriend?" Dana's eyes shine with mischief.

"No. I'm not sure who gave me this coffee, but it was probably Ms. Church."

"Then you shouldn't drink something from a stranger. That's what Deputy Moore taught us." Stephanie crosses her arms, full of sass.

"Boys and girls." I slightly raise my voice. "We have work to do. The coffee was from a friend, and that's all that matters. We're here to learn." I widen my eyes, pretending to be in control, when in reality my heart is pounding so hard.

Of course Walker would recognize his uncle's handwriting. Children are smart and perceptive. I pray he doesn't bring it up to anyone else, or that any of the other students tell their parents that Deputy Moore gave me coffee.

I'd rather leave my personal life outside of these doors where it belongs.

GUARDED DEPUTY

By the time the school day finishes, I'm anxious. My classroom door opens, and I look up from my computer to see the man who's tortured my thoughts all afternoon walk in with a grin.

"I was expecting a thank you text at the very least." He gives me a lopsided smile.

I stand, walk around my desk, and cross my arms.

"I was being interrogated by my students, so I didn't have a chance to text you."

"Oh?" He tilts his head, getting closer.

"They had questions about who gave me the coffee, if it was my boyfriend or Ms. Church. Why it said you're my cup of coffee on the cup when the writing should've specified *I* since the cup is the cup." I'm rambling and making no sense, but Nate chuckles.

"Kids definitely have a way of observing things in black and white."

"Tell me about it."

"Did you tell them who it was from?" He's challenging me with his raised eyebrow and smirk.

"I didn't have to. Walker recognized your handwriting." I shoot back.

His eyes widen slightly before a curse falls from his lips. "I didn't think about that."

"Apparently your sister calls your handwriting chicken scratch."

"I'm going to kill him," Nate mumbles.

"He's a kid. He said what he knows." I shake my head. "I diverted the conversation, but he might ask you about it."

Nate nods with his lips pressed into a straight line. "I'm sorry. I didn't think he'd realize it. I don't want you to feel awkward or uncomfortable."

I smile, reaching out for his arms.

"No need to apologize. I owe you a thank you. That was a sweet surprise."

"I did good, right?" He smiles.

"You did." I lean against my desk, my own smile wide.

"I'm glad you liked it. Since we couldn't grab coffee on Saturday, I thought I'd bring it to you today. Although, I wish we were having it together."

"I would've liked that."

He steps closer, almost encasing me against my desk. "I like hearing you say that. I'll make it happen. We can't hide our relationship from others forever."

"Relationship?" I tease him. "We've only gone on one date." I bite back my smile when his eyebrows quirk.

"One date or a hundred, it's the start of our relationship. And the kids were right, I am your boyfriend."

"Already?" I smile teasingly.

"I'm not looking for anyone else, babe. You're who I want."

I love hearing him say that. What I do know about Nate is that he's not one to show his emotions to many people. He can be mistaken for a grump, but he's open with me. It makes me want to hug him tightly.

Okay, not true. It makes me want to do a lot more than hug.

"By the way"—his voice drops—"the color pink suits you."

I lean my head back, eyebrows furrowed and look down at my outfit.

"I'm not wearing pink."

GUARDED DEPUTY

"Not up here, but..." His fingers softly stroke my knee where my dress ends.

My heart lurches as my eyes bug out. "Oh, my goodness."

Nate laughs, wrapping his arm around my waist.

"Don't worry. I think I'm the only one who saw it," he whispers in my ear.

"I want to die. I was so mortified when it happened and relieved none of my students said anything."

"I'm not your student, and I couldn't tear my eyes away from you as you played with them. It's sexy seeing you be so kind to these kids."

My breath falters, heat consuming me. If we weren't at work, I'd sit back on this desk and kiss him until we were both breathless.

"Oh, sorry!" Nate and I snap out of our bubble, and I look over his shoulder to see Andrea standing inside my classroom.

Nate jumps back, hands in his pockets, and takes a deep breath.

"We were just, uh, discussing a lesson."

"A lesson in chemistry," Andrea says.

"Andrea," I hiss.

"What? You two were making fire or something. Is it hot in here?" She fans herself as she laughs.

"I'm gonna go." Nate grimaces.

I shake my head so he doesn't worry about it.

"Goodbye, Deputy." Andrea wiggles her fingers at him, and his cheeks turn pink. Straight out blushes. I think this is my new favorite version of him. Who knew Nate Moore, Hot, Broody, and Packing Deputy would ever blush?

Once he leaves, Andrea raises her eyebrows.

"I knew something was going on when I saw him sneak out of your classroom earlier."

I sigh, biting my smile. "Don't tell anyone?"

"Your secret's safe with me, although I'd be more careful. You wouldn't want a parent to walk in and get the wrong impression of what you do during work hours."

"I know. He came by to say hi, and we got a little carried away."

"I could see that." She giggles. "You and the deputy. I must say that I saw this coming a mile away and very much approve." She nods with a smile.

"I like him a lot," I confess.

"What's not to like?"

"I know. He brought me a caramel frap today just because. He's sweet beneath that tough exterior. And man, can he kiss."

"Tell me more!" Andrea teases.

I shove her shoulder and shift on my feet.

"What's going on?" I switch subjects.

"Nothing. I was bored."

"Lucky you. I need to grade and don't feel like it." I sit at my desk and she grabs a student's chair.

"I caught up during music today. It feels like Thursday and it's only Monday. This week is going to drag."

"I thought it was just me," I tell her. "I'm ready for summer break."

"Two months." She smiles.

"Two very long months." I lean back in my chair and sigh.

"Which you will spend with your hottie deputy." Her eyebrows dance on her forehead.

"Stop." My cheeks burn, and I shove her shoulder.

GUARDED DEPUTY

"I'm only speaking the truth. Anyway, I'm going to go. I'd say don't miss me, but we both know your mind is on a certain hunk in uniform."

I laugh as she walks out of my classroom and I slump back in my chair. My mind is definitely on Nate. On the way he kisses me, his confident hands holding me, and the deep husk in his voice when we're close. He gives me the sensation of being on a roller coaster. My stomach bottom's out as I drop into the unknown, and yet it's exhilarating.

chapter 22
LIZZY

"I DIDN'T PEG YOU for someone who loved kayaking," Nate says behind me as we paddle through the water in Emerald Bay State Park.

It's been a long week, but spending my Saturday with him was worth the wait. Not to mention the few stolen kisses at work. Even when he's at the high school on Tuesdays and Thursdays, he sends me messages that make me smile.

The sun shines down on us, heating my shoulders. The water is still as we slice through it with no real direction. Mangroves are in the near distance, creating a forest that looks peaceful from the outside if it weren't for the mosquitoes that surround them.

"That's quite a stereotypical observation," I toss back at him.

"It is," he replies honestly. "But after our awkward run-ins and your accidental call I would think you were better off on land." His tone is teasing, and I smile, splashing water behind me.

"Hey!" he argues.

"Oops, I must've calculated wrong. It's my incoordination." I feign innocence, smiling over my shoulder.

"Right."

Water hits me a moment later, and I jolt.

GUARDED DEPUTY

"What in the world, Nate!"

"It's my strength. I pushed too hard." He mocks me.

"You little..." I try to splash him again but miss, making the kayak rock. My heart drops. Tipping over in the middle of the bay is not my idea of safety first. That and I have terrible lungs when it comes to holding my breath for a determined period of time.

"Whoa..." Nate calls out.

"Sorry," I squeak. "I'll behave."

"At least until we get to land." His double meaning hits me, and I shiver. "You naughty girl," he says when he sees my reaction, his fingers brushing along the back of my neck to my right shoulder.

"You totally meant it in a naughty way." I hate that I'm not looking at him.

"I can't help that you drive me wild." His finger strokes my top vertebrae, and who knew that that spot would cover my skin in goosebumps? "I see you reacting to me." His voice is husky.

"You could look at me and I'd react," I mumble.

The man has a direct line to my sensitive spots. One look, one arched eyebrow, one tiny tilt of his lips, and my internal Nate alarm goes off like I may die if I don't respond.

He's not good for my health.

"I heard that," he says.

"You're lucky you're cute."

"Cute? I thought I was hot?" I hear a smile in his voice.

"Goodness, I need to stop telling you things that will feed your ego."

"My ego is the perfect size and so is my—"

"If you finish that sentence, we end here."

Nate's laughter booms around us, rocking the damn kayak to the point I grip the sides because it feels like we're about to tip.

"Nate!" I yell, but he keeps on laughing.

"Babe, the fact that you thought I was actually going to say that shows how much you still have to learn about me. I'm a man of action not words. I think it's time we go back to shore and enjoy the beach."

"Okay." I'm at a loss for words based on his previous comment, and I'd rather him show me what he means instead of asking.

We paddle back to the shore, turn in the kayak, and then Nate's dragging me down to the beach area a few feet away. He rips his t-shirt off, giving me an uninterrupted view of his very defined chest and abs. I mean, wooheee. I knew he had to be fit and muscular, but he is on another level.

Each muscle on his body is defined and perfectly sculpted. I need to meet the artist who created this fine man and thank him. Oh right, that would be him and his workout regime.

"Are you going to stare or strip?" One side of his mouth lists in a smile.

"You are sassy today." I point a finger at him before unbuttoning my shorts and sliding them down my legs.

Nate's eyes don't leave my body, trailing my movements as if he were the one undressing me. It feels like foreplay.

Once I've removed my clothes covering up my bathing suit, he grabs my hand and leads us to the water. The soft waves crash on the white sand, and the smell of salt infiltrates my senses. The beach is my home. If I could turn into a mermaid and live forever in the water, I would.

GUARDED DEPUTY

As soon as my feet hit the water, I sigh. It's a hot spring day, and I could use a reprieve from the heat.

"The water feels amazing." I look at Nate, covering the sun from my eyes.

"It does." His smile is dazzling.

We go deeper in until we're mostly covered by the ocean. I smile at Nate as I bounce from foot to foot, staring at his gorgeous face. This man does things to my heart, making it flip and soar.

His hands reach for my waist, pulling me to him.

"Hi." He smiles timidly, and for a moment he looks like a vulnerable man.

"Hi," I whisper, placing my arms around his neck.

"Have I told you how beautiful you are?" He brushes away a strand of hair stuck to my cheek.

"I'm always willing to hear it." I smile.

"You're beautiful." He brushes his lips against mine.

I pout when he pulls away, and he chuckles.

"We don't want to make a show out in public. After all, you're an admirable teacher and I'm a man of the law."

"We are quite the example of morality in our town."

"But behind closed doors we can break all moral codes," he leans in and whispers, and my body heats to the point where the water may boil around us.

"You really are trouble." I jab his chest.

"Trouble is fun."

"And dangerous." I lift a brow.

"Nah." He shakes his head. "All fun." His hand flattens on the center of my back, the rough pads of his fingers tingling my bare skin. "Wanna bet?" He smirks like a sinner trying to lead me down the path of no return, and I'd follow him without a doubt when he looks at me as if I'm his favorite meal.

"By all means." I play along.

His hand moves further south, stopping at the base of my spine.

"Is this okay?" he whispers.

I nod, staring into his eyes. I love that he asks.

He rubs his nose back and forth on mine, and I pull him closer, enjoying this quiet, intimate moment. Our bodies are flush, and I can feel his chest against mine, rising and falling peacefully with each breath. I tilt my head and smile at him, wanting nothing more than to freeze this perfect moment and frame it so I can look back on it in the future and remember what it felt like to be cocooned in Nate's arms.

Until a stinging pain hits my leg.

"Ow!" I yelp and jump away, grabbing my foot and looking at the water.

"What happened?" Nate's eyebrows pull together as he stares at me while I hop away on one foot and release a slew of curses.

I see a jellyfish a few feet away and scream, running to the shore, which is almost impossible in water and with an injured leg.

"That's colorful language and all, but you need to tell me what happened. Are you hurt?" Nate is right behind me.

My leg throbs and stings at the same time. It's a pain I've never felt before, and I stare at Nate with my mouth open. He looks at my leg and drops to his knees to check it out. Welts are already forming on my skin. I take a deep breath to try to ease the pain, but it's pointless.

"A jellyfish stung me." I get out through my heavy breathing.

GUARDED DEPUTY

"What?"

"It hurts." I cringe. "Pee on it!" I stare at him as if he could be my savior.

"What? Why?" He jumps on his feet and backs away as if I'm going to grab him and milk pee out of him.

"That's what they do in *Friends*." I pierce my nails into my skin right next to the sting in hopes that the pain from my nails will ease the other. It's a stupid attempt.

"This isn't a sitcom!" he yells.

"My skin feels like it's on fire. Nate, help!" Tears burn my eyes from the pain. "Just pee on me."

"I'm not about to whip out my dick and pee on you. We haven't even gone to second base." He throws his hands in the air.

"What does second base have to do with anything? This is a medical emergency. Come on. This stings like a mother..." I trail off when I see a family with young kids staring at us.

Great, I can't even curse right now.

"I'm taking you to the doctor."

"Fine." I huff and limp away while Nate grabs our things. Just my luck to get stung by a sea creature. If I were a mermaid, this shit wouldn't happen.

I'm silent on the drive to the doctor's office, focusing on my breath and shaking my leg. What if I'm allergic to jellyfish and never knew it? Is my chest tighter than before? My hand presses against it, hoping that'll help me breathe easier, which makes no sense. Maybe the poison or whatever jellyfish release into my system is going to my brain and frying brain cells.

"Are you okay?" Nate asks quietly.

"I am not okay. I want to cut my leg off."

205

"You don't mean that."

I glare at him and squeeze my leg. "Does it look more red to you? I think the swelling is worse. Does their venom affect the nervous system or something?" I swear I've become a hypochondriac with age.

"Take a deep breath, Liz." Nate's hand lands on my thigh, squeezing comfortably.

"I'm trying, Nate, but someone didn't want to pee on me to ease the pain," I grit out.

"Again with the peeing. That probably doesn't even work."

"It does," I argue.

We pull into the parking lot in front of the practice, and I struggle to step out of his truck. Nate bends and carries me.

"What are you doing?"

"Making this easier for you."

"Now you react to help me."

"Lizzy," he warns. "I'm not peeing on you."

"Whatever." I sigh, shaking my head.

He walks straight to the counter, and I groan when I see there are quite a few people here. Everyone looks at me, and embarrassment consumes me. I'm tempted to hide my face in Nate's chest, but that might raise even more questions, starting with why our new deputy is carrying me while we're both wet.

"Lizzy, are you okay?" Mrs. Williams, one of my mom's friends asks with wide eyes.

"Uh, huh."

"She got stung by a jellyfish," Nate offers.

"Oh no, dear." Her hand lands on her chest.

The woman sitting next to her frowns and looks at Mrs. Williams, both of them talking about how unfortunate it is to

GUARDED DEPUTY

get stung but how lucky I am to have a strong man help me. Nate snickers upon hearing them, and I roll my eyes.

"This is going to feed your ego," I whisper.

"I'm glad you're back to joking. Honestly, how are you?" His eyes reflect concern.

"I've been better." I try for a smile. "But I appreciate having a strong man help me," I tease.

"You'll be okay."

"What's going on, Lizzy?" the receptionist asks.

"I got stung by a jellyfish." I frown. "Any chance Dr. Grant can see me?"

"Of course. Take a seat, and he'll be with you as soon as he can."

I thank her, and Nate walks us to a set of empty chairs. He carefully drops me on a seat before sitting down himself.

I take deep breaths, trying to keep my mind off the pain while Mrs. Williams sparks conversation.

"Deputy Moore is kind to take care of you," she tells me.

"Mm-hmm." I nod.

"Your mother didn't tell me you two were dating."

"I'm sure you will both talk about it soon." I just know that everyone is town will hear about this.

I try to keep polite conversation with Mrs. Williams, and I'm grateful when they call her name.

"She's nosy, huh?" Nate whispers.

"Yup. Get ready for people to talk even more about us." I shake my head, keeping my voice down.

After another few minutes, Dr. Grant calls me in. I stand carefully and wobbly toward an exam room with Nate holding most of my weight.

207

Dr. Grant smiles and takes a look at my leg. "I heard you got stung by a jellyfish."

"Yeah."

He starts observing the sting and plucking the visible tentacles. Then, he gives me an ointment to apply to the affected area after I soak it in hot water at home to ease the pain.

"Can you tell my friend here that he could've helped by peeing on me and it isn't a weird petition?" I tell Dr. Grant.

"Actually, that's a myth. Urine would make it worse."

My face falls as he says this and Nate smirks.

"You see. Don't take medical advice from TV shows." He crosses his arms.

"I can't even right now." I hide my face with my hands.

"Make sure to stop by the pharmacy and buy the ointment you need. Apply the cream twice a day." Dr. Grant instructs before I thank him and leave.

Nate carries me back to his truck, tucking me into the seat before pulling out of the parking lot.

"Aren't you glad I didn't pee on you?" Nate asks once we're on the road.

"Shush." I lean back in my seat, squeezing my eyes shut at the pain and hoping the cream Dr. Grant put on kicks in soon.

This is a nightmare. Not only did I ruin an amazing date, I likely got the rumor mill running wild with him carrying me into the doctor's office.

"We'll stop by the pharmacy to grab the cream and then head to your apartment," Nate says.

He pulls into the pharmacy parking lot a few minutes later and looks at me. "I'll go grab it. Wait here."

"Don't think I'll be moving much." I shake my head.

GUARDED DEPUTY

He smiles and steps out of the truck, walking into the pharmacy. I check my phone to see if I have any messages from my mom about people seeing me with Nate, but it seems the news hasn't reached her yet.

Nate's back out in a few minutes with a small bag. His steps are confident, and he aims a smile my way.

He opens the car door and gets in before driving to my apartment and parks in a guest spot.

I'll help you soak your leg." He opens the car door, ready to step out.

"You don't have to."

"Don't argue with me, Lizzy. I'm taking care of you."

My shoulders slump, releasing tension, and I nod. "Thank you."

"No need to thank me."

He comes around and helps me down from the truck, keeping his arm around my waist as we make our way to my apartment. Despite the sweetness he's giving me, I am still so humiliated.

"In you go." He kisses the side of my head when I open the door and limp into my home.

Nate doesn't hesitate to walk straight for the bathroom and fill up my tub with hot water, using my kitchen thermometer to measure the water temperature. Once he's certain it's at the temperature the doctor indicated, I sit on the edge of the tub and soak my leg. I jolt at the heat but immediately get used to it, especially when the water starts to ease the pain.

"Better?" he asks after some time.

"Yes. Thank you." I reach my hand out to hold his. "I'm sorry for being such a jerk."

"It's okay. Not everyone is cool when injured," he teases.

"I'm uncool most times, but especially around you." I shake my head. He chuckles, squeezing my hand.

"Relax, babe. I'm going to get you some water." He kisses my forehead and leaves me alone in the bathroom, sighing softly.

chapter 23
NATE

I'VE DISCOVERED SOMETHING NEW about myself that I had no idea was hidden beneath layers of cynicism. I would kill anyone or anything that hurts Lizzy. I've never felt this need to protect someone, make their pain disappear.

Except you wouldn't pee on the sting.

My conscience isn't letting that one go. Of course I wasn't going to pee on her. I knew it likely wasn't a solution, and there were people watching. I don't think Emerald Bay's deputy should be swinging his dick around, urinating in public.

My priority was making sure Lizzy was okay, and a professional was the most apt person to care for her in that moment. Now, I'm the one that will be certain she fully heals. I'm not leaving until I'm positive she's okay.

I grab two water bottles from the fridge and head back to the bathroom. Lizzy's eyes are closed, her hands on either side of her, gripping the side of the bathtub. Her face is sun-kissed, and the bridge of her nose and her cheeks are a darker shade of red.

She looks beautiful and innocent. She looks like the woman you bring home to mom. Hell, she is the woman I would've taken to meet my mom, and I know my mom would've loved her.

GUARDED DEPUTY

I clear my throat, swallowing down my emotions, and Lizzy blinks her eyes open, smiling over at me. My heart beats to a faster rhythm as our eyes make contact.

"Didn't mean to disturb you." I awkwardly stand by her, handing her the water bottle.

"Thanks, and you didn't disturb me. I was just resting my eyes."

I chuckle, finally moving to sit beside her but facing the opposite way. "Are you feeling better?" I bump my shoulder with hers.

"Yeah, the warm water surprisingly helps a ton." She takes a sip of water and then places it on the ledge between us.

"I'm happy to hear that. It wasn't that I didn't want to help you when you asked me to pee on you, but I just didn't think that was the right move. I'd never want you to think that I wouldn't help you if you were hurt."

Lizzy's cheeks turn a deeper shade of red that has nothing to do with the sun, and I smile.

"Have I already told you how mortified I am?"

"A few times." I chuckle. "It's okay, Murphy." I hold the side of her face, brushing her cheek with my thumb.

"Murphy?" Her brows dip.

"You're the embodiment of Murphy's Law."

"I am, aren't I? I need to think before I speak or act." She shakes her head.

"Nope. I like you the way you are."

"Even when I call you a stripper and Mr. Hot Deputy?" She bites her bottom lip.

"Especially that." I wink, pulling her to me and kissing her lips.

213

Lizzy leans back with a lazy grin.

"How's your leg? Do I need to add more hot water? The doctor said to soak it for about thirty minutes, and it's only been fifteen." I stick my hand in the water to test the temperature. "The water's getting cold. Let me turn the hot water back on."

I move toward the faucet, and Lizzy tugs me toward her by my shirt.

"I'm okay." Her smile grows.

"Just let me." I lean toward the faucet.

"Honestly." She pulls me toward her, and I lose my balance, sliding back and into the tub, hitting the back of my head with the wall. My legs hang over the edge in an awkward position. Thankfully I'm still in my bathing suit.

"Oh, damn." Lizzy slides into the tub, water sloshing over the side, to look at me. She grabs my head. "Are you okay? I didn't mean for that to happen."

I rest my head against the wall and laugh. Lizzy is trying to get to the back of my head, but I can't catch my breath or stop laughing.

"Are you hurt? Did you get a concussion and now you're delusional?"

"I'm okay. My back might be a little sore but at least I'm already soaking it in warm water." I reach for her.

"I'm sorry. I just wanted you to relax and not worry about me, and look what happened."

"Let's get one thing straight right now." I look into her eyes and make sure she's paying close attention. "I'm always gonna worry about you."

Her eyes widen and lips part before a smile takes over. "Really?"

GUARDED DEPUTY

"Yeah, so let me take care of you and stop being stubborn."

"I think you're the one that might need some taking care of." She places her hand on my chest and leans closer. My body buzzes where her hand is, an odd sensation that's beyond being physically turned on.

Her lips timidly brush along mine at first as if testing my reaction. Or maybe she's testing her own boldness. I wait for her next move, and her fingers clutch my soaked shirt as she leans in again. When her lips touch mine, I peek my tongue out and run it along her lip.

"Nate," Lizzy whispers.

"What do you want?"

"You."

I wrap my arm around her waist and pull her to me so she's on my lap. It's the most uncomfortable position I've ever been in while kissing a woman, but I don't give a shit. I could be suspended upside down and so long as Lizzy's lips are on mine, I'd be happy.

Our lips fuse together, tongues stroking one another as we devour each other. I can't get enough of her and neither can my body as it reacts to her soft moans. I kick off my shoes before sitting up in the tub and bringing her over my lap so she's straddling me.

"You're beautiful, perfect for me. God, I love your curves." My hands roam up and down the sides of her body as my lips kiss along her jaw to her neck, sucking her sensitive skin.

"Hmm..." Lizzy sighs, scraping my scalp and tilting her head away so I have better access to her neck. I feel her shiver, and smile against her skin.

Suddenly, she tenses before screaming in my ear.

"Fudge cakes, mother effing crap." Her cursing is creative as she stumbles off my lap, kneeing me in the groin.

"Ooof! What the…" I cup myself and close my eyes, breathing slowly. Fuck my life right now. What in the hell happened to take us from making out to her attacking me in my most precious area? Is this payback for not peeing on her leg?

"A-a-a…" Her voice trembles, and I open my eyes to find a terrified expression on her face. She's already out of the tub, the red sting mark looking angry, but Lizzy's arms are flailing.

"A lizard, Nate! A freaking lizard is on the ceiling staring at us like a peeping Tom. Please get it and take it outside."

I scrub a hand down my face to hide my smile and stand. Sure enough, a small lizard is looking at us, or at least it seems to be.

"This little guy?" I can't help but tease her.

"Nate." There's a panicked desperation in her pleading voice. "It's running away!" She points at it, jumping on the toilet seat cover.

I cup my hand over the small animal, but it's a fast little fucker. I chase after it from side to side on the ceiling, and when it climbs down the wall, I cover it with my hand, feeling the coolness of the animal against my skin.

"I got it." I smile triumphantly at Lizzy, who's clutching her hands together, eyes round with fear. I swear I see tears forming.

Taking the lizard, I step out of the bathtub, leaving a trail of water as I make my way toward the front door. I'll clean her floor after releasing the intruder. I let go of the little guy, or gal, feet away from the apartment on a bush so it doesn't find its way back to her house.

GUARDED DEPUTY

When I return, I find Lizzy in the same spot, eyes roaming all over the bathroom as if a million lizards might appear from the walls and attack her.

"Thank you." Her voice is quiet.

"You're welcome. Are you okay?"

She nods, slowly stepping down from her perched position. I wash my hands with soap and water and then turn to look at her.

"You're really terrified of them."

"I am. It's not just because they're gross, I hate them. I'm sorry for kneeing you in the balls. If you want an exit plan to escape my crazy, you've got it. I'll turn around while you leave and will never speak to you again unless work requires it."

"What are you talking about?" I walk toward her, holding her hips.

"Let me see... I am a disaster and pretty sure I'm crazy. You don't need to feel sorry for me."

"I'll admit you scared the shit out of me. I was wondering why you kneed me, but I get it. You have a phobia, that much is clear, but I don't scare easily and neither does my guy down there." I nod toward my crotch.

Lizzy covers her face, hiding herself from me. I hate that she feels that way, that she thinks I won't accept her for who she is.

"Hey." I pull her hands away. "Come on, let's get dried up and put that ointment on your sting before it becomes irritated again."

She remains rooted in place, so I bend to stare into her eyes.

"Lizzy Andrews, look at me. Do I look like I'm ready to walk because a few awkward incidents occurred? I'm not going anywhere unless you kick me out. But please don't do that because I really like you, quirks, fears, and all." Using my thumb, I lift one side of her lips in an attempt to form a smile, and Lizzy giggles.

"I am not going to get over this. I'll think about it and remember it and get embarrassed all over again. I still can't believe how today's gone. This is by far the worst date ever."

"I'm offended by that," I say.

"No, I didn't mean you. For fuck's sake, shut up, Lizzy." She shakes her head, chastising herself.

I toss my head back and laugh loudly. "I'm kidding, babe. I know what you mean, but I was trying to lighten the mood. Now, do you have a towel I can borrow?"

"Of course." She walks out of the bathroom and opens a small closet on the adjacent wall. "Here you go. Do you, uh, need clothes because I don't think mine will fit you?"

"I have a bag in the truck. I'll be back." I kiss her cheek and pat down my clothes to prevent making more of a mess in her apartment, then head to my truck for my bag.

"I'm changing in my room, feel free to use the bathroom," Lizzy calls out when I enter her apartment again.

I walk into the bathroom and dry myself quickly before putting on shorts and a T-shirt. When I step out, Lizzy is mopping the floors.

"Let me do that. I was going to do it anyway."

"It's okay. I'm done." She leans against the stick and smiles.

"Did you put the cream on the sting?"

"Yeah."

"Good, good." I shift on my feet, wondering how I can delay my stay. "I should stay and make sure you don't have any kind of reaction." I run a hand through my hair. I'm usually smoother than this.

GUARDED DEPUTY

Lizzy laughs and nods. "Want to order pizza and watch a movie?"

"I thought you'd never ask." I breathe easily.

"Give me that, and I'll wash it with my stuff." She reaches for my clothes.

"You don't have to."

"I know, but I'm going to put my stuff in anyway."

"Okay. I'll order pizza then. Same as the other night?" I look over at her, grabbing my phone.

"Yeah, thanks."

I smile at her, feeling very domestic, and I like it. I don't usually want this, the homey feel of a relationship, and yet with Lizzy, I can't get enough of her. I want to mark her and this place like a fucking animal. I'm pretty sure that's not sexy, but my instinct takes over when I'm with her.

She meets me on the couch and takes a seat, careful not to injure her leg more than it is. We look at each other for a moment before I pull her to me and kiss the top of her head and hug her tightly. Lizzy leans against my chest and inhales deeply.

"You smell good, like fresh cotton."

I laugh at her comment. "That's my detergent."

"I like it." She glances up at me.

"I like you."

"Thank you again for getting rid of the peeping Tom."

"Stop thanking me." I squeeze her.

"Other guys in the past have laughed at me and made me sound crazy. I know it is crazy, but I can't help it. It's something beyond my control."

"I know how fears work, so don't excuse yourself. Those guys are assholes."

"Yeah." She sighs, looking away as she blinks rapidly.

"Let's watch a movie." I tap her back and smile at her.

"Action or RomCom?"

"What's your favorite movie?" I want to know everything about her.

"*Sweet Home Alabama.*"

"Then, let's watch that one."

"Really?" Her eyes light up.

"Really." I nod, kissing the tip of her nose.

That unfamiliar feeling from earlier where I'd do anything to protect her has expanded into doing anything that would make her happy, at peace, and safe. Lizzy has wormed her way into my heart, breaking my guard and making me believe that maybe a relationship could have a happy ending.

Just because I'm a product of my father doesn't mean I am him.

chapter 24
LIZZY

NATE'S FINGERS CARESS MY arm while I lean into him, watching Melanie and Jake go from hating each other to slowly rekindling their romance. I sigh with a smile. No matter how many times I've watched this movie, it feels like the first time.

To watch it with Nate holding me makes it a whole new experience. My heart expands and drums to a different beat. My skin pebbles, and my stomach clenches with the desire to crawl into him and stay there forever.

He's amazing, sweet, gentle and caring. The way he's made sure I'm okay all afternoon speaks volumes. Instead of high-tailing it out of here like my craziness might be contagious, he's stayed. It says a lot about a man when he stays.

I shift and look up at him, to find him staring at the TV, but his eyes glance down at me as soon as he feels me move.

"Are you okay?" His other hand brushes away the mess of hair from my face.

"Yeah."

"Is it time to reapply the cream?" He scoots back to sit up straighter.

"No." I hold him down, placing a hand on his chest. His heart has a steady beat I can get lost in like the bass of a techno song your body can't help but move to.

"Are you sleepy? I can go so you can rest. You've had an exciting day."

I snort at his word choice and shake my head. "Can you stay? I mean, I don't mean that we have to you know, and you live with your sister so it'd probably look bad, especially since I'm her son's teacher. Ugh, this is so awkward." I ramble.

"Lizzy." His voice is firm.

I look at him, waiting for what he's going to say.

"It's not awkward. Yeah, it's a little unconventional since I'm related to one of your students, but it's not a big deal. We live in a small town where it's almost impossible to not have like a two degrees of separation situation on our hands." His eyes search mine. "You're a professional, and you'll keep your personal and professional life separate."

"I will," I quickly say.

Nate leans in, his lips a centimeter away from mine. "I'll stay."

A smile curves my lips and I close the gap, kissing him lazily. Nate groans, wrapping his strong arms around my waist and pulling me until I'm sitting on his lap. The feel of his arms around me never ceases to make me feel cared for and yet wanted and desired.

His lips move with mine, finding our rhythm. Tentatively, I peek my tongue out and instantly find the tip of his. All modesty dissipates, and I shift on his lap so I can kiss him better and lose myself in this man.

His hands roam up and down my body in a way that makes me feel sexy. Like if his hands were kissing me the way his lips are.

They hold me close, pull me to him, touch with desperation. It's everything I've always fantasized about and yet better because Nate couldn't be conjured by my thoughts.

I moan into the kiss, gripping the back of his shirt. My body buzzes with desire as his tongue tangles with mine.

Nate slows our kiss and holds my face, staring at me.

"I can't," he says.

"Can't what?" I lean back to get a better look at him.

"I can't control myself around you. We need to slow down, take a breather."

"Why?"

"You're injured."

I laugh at his excuse and hold his face, smiling.

"I want to be with you. I want to do this, but only when we're both ready. If you want more time, need more of us together before we take that step, I'm perfectly okay with it."

"I don't want you to regret anything."

"I could never regret anything with you. You're my cup of coffee." I grin, using the words he wrote on my coffee cup.

Growling, he hugs me tightly, kissing my clavicle. His scruffy beard scratches my skin, and I love the sensation it brings about. Fire in the pit of my stomach grows.

"Are you sure?" He tilts his head to look at me.

"Positive," I whisper, brushing my hand through his hair.

"You make me crazy."

"Good crazy?" I tilt my head.

"Amazing crazy. The kind where I never want to be sane again." He takes my lower lip between his teeth and tugs.

I moan in surprise, pulling his hair.

"You like that." It's a statement, eyes alight with mischief.

GUARDED DEPUTY

"Seems like it." I lift a brow.

"I just want you to know that this means something to me."

"Me too," I whisper, leaning into him.

He doesn't hesitate to take my lips this time, our mouths fusing as if we were finally put back together and made whole. My heart lurches and drops, the sensation of being on a roller coaster taking over. It's exciting and scary and needy. I need him. I need his kiss, his touch, his masculine scent. I need his smile and laughter.

His lips kiss down my neck and along my shoulder. I shiver at the ticklish feel of his beard. When his teeth bite my skin, my core clenches and my entire body heats.

"Bedroom." His gruff voice vibrates against my neck, and I nod in a desire-laden daze.

He stands with me still on his lap, my legs clutching on at his waist. His lips kiss every part of my neck and chest he can reach as we make our way to the room. Every tiny part of my body is pulsing with anticipation.

His erection moves against my core as he walks, and I moan. I'm so sensitive, so ready for him. When Nate opens my bedroom door, he pauses and brushes away my stubborn hair from my face. There's a moment of silence, a quiet, intimate energy that passes between us as our eyes catch.

He walks to the edge of my bed and pauses, looking at the clothes I didn't put away this morning. He pushes all the clothes off my bed before laying me down.

"You already know laundry isn't my strong suit."

"Not a deal breaker for me." He chuckles, settling over me.

His body is like a weighted blanket that I never want to strip off. His fingers lace with my hand, and he moves it over my head on the bed, keeping our fingers intertwined as his lips crash against mine in a consuming kiss that makes me dizzy.

"I can't wait. I need all of you. To taste you."

I whimper and arch my back, squeeze his fingers tighter in my hand, and wrap my legs around his waist.

"You're needy. Don't worry. I'll make sure you feel completely satisfied."

Nate's lips pepper my jaw and neck, down to my chest. Instead of removing my shirt, he kisses over the fabric, a sensation of forbidden desire as he sucks my nipple through it.

He continues his descent, and with his teeth, tugs my T-shirt up my stomach. When he can't move it any farther, he uses his hand, holding my waist and sliding the material up. My body tenses and wiggles beneath him. His lips, teeth, and beard create this swirl of sensations that make me crazy with a hunger only he can satisfy.

"I love how sensitive you are."

"You're making me mad."

"Mad like Mad Hatter, or mad like Hulk?"

Laughter bubbles out of me. "You can't make jokes like that right now."

"I'm sorry?" He glances up at me.

"You're not."

"I'm breaking the ice."

"I'm not sure we need an ice-breaker at this very moment."

"You're right." He licks a path along the waistband of my shorts.

"This is slow torture," I mumble, pressing my head into the mattress and closing my eyes.

GUARDED DEPUTY

"It's the sweetest kind." His words vibrate against my skin. I had no idea how wonderful that would feel until now. Words spoken against me, tingling my skin in a way that adds to my yearning.

Instead of removing my shorts like I think he will, he kisses back up my body, this time releasing my hand to remove my T-shirt and bra. Nate looks at me with darkened eyes, licking his lips. When his gaze meets mine, it becomes fiery.

His lips crash against mine in an all-consuming kiss. I claw at his back, wanting to rip his shirt off. Breaking away a moment, he allows me that small gift. He tugs it up and over his head, throwing it on the floor before leaning back down, and his chest smashes against mine with no barrier. We're skin to skin, heartbeat to heartbeat. His body moves over mine until he flips us and I'm on top.

He runs his hands up my thighs, and I shiver when his fingers sneak into my cotton shorts, finding my wet core.

"Fuck," he murmurs.

"Ditto." I moan when his finger brushes against my clit.

He does it again before sliding his finger into me, eliciting a drawn-out moan. His fingers move alternating between being inside of me and rubbing against me, brushing and stroking and bringing me to the brink. My body is already so sensitive that a touch from him is amplified. But Nate continues to push me until I'm begging him for more.

I ride his fingers like my life depends on it. I'm almost there, whimpering at the feel of a rising orgasm.

Abruptly, he slides his fingers out of me and leans his head up so he can look at me.

"Time for dessert." He winks and kisses me.

I slide off him and lie back. He trails down my body with his hands while I finish kicking off my shorts and underwear. He chuckles at my desperate attempt to get completely naked.

He moves toward the end of the bed, and his hands hold my thighs, spreading them open. His eyes blaze into mine as he smirks.

Jesus, I'm going to combust.

"Hold on." He tilts his chin toward my hands.

His mouth descends on my most intimate area, tongue slowly swiping along my clit. Each movement is deliberate and tantalizing. Nate is nothing if not aware of my body. He holds my hips down, keeping me in place, as his mouth devours me.

Everything in this moment becomes like a scene in a movie where it turns to slow-motion. My heart echoes in my ears, the sound dulling everything else around me. My hands go to Nate's hair, tugging the strands while at the same time keeping his head in place.

He doesn't relent. His tongue fucks me and teases me and swipes everywhere. His fingers move to where his mouth isn't, adding to my pleasure. It's too much. Too intense.

"Nate," I say tightly through a moan. "Don't stop."

"Don't plan on it. You're addicting. I can't get enough." His words fuel my desire. My head thrashes, moving from side to side as my fingers clutch my sheets.

My body tightens, core pulses. Heat swims inside of me, prickling my skin. I call out as he pushes me over the edge with no mercy. My legs shake as my orgasm takes over, making my cry out in pleasure. I will my body to relax, but it's so tight, so coiled, that until I release completely, my body remains like this.

"Get lost in me," Nate says.

GUARDED DEPUTY

And I do. I get so damn lost that I'll never find my way back because Nate has paved a new way that will never compare. I'm lost in him. Lost in us. And I have no intention of being found.

When I finally come down from the intense climax, Nate kisses up my thighs and stomach until he's at my mouth, fusing our lips together. In this moment, I know that I'll never be the same. This isn't just sex. It isn't just an orgasm. It's a connection. A union with a man I'm falling for.

"We're not done." Nate smiles, brushing my hair away so gently it's a contrast to the way he was eating me before.

"Good. I don't ever want to stop."

He chuckles, kissing the corner of my lips. "We'll have to take a break at some point."

I laugh, shaking my head. "You know what I mean."

"I do." He leans down to kiss me before moving away.

I complain, but he only looks at me and winks. I sit up and move toward him, placing my hands on his hips. His stomach clenches. I don't speak as I grab both sides of his shorts and tug them down his hips and legs, biting my lip when he stands before me naked.

I wrap my hand around his erection, feeling the hot smooth skin as I move up and down the length. My core clenches at the idea of him sliding into me, making me his. Nate's eyes glance down to my chest. I follow his line of vision to find my nipples hard.

"You make me this way," is all I say before tasting him.

"Fuck, Lizzy." His hands are in my hair immediately.

Instead of responding, I swipe my tongue around the base of his dick before taking him in my mouth. I take my time to slowly pleasure him. I want to torture him the way he did to me.

I want him to beg me for more. I want to be fully in control of his pleasure.

When his hands try to keep me in place, I pause, looking up at him with an arched brow. He smiles, shaking his head.

"You're bad." His voice is husky.

I remove my mouth from him. "I beg to differ. Does bad feel like this?" I cup his balls and suck him into my mouth, harder this time.

Nate groans and curses, his legs faltering. My other hand goes around to his hip, feeling his hard muscles.

He moves his hands to my breasts, twisting and pinching my nipples before cupping my breasts. I moan, and his legs shake. Deciding he's had enough, I suck him harder, taking him to the back of my throat and back out. My tongue traces the underside of his length before taking him again, relentlessly pleasuring him until I feel his dick grow harder.

"Stop."

I shake my head, wanting to make him completely lose himself.

"Lizzy, I want to be in you."

I pause, releasing him, and look at him. "Do you want that, or do you prefer to come like this? Because in all honestly, Nate, I don't want to stop but I will."

"Fuck my life. I have to choose between your mouth or pussy?"

"No. It's all yours. I'm all yours."

His hands tangle in my hair, pulling me to him. I willingly open my mouth and finish what I started. Nate loses himself in my mouth, orgasming until he has nothing left. He drops his head, shaking it slightly, and loosens his hold on my hair.

GUARDED DEPUTY

"You're amazing," he says gruffly.

I stand so we're closer in height and kiss him.

"Now, are you going to claim the rest of me?" I arch a brow.

He growls, wrapping me in his arms and leaning me back on the bed. We kiss until our lips are sore and touch each other until we need more. He starts to harden in my hand, and I feel a sense of confidence that I can make him react this way.

Nate aligns himself with my body and inches himself into me. I stare into his eyes, lips parted.

"Perfect," he whispers, kissing me lovingly.

We move together, finding our rhythm. I scrape my nails along his back, his muscles flexing beneath my touch. His hand is on my breast, massaging my sensitive skin to add to my building pleasure. The fire from earlier is back, heating me with intensity that feels like too much and yet perfect.

Our breathing is labored and my belly clenches with an impending orgasm. I'm overwhelmed in the best way until I'm calling out his name. My body pulses and tingles, my climax taking over in a powerful wave. I'm drowning in Nate, but I don't need a lifesaver because he breathes new life into me.

My heart and soul feel like they're soaring. I feel an immense amount of joy and need to memorize this experience.

"Baby," he whispers. "Fuck, you feel so good." He continues to thrust into me, extending my orgasm.

When he tenses, I know he's close. Leaning my lips to his ear, I whisper, "Lose yourself in me. I need to feel it."

Nate growls, stilling as his dick pulses inside of me.

"My heaven. That's what you are." He drops his body on half of mine, kissing me fervently and desperately.

I've never felt as content as I do in this moment. His arms wrap around me, making me feel safe as his lips kiss my shoulder, cheek, and lips.

The peace that fills me is otherworldly. It's inexplicable.

I look at him and smile. "Stay the night?"

"I'm not going anywhere."

I bite my lip as a smile takes over and lean in to kiss him. My heart is still racing, and I reach out to see if his heartbeat matches mine. My palm flattens on his chest, and Nate's expression softens.

"It's all yours."

His words make my breath catch. We stare at each other for a few moments before I grab his hand and place it over my heart.

"And this is yours."

chapter 25

LIZZY

"RUMOR HAS IT YOU'RE dating Deputy Moore," my mom says, sitting across from me at the dining table in her kitchen. I came over for breakfast today.

I sigh, surprised she hasn't been blowing up my phone about this. I have no doubt that the people who saw us together at the doctor's office started talking about it.

"We've gone out."

"Are you sure that's a good idea? I know I told you that you needed a man like him, but after what happened to your father..." Her words trail off.

"Mom, what happened to Dad was sick and cruel. I hate thinking about it, but we can't live our lives stuck on that experience, making decisions based on it." I reach out and squeeze her hand.

"I just don't want you to live through something like that, and this line of work is uncertain."

"I get that, but just because it happened to Dad, doesn't mean I'll live through it with Nate."

"You're right." She smiles. "Nate is quite the looker, too." She winks and takes a drink of her coffee.

"Mom." I groan but can't help but laugh.

GUARDED DEPUTY

"Tell me about this man."

I jump into the conversation, telling her about Nate, the dates we had, and my sting. Her eyes widen when I mention the jellyfish, but she smiles when I show her it's healing.

"You look happy." My mom interrupts me as I'm telling her about the work Nate is doing at the school.

"I am." I lean back in my seat with a smile.

"Then, I'm happy."

"Hello, ladies." Gary enters the kitchen with a grin and kisses my mom's cheek.

"Hi, darling. How was breakfast?"

"It was good. Steve says hello. He wants to get together soon. With you, too, Lizzy. He's going to propose to Ana."

"Wow," I say. "That's exciting. I know siblings are usually involved in each other's weddings, but is there a code for step siblings?" I jokingly ask.

"I'm sure there is. It'll be exciting." Gary's eyes sparkle.

How's Jessica?" I ask about his daughter. She's in college, so I haven't seen her in a while.

"She's great. She'll be starting nursing school in the summer." Gary serves himself some orange juice and takes a seat.

"Awesome."

I look at my mom and her face is lit up. I'm glad she found someone like Gary to give her a second chance at love after my dad passed away.

"I'm going to go." I stand.

"You don't have to." My mom's brow furrows.

"I know, but I'm going to run some errands and try to meet up with Dani and Avery. Thanks for breakfast." I stand and kiss my mom's cheek and then hug Gary.

235

FABIOLA FRANCISCO

I leave their house and open my group chat to ask my friends if they're free to have some coffee after I run some errands. I could use girl time, and between our demanding jobs and getting to know Nate, we haven't seen each other much.

Once I finish buying some things for a science experiment, I walk to Bay Brew to meet Dani and Avery. I'm looking at my phone, reading a text message from Nate and smiling. Every time he writes saying he's thinking of me, I can't help the wide grin that spreads on my face.

"Looks like someone is in love."

I startle, looking up from my phone and sigh when I see Dani. She chuckles, and I shove her before pocketing my phone in my jeans.

"You're a jerk."

"You had this googly in love look in your eyes. Were you talking to Mr. Hot Deputy?"

"Yeah, I got a message from him." I bite my lip and continue toward the coffee shop with her.

"What's going on with the hottie?" She hooks her arm in mine as we walk. "Everyone in town is talking about seeing you two together."

"Ugh." I toss my head back. "We were on a date and I got stung by a jellyfish so he took me to the doctor. Of course, he carried me in so I wouldn't be in more pain."

"You got stung? Are you okay?" She grabs my arm, almost ripping it off to check me for any marks.

"Hey! Uh, what is Dani doing?" Avery catches up with us on the way to the coffee shop, looking at Dani as if she's crazy.

"She's looking for my jellyfish sting," I explain.

"What?" Avery screeches.

GUARDED DEPUTY

"I'm fine." I wave my hands at both of them to calm them down.

"She was on a date with Nate when it happened," Dani tells Avery conspiratorially.

"Oh, is that why you were at the doctor?" Avery eyes me.

"Small town rumors are the worst." I toss my head back. "Yes, that's exactly why I was there. The sting was on my leg and I'm okay now." I open the door to Bay Brew and shake my head.

"Good, good." Dani nods, looking at me with curiosity. "So he took care of you." A devious smile lifts her lips, and her eyes cut to Avery.

"Yup." I bite down my smile.

"Look at her face." Avery elbows Dani. "And this was the woman who told me a few months ago she was done with dating."

"She's swooning," Dani says.

"He's great." I sigh, proving them right.

"I'm glad. Let's grab coffee and you can tell us all the dirty details." Dani's eyebrows waggle.

"I'll keep it PG-13."

"You're no fun." She pouts and laughs. "I'm only kidding, but you do have this glow about you."

"Glow?" I lift my brows. "You're insane."

"It's like you put shimmer on your skin," Avery adds.

"Stop it." A blush fills my cheeks.

Standing at the counter once inside, I order a latte and chocolate chip cookie. The girls orders after me, and we sit at a loveseat in the back of the coffee shop.

"Okay, spill." Dani tucks her leg beneath her and blows her steaming coffee.

I look between my friends and break out in a wide grin, ready to gush.

"Things are great. We went to the state park yesterday and kayaked. That's where I got stung by a jellyfish though and made a major fool of myself. Somehow, he stayed and made sure I was okay instead of running for the hills. I went with the pee remedy and practically begged him to pee on me." My face scrunches up.

"Oh, my goodness!" Dani shouts and laughs.

"You didn't." Avery's eyes widen.

"I did." I nod in embarrassment.

Dani keeps laughing loudly, drawing attention to us.

"Shhh..." I widen my eyes and shift to stare at her. "D, stop making so much noise."

"Sorry, but I can't believe you did that," she guffaws, holding her belly.

"I know, but I was desperate. I've never felt pain like that before. Anyway, besides that hiccup where I embarrassed myself, it was great." I stare off, reliving last night.

Although Nate and I had sex, the best part was waking up with his arm around me in a safe embrace. When I saw his sleeping face, this pang of nostalgia hit me. As if I've been missing this my whole life, wasting the opportunity to be with him by dating duds.

"You totally did it!" She calls out, punching my shoulder and making coffee slosh over the side of my mug and onto my jeans.

"Dani!" I hiss.

"Oops, sorry, but you totally did it." Her voice drops, thankfully so.

I nod, unable to contain the giddy feeling that's conquered me all day. If I can't confide in my best friends in times like this, who can I talk to?

"It was amazing." I grab a napkin and wipe myself. It won't get rid of the stain or coffee smell, but at least it'll help.

"No shit," she snorts.

I shake my head, heat filling me as I remember last night and from the embarrassment.

"Honestly, Dani. Can you be mature for a moment?"

"Okay, okay. I'm just teasing you because I know how you get with these things, but Nate honestly seems like a nice guy. I know you like him a lot."

"I do." I grab my mug when I realize I'm in no more danger of spontaneous attacks from her and finally take a drink. I sigh happily as the caffeine hits me. It may be my third cup of coffee for the day, but who's counting?

"How was the rest of your date minus the jellyfish sting?" Avery leans in as if I'm about to tell her the most scandalous gossip. My dating life isn't that interesting. Or it hasn't been until now.

I dive in, telling them details about my date and how he took care of me afterward, including removing the lizard from my bathroom. Dani howls with laughter at that part, making me want to put tape over her mouth.

"You ladies having fun?" A deep voice breaks up the conversation, and my head snaps up with wide eyes.

Dani and Avery smile like the devil when I glance over at them.

"Absolutely. Take a seat, Mr. Deputy." Dani winks at him.

"Just Mr. Deputy today?" He smirks at me, sitting on an armchair across from us.

I take a deep breath and close my eyes, knowing my friends are about to make this awkward.

"Are you tired, Lizzy?" Humor tints Nate's voice.

I open my eyes and glare at him. "Nope, I slept like a baby."

"Really?" His brows lift. "Me too." He leans back, crossing his leg over his knee.

Dani's eyes bounce between us with glee. She's enjoying this way too much.

"Are you here for coffee?" I ask.

"Yup, but then I saw you here and couldn't resist saying hello. It seems as you're wearing your coffee today." He leans forward and looks at me.

"Blame this one." I point to Dani, who shrugs unapologetically.

"You look beautiful any way, Murphy. Coffee stains and all."

My smile breaks through like the sun at dawn, and I can no longer keep up with the banter.

"Thanks, Deputy."

"I missed something." Dani points at us. "Who's Murphy? Do you know?" She looks at Avery, who shrugs.

"She is because disaster follows her, but it's cute."

"You know, like Murphy's Law," I add.

"Wow, you have pet names for each other. This is serious." Dani leans back, crossing her arms and nodding to herself.

"It is." Nate looks over at Dani before back at me, his expression intensifying. "I'll go so you can have your girl time. We'll talk later." He hesitates as if he wants to kiss me, but people in

GUARDED DEPUTY

the coffee shop are staring as if we're their newest reality show stars.

"Bye." I shoot out way too fast and unromantic.

Now that I've snapped out of our bubble and realize we're on display, my heart jerks in an uncomfortable way. Nate chuckles and stands, winking at me.

"You went from witty banter to really awkward." Dani raises her eyebrows.

"I realized how many people are staring and got nervous." I fall back on the sofa with a sigh.

"Who cares?" Dani shrugs. "Live your best life and forget the rest." She waves her arms out like she's on Broadway or something, and a few people laugh. "That's what I do. Ah, fuck." Her arms and smile drop instantly.

"What happened?" Avery looks around.

"I'll accept a Nate interruption, but this is too much for me." I follow her line of vision and see her next door neighbor in line with a woman beside him.

Dani scowls at his back, though he's oblivious to her. All I've heard are complaints about him ever since he moved next door to her. He looks over his shoulder as if her laser-beam-stare was burning his back and narrows his eyes in her direction. The glaring competition is intense.

The woman beside him says something, stealing his attention, and Dani exhales.

"He's such a jerk." She leaves it at that and looks at us.

I press my lips together and remain quiet. I once asked Dani if her hatred toward him was actually attraction and she practically bit my head off. I would very much like to keep my entire

241

body intact, especially now that I'm dating Nate and would like to feel his hands and lips on me again.

Heat trails up my body, and I shake it off.

"Are you thinking about Nate again?" Dani laughs.

So much for trying to hide the direction my thoughts went in.

"No," I lie.

"Right. And I secretly love my neighbor." She rolls her eyes.

That's questionable, but I keep it to myself. Instead, I finish my coffee and tell them about the science experiment I'm going to do this week and hear about the recipes Avery and Gabriel are creating for a new cookbook and the interview Dani has at the station with one of country music's up and coming stars.

In another life, I want to work in the music industry to meet all these musicians, although I'd likely be a rambling mess unable to get a full question out. Just observing me with Nate is enough to tell that my social skills with people I like or admire is questionable.

chapter 26

NATE

I SEE LIZZY DOWN the hall and smile. Looking around, I don't see anyone else in the area so I pick up my pace. She looks over her shoulder and spots me with wide eyes. I'm not sure why she'd react that way, but I keep walking toward her. I'm about to wrap her in my arms and kiss her cheek when she shifts, and I see a young boy in front of her.

I put the brakes on my plan and wait a few feet behind her. Thank God she moved or it would've been really bad.

When she finishes talking to the boy and he leaves, she turns to me with crossed arms and a crooked smile.

"Hi." I shuffle on my feet.

"Hi, Deputy Moore."

"I didn't realize you were busy."

"I could tell. I heard your heavy footsteps." She drops her arms and puts them in her pockets.

"I got distracted when I saw you and had a one-track mind." I shrug unapologetically.

"At work?" She arches her eyebrow in challenge, and it takes everything in me not to grab her and kiss her.

"There was no one around."

GUARDED DEPUTY

"Ah, but there was." She smirks, cracking her authoritative mask.

"Can't blame a guy for trying to kiss the woman he likes."

"Very true." She reaches her arm out and I take her hand, squeezing it. "How's your morning been?"

"Boring because I haven't seen you."

She laughs and shakes her head, looking at me.

"You already won me over. The cheesiness could stop."

"Cheesy? Me?" I look at her offended.

"Super cheesy. Like extra cheese pizza."

"Babe, there's nothing cheesy about my words. I speak the truth. Besides, a man should never stop wooing a woman, even if he *won* her." I step closer and kiss the top of her hand.

Lizzy sighs with a soft smile. I have the urge to always make her feel like she's wanted.

"Did I ever tell you that I love the way you look in your uniform?" Her free hand trails down my chest, making my body tight.

"No." I clear my throat.

"It's sexy. Gives me all sorts of ideas." Her smile is wicked.

"Lizzy, we're going to need to shelf this conversation for another moment when we're not at work."

"Will you still wear the uniform?" Her eyes gleam.

I growl and pull her to me, staring into her eyes as she breathlessly looks up at me. Her lips are parted in surprise.

"I'll wear whatever the hell you want me to wear." I press my mouth to hers.

Lizzy moans quietly, her mouth moving against mine. In the back of my mind, I know we shouldn't be doing this, but she feels so good against me that one minute won't make a different.

The clicking of heels echoes behind me, and Lizzy pushes me away, shaking her head as if she were in a fog. I furrow my brows and look at her and then behind me.

"Fuck," she mumbles.

The principal is looking at us with a stern expression.

"Ms. Andrews, don't you have class?" She lifts her brow at Lizzy.

"Yes." Lizzy's eyes briefly glance at me and then she walks away.

I blow out a breath, looking at Mrs. Sanders with pursed lips. I've gotten into trouble in my life, but it's never felt as grave as this. Maybe because I'm an adult and should know how to act properly.

"Deputy Moore, can we speak?"

"Of course." I close the gap and stand before her.

"I've heard you and Ms. Andrews are dating, however, I expect complete professional behavior when you're on school grounds. I'll be having the same conversation with her as well."

"I understand." I nod, expression impassive. "I apologize for not being professional. I promise to keep our personal life out of the school."

I can keep a straight face and not let others see how they affect me, but I hope Lizzy won't hold this against me.

"Great. Have a good afternoon."

"You too." I walk away, breathing deeply.

I lost control when I saw Lizzy, but my priority is making sure we both keep our jobs. Kissing her in the hallway at work is not part of that plan.

She's everything I've always wanted and thought I didn't deserve. When I see her, it's like my heart catapults toward her

GUARDED DEPUTY

and I act on impulse. I should get that checked. I've always been good at controlling my emotions.

The rest of the afternoon drags, and I have no more sightings of Lizzy. It's unfortunate for me, but the best thing for our work situation. When I grab Walker, Lizzy barely smiles at me. Taken aback, I tilt my head but she presses her lips into a straight line.

"Let's go, Uncle Nate." Walker tugs my hand before I can even find a way to ask Lizzy what's going on.

I look at him and realize he's not the same amped up kid he usually is. "Hold on. Is everything okay?"

"Yeah, just tired. I wanna go home." He pulls the handle on my car, but it's locked.

I grab the key fob and unlock the car, analyzing him as if searching for a lie somewhere. Walker seems upset. His shoulders are tense, and his jaw is locked. Something's up, but I'll have to ask Lizzy if something happened once I'm home and he can't hear me.

After giving Walker a snack and making sure he's doing homework, I sneak out to the backyard and call Lizzy. Her attitude at pick-up was off, and Walker is still in a bad mood.

"Hello?" she answers

"Hey. Is everything okay?" I pace along the patio.

"Yeah." Her voice sounds tight.

"I'm going to call BS on that." I run a hand through my hair as I wait for her to say something.

A deep sigh sounds on the other side of the line, and I pause.

"I wanted to talk to your sister first, but Walker had an incident at school today."

"What?" I growl. "What the hell happened?"

"Nate," she warns. "Right now you're a student's uncle, not my boyfriend." Her tone takes a professional lilt that equally turns me on and frustrates me because I am her boyfriend. I know the situation is delicate, though.

"Right."

"Some of the kids were teasing him about us, saying that I'm your girlfriend. He didn't take it well and got angry."

I frown and look into the house through the glass doors. Walker is sitting at the table with a deep furrow.

"How do kids even know that?" I begin pacing again.

"We live in a small town. Their parents probably talked about it and the kids overheard. It's not unusual." She sounds resigned.

"Freaking nosey bodies."

"Yup."

"I'll talk to him," I promise her.

"That would be good, yeah. I handled the situation about my private life."

"Did Mrs. Sanders talk to you as well?" I ask.

"Yup. We need to be professional at work, Nate." She sounds stressed, and I hate that it's because of me.

"I know. Sorry." I feel guilty for putting her in that position in the first place.

"I know I'm hard to resist, but you need to keep yourself under control." Her voice brightens.

"You're impossible to resist, but I will behave."

"Good." She breathes out.

"Are you free tonight?" I ask.

"You want to get your fill so you'll behave tomorrow at work?" I love that she challenges me.

"I'll never get my fill when it comes to you, but I'm not against trying."

"I have to grade some papers."

"Any chance you want some help to finish faster?"

"You? Grade tests?" Her voice rises in surprise.

"Yeah?"

"I'd love to see that," she teases.

"Game on, Murphy. I'll be over later tonight with some dinner."

"A man after my own heart."

"Always."

Feeling more positive about what happened earlier, I hang up and go inside to talk to Walker. I hope I'm still the owner of Best Uncle Award by the end of our conversation.

"Walker understood the situation. He was more upset that people were teasing us than us actually going out, although he asked if he'd have to call you Aunt Andrews instead of Miss Andrews."

Lizzy chokes on her bite of pizza, covering her mouth as she sputters.

"What did you tell him?" Wide eyes stare at me.

I bite back my chuckle and shrug, leaning back on the couch. I'll admit that Walker's question caught me off-guard, but I recovered by laughing at his absurd question and explaining that he should continue to call her Miss Andrews.

"That we aren't married so you aren't his aunt."

"That evenly?" Her eyes are still like saucers.

"I was surprised," I admit. "But I understood his confusion."

"Kids crack me up." She shakes her head and wipes her hands on a napkin. "The pizza is great and all, but I do need to grade. That wasn't an excuse." She arches an eyebrow.

"Put me to work, boss." I place my plate on top of the mostly empty pizza box sitting on the coffee table.

Lizzy snorts and fights back a smile.

"Too much enthusiasm?"

"Too much *false* enthusiasm," she corrects.

"No such thing as false enthusiasm when I'm with you." I grab her hips and pull her until she's sitting on my lap. Brushing her hair away from her face, I smile and lean in for a kiss.

Lizzy relaxes against me as I kiss her slowly. When I feel her smile against my lips, I decide it's the best experience of my life. Not true, actually. The look in her eyes as if I were the world's best hero when I removed the lizard from her bathroom was the best experience. I felt like a king.

"We need to work," she murmurs against my lips.

"You sure?"

"Yes." She pushes back, but her smile is blinding. "Bad influence." She scoffs.

"I call bad influence a good thing." I wink.

"Okay, Mr. Deputy."

"You hurt my feelings. It's Mr. Hot Deputy to *you*."

She rolls her eyes. "Fine, Mr. *Hot* Deputy. Here is the list of the spelling words. Check mark if they're spelled correctly, and an X if they're not."

"I've got it. I was a first grader once and had spelling tests."

"Smart ass." She laughs.

"But I'm a hot smart ass, right?"

GUARDED DEPUTY

"I'm going to starve your ego."

"Don't do that." I pretend pout.

"You're ridiculous." She shakes her head and sits on the floor, using the coffee table as a surface. I lean back on the couch and use the clipboard the tests are on.

My eyes wander to Lizzy every so often and catch her biting her lip or concentrating with her tongue peeking out. She's focused on her task while I'm here trying to help and wondering if these really need to be graded tonight. I have another type of lesson in mind. Anatomy of the sexual kind.

Yeah, I much rather be leaving marks on her skin than on these papers.

"Are you working?" She doesn't even look up at me when she asks.

I smile and place the clipboard on my lap. I love that she's attuned to me without even watching me.

"Of course. How dare you question my commitment?"

She finally lifts her gaze and looks at me. "If you were one of my students, you'd be the one to give me gray hairs."

"I'm glad I'm not your student. I'm the man who gets to do this." I scoot down beside her and move her hair over her shoulder, leaving her jaw and side of her neck exposed.

Lizzy is motionless while my fingers trail along her jaw and down the center of her chin to her neck, stopping right under her collar.

Her breath catches, and I smile at her reaction. I lean in close enough to tease her but too far to taste her. Inhaling, I allow her sweet scent to consume me. Lizzy grips the pen in her hand, the only sign that this is affecting her.

251

My girl has willpower, but I'm here to make her break in the best way possible. It'll be fun to watch her come undone.

chapter 27
LIZZY

IF NATE DOESN'T DO something soon besides stare at me, I'm going to jump on him and take matters into my own hands. With my luck, I'd kick him in the groin again—Murphy's Law and all—so I'm being as patient as possible.

His lips *finally* touch my skin. My jaw, but I'll take it. I'll gladly accept a kiss on the cheek at this point to have some real contact with him. So much for being a responsible adult.

A soft skim moves along my jaw. It's almost too soft. Too subtle. I lean into him and feel him smile against me.

"You want more?"

"So much more." I don't hold back.

"I love that you do." His strong arms wrap around my waist and tug me onto his lap.

Nate continues his gentle exploration, moving up to my neck. Goosebumps rise on my skin. My belly clenches. My chest expands. A slow simmering builds beneath my chest. Even and heating.

He nibbles my ear, pushing me beyond patience. My hand lands on his thigh, and I squeeze.

"Don't control your reactions. Surrender. Be mine. Show me how you feel." His words are fuel that push me forward.

GUARDED DEPUTY

Sighing, I turn to look at him. His smile is sweet, a contradiction to the way he's making me feel. When his fingers comb through my hair, I sink into his chest.

"I really did have plans to grade papers."

"I did, too, but then I saw you and knew I'd rebel. I can't help it. If I need to behave at work, I'm going to enjoy every inch of you outside of it."

I whimper at his words, feeling my resolve strip away much like I'd like him to strip me out of my shirt.

"I like rules, but you're proving that they're fun to break."

"So fun when it involves you, naked and beneath me." His gruff voice vibrates against my skin.

I moan, moving my face toward his. I look into his eyes and cup his cheek, leaning in to kiss him as if he was my light in a dark tunnel. My body flames with need. Not just for his body but for his heart and soul.

I want him in a way I never imagined. A way that felt far off in the land of talking animals and fairy godmothers.

"Lizzy," he groans like he's in pain. Like he needs me just the same.

"I know." I move my hand around his shoulder and comb through his hair. "Let's go to the bedroom."

"You sure? Your work."

"I feel like the tests are judging me. Not only for not grading them but for doing the deed in front of them."

"That makes no sense," he mumbles against my neck.

"Go with it." I grip his shoulders, my body taut.

I force myself to stand before I have to get in some acrobatic position between the couch and the coffee table. Nate complains but slowly gets up.

My eyes wander to his nether region and find his tented shorts.

"Don't lick your lips like that until we're in the room."

"Like what?" I scrunch up my nose.

"Like you're starving and I'm the only meal in a million mile radius."

I smile, pressing my hand against his chest. His heart is thumping quickly.

"I'm definitely starving for you."

"Fuck," he breathes out.

"We will soon." I taunt him.

Nate growls, grabbing my legs and picking me up over his shoulder while I squeal in surprise.

"I need to taste you, Murphy. I feel like I might die if I don't get my mouth on that pussy."

My thighs clench together.

"I feel you squirming." His voice is deep and dark.

"Can't control my body around you."

"Good."

I land on my bed with a bounce and Nate smirks down at me like I'm his prey. Lucky for him, I like this game.

"I love seeing you lying there, assessing my next move, wondering if I'll surprise you or if you'll guess it." His eyes darken.

I stare up at him unmoving except for my chest rising and falling unevenly. Nate in the bedroom is exactly how I imagined him—direct, in control, and oh, so hot. Fiery. So...

Man, it's really hot in here.

I shift, feeling like my skin prickles with heat. What in the world? I look around my room as if the walls had the answers to what I'm feeling. My breathing comes in faster and I sit up.

GUARDED DEPUTY

"Are you okay?" Nate steps forward.

"No." I put my hand out and then tie my hair in a bun.

Why is it so hot in here all of a sudden?

"What's wrong? Lizzy?" He looks at me with wild eyes. I get it. We were about to get it on in a great way and I am acting crazy.

"It's really hot in here. Aren't you hot?"

"I was until I saw you panicking."

"Not like that." I shake my head and stand. "It's suddenly uncomfortably warm in the house." God, is this a pre-menopause hot flash? I'm too young for that, but my mom gets this way. "You don't feel hot?"

"It's a little warm in here, but I thought it was just me and figured the AC was high."

"No." I move to the door. Why does this happen now? Right before we get to the good part.

I stand by the thermostat in the hall and point to it. "See? Seventy degrees."

"It's not seventy here. Maybe eighty," Nate says.

"Why are you just telling me now?"

"I don't know. I'm not going to tell you to lower your air. How are you just noticing?" His eyes round and brows rise a bit.

"I wasn't moving so didn't notice it. You got me all hot and bothered and my temperature rose." I scratch my arm and then fan myself with my hand.

"I do have that effect on you." He gives me a crooked smile.

"Not the time. I mean, totally the time if it weren't that my AC likely broke."

"I'll take a look at it. Why don't you turn on the tub with cold water and soak?"

"You don't think I'm crazy?" I stare at him as if he has five heads with different expressions.

"Why would I think you're crazy?"

"Because I stopped us right before sex, complaining about the temperature."

Nate frowns and steps toward me, grabbing my hands. He ducks his head so we're at eye-level.

"Lizzy, if you think I'm going to get pissed because you're uncomfortable, then I'm going to be disappointing you a lot. Yes, I wanted to move onto the bedroom, but this isn't a dealbreaker. I want to be with *you* in any capacity not just for sex."

"But—"

"Nope. No excuses. I don't know what kind of men you've dated in the past, but I'm not going to get upset because you interrupted foreplay due to this." The men from my past were not as understanding when it came to my quirks.

"Technically, we hadn't started foreplay." I shrug with a smile.

"Babe," he groans. "I was so hard that my body felt like we had. You are my foreplay." He wraps his arm around my waist and kisses me "Get in the tub, and I'll meet you there after checking on the AC."

"Tub sex?"

"Cold water. It is hot as fuck in here."

"It really is. I need to get a fan if it's broken. Someone won't be able to come out here until tomorrow the earliest. I should call my landlord."

"Do that while I take a look, then go into the bathroom."

GUARDED DEPUTY

I smile and nod, heading to the living room where my phone is while Nate opens the closet door where my AC is and squats.

He continues to surprise me.

After telling my landlord that my air isn't working properly and agreeing to send someone out here to take a look, I turn on the water in the tub to colder than usual. It will help remove this sticky feeling on my skin.

Once the tub is filled, I slide in and shiver at the welcomed coolness of the water. I don't even bother putting soap since I just want to cool down. Closing my eyes, I take a deep breath. My mind wanders to the man out in the hall looking at my air conditioning without a second thought.

I could lie to myself and say that what I feel for him is trivial, but Nate has stolen my heart and mended its pieces. It beats for him. For his kindness and gentle heart beneath that tough exterior. For the way he cares for me and treats the kids in school.

The echo of footsteps interrupts my train of thought, and I open one eye to find Nate standing in the doorway, already stripping off his shirt and staring at me with flared eyes.

"You look stunning like that. The water trying to blur your body but not quite accomplishing it. Are you feeling better?"

I nod, staring at him as his hands move to his shorts.

"Good. I couldn't figure out the problem, but hopefully you can get someone out here tomorrow."

"My landlord said he'll get it fixed."

"I'm glad. I'm gonna get in there with you, babe."

I scoot up and his eyes zero in on my chest. When he strips, there's nothing hiding his erection. I shiver at the view of his naked body before me, unabashedly exposed for me to admire like a work of art.

His body is my favorite masterpiece. It belongs in a museum, but I'd get jealous of everyone ogling him. Possessiveness consumes me, wanting to keep this man completely to myself.

He settles behind me, long legs stretching on either side of me. I grip his knees and use them for leverage to scoot back against his chest and sigh happily.

"Thank you," I whisper.

"What for?" His arms are around my body, hands lazily cupping water and letting it slip through is fingers.

"For being you." I turn my head and kiss his arm wherever I can reach.

He, on the other hand, leans forward and kisses the back of my neck in response. We stay like this for a bit. When the water warms up, I turn on the tap again and fill it with cold water, balancing the temperature.

"You know what?"

"What?" I turn my head to look at him.

"This turned out better."

"Really?" I furrow my brows. "Because I'm not about muggy heat indoors."

His chest rumbles with laughter against my back, and it's oddly soothing.

"But being here is much better than rushing to have sex. This is slow and steady." He fingers brush along my leg up my thigh.

"So sex in cold water to counteract the heat in the apartment?"

"Bingo," he jokes.

GUARDED DEPUTY

I turn around and straddle him so we can see each other. Nate arches an eyebrows and smiles.

"I'm going to hurt my neck by turning it to look at you. This is more effective and your thighs are a comfortable chair."

"You can sit on me whenever."

"Noted." We stare at each other with borderline cheesy expressions.

"You really are Murphy's Law," Nate says as he leans closer to me.

"I hate it."

"I don't. It wouldn't have brought us to this point. I very much approve. Please continue to always be that way." A smile brushes his lips in the sweetest way.

"I don't have a choice. It's a part of my DNA."

"I like your DNA."

I run my fingers along his chest and shoulders, feeling the hard muscles beneath my touch. His hands are on my back, fingers softly brushing my skin. We lazily trail each other's bodies, avoiding the obvious parts. Regardless, my breath hitches when he strokes my ribs, and his eyes darken when I trace his abs.

Scooting closer, I feel his length between us. I'm so tempted to reach into the water and stroke him, but I like this game more. It's a slow build-up, almost innocent. Time becomes a nonexistent thing.

His lips finally brush mine, and I sigh. We kiss and touch and breathe each other in until he can no longer control himself and cups my breasts. I tremble as his thumbs brush my nipples and his tongue invades my mouth.

I reach into the water and wrap my hand around his length, stroking him in measured movements. His hips jerk, and I smile.

"You mean so much to me," he says as he moves his lips from mine and stares into my eyes. The gold in his hazel eyes shine brighter, almost like flames dancing in his irises.

"I feel the same way." We aren't coming out and saying the words, but the emotions are laid bare.

He smashes his mouth against mine and steals my breath, my kisses, my heart. I allow him to take all of me. We shift and water sloshes out of the tub, but I couldn't care less.

His hands move down my body, finding my core. I moan as he touches me, my body quivering with need beyond his fingers. Moving over him, I position myself and look at him, waiting for his approval.

"Take me," he says, so I do.

I sink down on him, arching my body as he fills me. Nate's eyes close for a moment before blinking them open with intensity. His hands grip my hips and we move together, finding our rhythm. All I see and feel is him.

Our lips meld and we kiss until we're both panting and moaning. I could do this my entire life. Get lost in this man and forget the world. I shatter above him, hips jerking as my orgasm washes over me. Nate continues to thrust upward, prolonging my orgasm by taking my nipple between his teeth. When he stills inside of me, he curses and grips the back of my neck, swallowing my moans.

I vow to myself never to lose this. To work every day so we're always so attuned to each other. I promise myself to love this man until my last breath. No one else has ever taken out a

GUARDED DEPUTY

lizard without complaint, tried to fix my AC, or put up with my awkward and inappropriate comments.

When I told myself that I was going to remain single and focus on my career, this man shows up in my life and tempts me to break all my rules.

He's worth it, though.

chapter 28
NATE

I STAND OUTSIDE THE station and pocket my phone after reading an unwanted message. Things are going great, so the last thing I need is my past to knock on my front door. As it is, I have a meeting with Sheriff McCall, which I doubt has anything to do with work.

I run a hand down my face and walk into the station, ready for a lecture. I'd be lying if I said I didn't expect this. I actually thought the sheriff would call me sooner.

"Hey, man." Luke waves from behind the counter with a smile.

"Hey, how's it going?"

"Good, good. All is calm. How's the school?" Luke grins and winks.

"All good."

I haven't hung out with Luke in a couple of weeks. I spend the free time I have with Lizzy, but maybe we should go out with our friends. I wouldn't mind getting her on a dance floor.

"I'm going to go in and see Sheriff McCall."

"Good luck." He laughs as I walk back toward the office.

Knocking on the open door, Sheriff looks up at me and waves me in.

GUARDED DEPUTY

"Come in, Nate."

"Good afternoon."

Rubbing my hands down my pants, I enter and sit on a chair. I don't know why I'm nervous. I've never been nervous confronting anyone in my life, even if it has to do with my personal life.

Because Lizzy means a lot to you.

"I'm sure you can imagine why I called you in here."

"Pretty sure I have an idea." I sit straight, waiting for him to speak more than a few words.

"Lizzy is my niece. I love her as if she were my own daughter, especially after we tragically lost her father." McCall frowns, taking a deep breath before continuing. "I hear you two are seeing each other."

"Yes, sir."

"I've never been in a situation where one of my employees has a direct tie like this to a family member. I hope this doesn't affect your work here or the work you're doing at the school." He lifts a brow.

"Not at all. I understand the difference between my professional and personal life." I hope to hell he hasn't spoken to Principal Sanders.

"That's what I like to hear. I'm not going to throw threats your way. We're both grown men, and I trust you know how to respect a woman."

"I do." I finally relax, leaning back in my seat and breathing out the tension coiling through my body.

"Great. Now that we're over that awkward conversation..." He chuckles. "Tell me how things are going at the school."

265

"They're going well. The kids seem to be receptive to the classes, and the teens have started to take it seriously." My knee bounces.

"I'm happy to hear that. Remember how important this pilot program is for us. We need it to go well so the county allows us to implement it across public schools. I'll be going by some time in the next week or so with the superintendent so she can see how the program is run, observe you in action, all that." He looks at me seriously.

"Okay." I nod, hoping like hell that I impress the superintendent. A lot is riding on this, including my job.

My jaw tightens when my phone buzzes in my pocket, and I press the side button, ignoring the call.

"Is everything okay?" Sheriff asks, way too perceptive for my liking.

"Of course. Is there anything else?" My leg shakes some more.

"That's all. I'll let you know what I plan to go to the school."

I nod, standing. "Thanks, Sheriff."

"Don't thank me. I'm doing my job, and I expect the same from you." He gives me a pointed look.

"Right."

Nodding, I walk out of the office and find a few co-workers, who I say hi to.

My phone vibrates again in my pocket, interrupting my conversation, and I can barely contain my anger. I already know it's another string of messages I don't want from a person I have no interest in seeing.

I say goodbye and head out before I read the messages, blood pumping.

GUARDED DEPUTY

Unknown number: Hello, son. How are you? I know it's been years since we've spoken, and I want to mend that.

Unknown number: I can understand if you're upset or hesitant to meet with me.

Unknown number: Think about it. I'll wait for your call, but life has passed me by and I've realized how important family is. I want to get to know my kids again.

That son of a...

I take a deep breath, staring up at the blue sky. I wish it would calm me, but my body is shaking with anger. How dare he contact me as if nothing happened? As if apologizing for being a shitty father is acceptable through text message.

He abandoned us. You don't come back from that.

I kick a rock on the ground when what I really want to do is punch something. I take a few more deep breaths before getting in my car. Maybe driving right now isn't the best decision, but it's always been something that's soothed me. My knuckles turn white by how tightly I'm gripping the steering wheel as store fronts pass me by. When I make it to Bay Drive, I slow down. Lowering my windows, the saltiness of the ocean to my left soothes me. In a short time, the beach has become home. Become a familiarity that fills me with peace.

My phone rings, and I sigh when I see Lizzy's name on the screen. I hit the side button and ignore the call. I'm in no condition to talk to her. My mood will scare her away, and another person who's left me will be added to the list.

I scrub a hand down my face. I only saw my dad once after he left us. I was a teen. He was with another woman and didn't see me, but it was enough to realize he moved on with his life, forgetting all about us.

The last thing I need is that man to re-enter my life. What would Brooke think? I don't know about her, but I'd hate Walker to meet him, get close. If I can prevent him from living with the disappointment like what we went through, I will.

When my phone rings again, I reach for it and answer the call.

"Hello?" My voice comes out gruffer than I mean for it to.

"Hi." Lizzy's voice is soft. "Sorry, is this a bad time?"

"No, what's going on?" I pull over when I get a chance and put my car in park. I can't drive and have a conversation right now. My mind's all over the place.

"Are you okay?"

"I'm fine, Murphy. I'd be better if you were with me."

She giggles, and I imagine her shaking her head. The sound helps me relax, and I lean my head against the headrest and close my eyes.

"Well, I was calling to see if you're free tonight." Her voice holds a hint of teasing that makes me want to rush to her place and kiss her.

"Do you need a brave man to remove another lizard?" I joke.

"Thankfully, no. I should've rented an apartment in the top floor to make it harder for those devils to enter my apartment."

GUARDED DEPUTY

I laugh at her comment, stretching my neck to ease the tension there.

"What were you thinking for tonight?" I ask.

"My friends invited us out. They're going for drinks at Sips and Beats."

"Does that mean I get to dance with you?" It's exactly what I was thinking about earlier. Getting her in my arms is the perfect remedy to the shit my father makes me feel.

"Maaaybe."

"I'll take that maybe as a, 'Yes, Mr. Hot Deputy.'" I smile.

This woman is exactly what I need. She's my solace on dark days. My joy when I feel like life is spinning out of control.

"Don't forget packing."

I laugh at her comment. "I'll pick you up. Is nine okay?" It'll give me time to talk to Brooke about daddy dearest.

"That's perfect. Are you better? I could tell you weren't okay when you answered the phone."

"I'm good, Murphy. Talking to you makes everything better." It's the truth.

"You're making me swoon, Mr. Hot Deputy."

"Good." I put my phone on the loudspeaker and start driving home. "Remember that when I ask for a dance tonight."

"You know I'll save all my dance moves for you. Just be warned, they can be a bit awkward and jerky, especially if Luke Bryan comes on."

"Luke Bryan?"

"Yeah, his music just gets me excited. If only my dance skills were up to par." She sighs.

Chuckling, I vow to ask the bar to play Luke Bryan so I can witness this.

"I'll see you later. I'm getting home."

"Now? I mean, who cares? It doesn't matter when you get home. It's not my business to keep tabs on you," she rambles.

"Breathe, babe. I had to go to the station after work. Your uncle wanted to have a little chat."

"Oh. No."

"Oh, yes. Don't worry, though. We cleared a few things up, and then he put the pressure on about the program at school. I'm pretty sure that overshadowed our relationship status. Although, it's the first time a girlfriend's uncle confronts me about dating his niece."

"Thanks for letting me know," she deadpans. "Just what a girl wants to hear. I'll go into hiding now. Don't bother showing up at my place. My dance moves and I are staying in tonight."

"You're ridiculous. I'm seeing you tonight regardless. We gotta show the town those moves."

"Ohhhh, the town's seen them. On more than one occasion. Especially when vodka's been involved. I think they'll be happy to never witness them again."

I laugh at her comment, wondering how many times they've witnessed her moves. "But I haven't. I'll see you later. Don't stress about the sheriff. I told him my intentions are pure and honest."

"You're enjoying this way too much." If she only knew this was the distraction I needed. "I gotta go. Brooke is staring at me from the front door with a weird expression. See you later."

"Bye, Deputy." She blows a kiss, and I wish I were in person to savor her lips.

Stepping out of my car, I nod at Brooke.

GUARDED DEPUTY

"Hey, what's going on?" My steps are tentative in case she's also heard from our father.

"Wondering where you were. Dinner's almost ready."

Hooking my arm around her shoulder, I guide us into the house and close the door.

"I had to go to the station to talk to Sheriff McCall. I do need to talk to you about something, though. Is Walker in his room?"

Brooke looks at me with furrowed brows, concern lining her forehead.

"He is. What's going on?" She steps away to stand in front of me and stares at my face.

"I got a surprise and unwanted message today." Brooke's brows dip and she tilts her head.

"What was it?"

I don't even know how to tell her or find the right words without cursing the world, so I grab my phone, open the text message, and hand it to her.

Her wide eyes scan the screen, chest rising and falling rapidly.

"Is this real?" Her head snaps up.

"Seems so. Don't think anyone is playing a practical joke on me. Can you believe the guy?" I throw my hands in the air.

"What are you going to do?" Brooke's eyes glance up at me with concern.

"Ignore him until he gets tired of writing to me." I shrug, running a hand through my hair.

The amount of pain that man caused my mother. She never got over him leaving. Until her last breath, she questioned what she did wrong to push him away. Not to mention the trauma Brooke and I had from waking up one day and not having our father in our lives.

"I hope to hell he does. I have no intentions of seeing him again. Who the fuck does he think he is?" She clenches her fists.

"What's wrong, Mom?" Walker comes into the kitchen. His eyebrows furrow before he looks at the stove. "Is dinner ready?"

"Yeah, we'll eat now. Help me set the table."

"Do I have to?" Walker drops his arms and groans.

"Yeah, you do." Brooke nods and arches her eyebrows in a stern mom-look.

"Fine." Walker sighs. "I need the plates." He lifts his arm up limply as a sign that he's too short to reach the top cabinet where the plates are.

I shake my head, grab three plates, and hand them to him. Then, I look at Brooke.

"We'll talk about this tomorrow. I'm going out after dinner."

"With Lizzy?"

"Is Ms. Andrews coming?" Walker looks at me with wide eyes.

"No, buddy." I cut my gaze to Brooke.

"Uncle Nate is going out with her tonight. It's you and me at home, sweetie. How about we make cookies and watch a movie?"

"I guess." Walker shrugs. "I can't go with you?" He looks at me, and I chuckle.

"Not tonight. Why don't the three of us do something tomorrow? Breakfast?" I give Walker my best smile. He's gotten used to having me around at all hours, and I don't want him feeling like he's being pushed to the side.

"Okay." He smiles, going to the drawer to grab forks and knives.

"Thanks." Brooke squeezes my arm.

GUARDED DEPUTY

"Anything for y'all. Don't worry about what I told you. We'll figure it out." I kiss the top of her head and help Walker set the table.

chapter 29
LIZZY

"Did my uncle really question you?" I ask Nate as he drives to Sips and Beats. As soon as he told me that Uncle Roy spoke to him, I wanted to die.

It shouldn't surprise me, but I can't help but feel embarrassed.

"He sure did." Nate smiles my way while keeping his eyes on the road.

"Is it too late to melt into a puddle and evaporate in the heat?"

Nate chuckles, shaking his head.

"I get it, Murphy. You mean something to him, and I'm glad you have family that cares about you."

"You don't mind?" I shift in my seat, pulling the seatbelt a bit and turning to look at him.

"Nah. Besides, Sheriff McCall is a simple guy. We spoke a bit, cleared the air, and moved on."

"Guys are easier. They say what they need to without run-arounds or feeling like they might offend each other." I sigh, falling back in my seat.

Nate laughs, reaching out to squeeze my thigh.

GUARDED DEPUTY

"If it means I can be with you without any problems, I'd talk to your uncle about my intentions every day." His words hit me straight in the heart.

Nate gets to the street Sips and Beats is on and finds a parking spot a few feet away.

"Ready to dance with me, Ms. Andrews?" He gives me a lopsided smile.

"I'm still deciding, Mr. Deputy." I wink and step out of the truck.

Nate gets out and meets me by the passenger side, caging me against the door.

"I'll be the happiest man if you do." He leans in and kisses me.

I melt against the metal door and wrap one arm around his neck. Kissing him back, I close my eyes and sink into this feeling.

"Is that a yes?" Nate asks against my lips.

"No one else I'd rather dance with." I comb my fingers through the back of his hair, and he moans.

"Let's go inside before we head back to your place." His husky voice makes my belly clench.

"I expect you to spin me around the dance floor before you get any loving." I jab his chest teasingly.

"You got it, babe." He kisses the corner of my mouth and pushes off the truck, reaching his hand out for me to grab.

I hold his hand and walk into the bar feeling like the main character in one of my beloved romance novels. I've got the best guy by my side. Nate looks over at me and winks as we reach our friends.

"I've gotta say, this is quite the view," Dani says, wiggling her fingers at us. I roll my eyes and shake my head.

"Hey." Nate smiles at her.

"Don't 'Hey' me Mr. Deputy. You've stolen my best friend and think a smile with dimples is going to win me over. No, siree." She shakes her finger at him.

"Don't listen to her." I look up at him.

"I guess your talk with Sheriff went well today," Luke adds, smirking.

I roll my eyes before looking at him. Nate chuckles, squeezing my hand.

"It went great." He nods.

"I need new friends," I say.

"Nonsense." Dani waves her hand. "We're the best you'll find. Right, Lukey?" She gets on her toes and hooks her arm around his neck.

"I hate when you call me that." He glares at her, and I laugh.

"You secretly love it." She blows him a kiss and releases him.

"Hey, guys." Avery comes up behind me.

I turn around and smile at her and Gabriel.

"You made it," I tell her.

"Yup. I might fall asleep on the bar, but we're here for a one drink." She holds her finger up. "We really need to plan these outings on Saturdays since I close the bakery on Sundays."

"True," I nod.

"Life is short and we are young," Dani says. "We need to celebrate any chance we get."

"Is she already drunk?" Nate whispers in my ear.

"No, this is Dani in her element."

"Gotcha. What do you want to drink?"

"Can I go wild tonight since I have a DD?" I wink at him.

GUARDED DEPUTY

"You can go wild with me later tonight." His breath tickles my ear.

I giggle and shove his chest.

"No secrets, lovebirds," Dani calls out.

I sigh, taking a step back, and glare at her. She's smiling widely, though.

"I'll have a beer," I tell Nate.

"Coming right up." He steps toward the bar.

"Things seem to be going good." Avery smiles.

"They are." I nod. "We've gotten closer these last few weeks."

"I'm happy to hear that." She taps her elbow with mine.

"He seems like a nice guy," Gabriel says.

"He is." I bite my lip and look over at Nate. He's looking down at his phone when the bartender stops in front of him.

Sips and Beats has quite a crowd of people gathered tonight and country music plays through the speakers. The gray walls add to the dimness in the place, creating a cozy ambience. People love coming here to hang out and meet with friends. It's a guaranteed good time.

"Hey!" Andrea joins our group, and I smile at her and wave.

"Long time no see," I joke.

"It's been for-ev-er." She imitates Squints from *The Sandlot*.

I laugh and shake my head.

"How are you, Church?" Luke asks.

"Great. Ready to let loose." Andrea shimmies.

Luke lifts his brows and stares at her.

"Too much?" She scrunches up her face.

"A tad. Tone it down a bit."

"Jerk," she says.

"Here you go." Nate returns and hands me my beer. "Hey, Ms. Church." He smiles at her.

"I think we can stop with the professionalism here, Deputy Moore." She arches a brow and looks between us.

"Yup." He nods, wrapping his arm around my waist.

I take a sip of my beer, looking at my friends interact. Smiling, I move my head to the George Strait song and hum along.

Nate gets to know my friends more, especially Avery and Gabriel, who he's had less time to interact with. Dani smiles and wags her eyebrows. I chuckle at her and shake my head.

"You two look adorable together," she says beside me.

"Thanks." I grin, unable to hide my happiness.

When the song changes, Nate reaches for my hand. "Let's dance." He grabs my beer with his other hand and places it on the high-top next to us.

We move a few steps away where other people are dancing and move to the beat. He spins me around before placing one of his hands on my waist. My body tingles and warms under his touch.

"You're gorgeous." Nate looks into my eyes.

"And you're handsome." I reach up and cup his face.

He closes his eyes, turning his head to kiss my palm. His beard feels like home against my skin. My other arm goes around his head, and I step closer, looking into his eyes. The world fades around us as I connect with the man who's stolen my heart after telling myself that it was closed for business.

"I can't tell you enough how happy I am that we met," he says.

"Me too. I'm glad I made an unforgettable impression on you." I wink.

GUARDED DEPUTY

Nate laughs deeply, kissing my forehead. I'm happy he sounds better than he did when I called him earlier. I was worried when I heard the bite in his voice, but it seems he's okay.

We dance and laugh, Nate singing the song along with the musician. As perfect as he is, he does not have the voice of an angel, and I laugh at the way his voice cracks when he attempts to sing at a higher pitch.

When the song ends, we head back to our friends, who are talking, some of them dancing. I grab my beer and take a drink. Nate leans against the table and talks to Luke.

I glance at him from the corner of my eye, smiling at the way he fits in so well. His laughter when Luke says something makes me smile. Suddenly, Nate tenses.

He reaches into his pocket and takes out his phone, looking at it with a scowl. His fist clenches around the phone before shoving it back in his pocket. Luke seems oblivious, but I can't help but notice the way Nate's demeanor changes.

"Are you okay?" Avery asks.

"Yeah." I smile. "Just tired."

"Tell me about it." She suppresses a yawn.

"It might be time to take Avery back home, ladies." Gabriel wraps his arm around us.

Avery glares at him and elbows his ribs. "Hush, Grinch. You're alert because you decided to sleep in." Avery and Gabriel met during the holidays when he wanted to buy her bakery, and she nicknamed him her Grinch.

"I was also up until late with online meetings with my bakeries on the West Coast." He arches a brow.

"Whatever." Avery rolls her eyes.

279

Gabriel owns a popular chain of bakeries across the country, and now he helps Avery run her local bakery in town. They met a few months ago and are the perfect match.

I smile at their exchange and look back at Nate. He's once again looking at his phone, Luke nowhere to be seen.

"Excuse me," I tell my friends and go to Nate.

I wrap an arm around his waist. "Hey."

He jolts, snapping his head up at me. Well, that's not the reaction you want your boyfriend to have when you touch him.

"Hi." He forces a smile.

I furrow my eyebrows, surprised at his reaction.

"Is everything okay?"

"Yeah." His jaw ticks, and he looks at Luke again.

"Are you sure? Because you were giving your phone an awful glare."

"It's nothing Lizzy. Drop it," he says harshly.

I blink at him, surprised by his tone. His face is proof that he's not in a good mood with his flared nostrils and tight jaw.

A heaviness settles in the pit of my stomach. It's the same reaction he gave me over the phone.

So much for thinking it was nothing. Something's up with him. I try to focus on my friends again, but my eyes wander to Nate. This is the same version of the man who was at the concert. His hot and cold mood is back, and I swore we had overcome that. I know we have.

"You're not okay." I push.

"I'm fine. I need to go, though. If you want to stay and have Dani take you home, that's fine."

GUARDED DEPUTY

"Whoa, whoa. What?" I tilt my head and hold my hand out. "Are you trying to get rid of me?" I point to myself. Tears burn my eyes, but I take a deep breath to keep them at bay.

"No." He sighs. "But I understand if you don't want to leave yet. I'm just..." He shakes his head.

"Talk to me. Why don't we get out of here and you tell me what's going on?" I reach out to squeeze his hand but drop it when Nate shakes his head.

"I just want to go home."

"I can walk back to my apartment." Sips and Beats is within walking distance to my apartment. It's the plus side of living in a small town.

"I'd rather you didn't." His eyes shine with frustration and sadness.

"I could use the fresh air." I'm so confused.

"Let me drive you." He nods.

"I have no idea what's going on with you or what you're hiding, but I notice the way you react each time you look at your phone. We were having fun, dancing, laughing." I blink quickly to dry the tears. "I'm not going to apologize for feeling hurt that my boyfriend can't trust me or the tone you're taking with me. Or think that what you're hiding is evidence for me not trusting you." My lower lip trembles, so I tuck it in and bite down on it.

"You can trust me, Lizzy." His voice is pained, his eyes sad. When his hand squeezes mine, I take a stabilizing breath to keep my emotions at bay.

"Are you sure?" I can't keep my eyes on his, though, because I'm about to lose it in this bar and the last thing I need is to be front page on Emerald Bay's gossip cycle tomorrow.

"I am. I just need some time to figure something out, but it has nothing to do with you or us."

I laugh humorlessly because it sure as hell feels like it. "Whatever. I'm gonna go." I signal Dani and let her know I'm leaving. Her brows pull together, but I walk away before she can question me. Nate walks behind me.

Maybe I'm overreacting, but something about this feels wrong in my gut. I want him to trust me, not put up his walls again when something comes up.

"Lizzy." He reaches for my hand and tugs me toward him. When he stands before me, I keep my eyes on his chest. "Trust me." He brushes my hair away from my face.

"It's a family matter. I need to talk to Brooke."

I nod because there's nothing else to say.

"Come on." He opens the door on the passenger side of his truck.

I look at him for a beat and then get in. I'm not in the mood to argue about him driving me, and my feet would hurt to walk in these heels. So much for dressing up more than usual and hoping to have the best time with my boyfriend.

A piece of me feels like we have a brick wall between us no matter how much Nate says that what's going on has nothing to do with us.

I hope he's right, but my stomach feels like lead. Like dead moths are lying in the pit of it, making me nauseas. It's like the happiness I found is being stripped away.

If this isn't the epitome of Murphy's Law, then I don't know what is.

chapter 30
LIZZY

My weekend only got gloomier when I barely heard from Nate except a couple of short text messages. He asked me to trust him, but I don't know how I can if he's shutting me out.

When Dani called me to have coffee Sunday morning, I desperately agreed. Apparently, she wasn't oblivious to Nate and my argument at Sips and Beats because it was the first thing she asked me about.

Her words of encouragement didn't help a ton, but I appreciate her being there for me and letting me vent.

Hopefully, the day goes by quickly so I can go back home. Thankfully, being at school has provided a small distraction from my feelings.

"Ms. Andrews?" Stephanie asks.

"Yeah?" I lift my head to look at her.

"Are you okay? You look sad."

"Of course." I nod, shaking off this mood. Kids are too perceptive. I need to feign being happy or they'll figure out what's going on.

"Did you break up with your boyfriend?" Dana asks.

"What? No." I shake my head. "I don't..." I pause and look at Walker, who's staring at me with squinted eyes. I don't want to

GUARDED DEPUTY

say something that he'd misinterpret since he knows Nate and I are dating.

This is why people recommend not dating someone you have some sort of connection with, less so if it's in your professional life.

"Let's get to work." I clap my hands, not sure why, and guide them to the page they're on in their reading book.

I distract myself in the lesson, going over vocabulary, asking my students comprehension questions, and being amazed at how smart and interested they are in this lesson.

Seeing them flourish is one of the reasons I love teaching. Listening to their ideas and thoughts, the individual people they are at such a young age, is the best feeling in the world.

I may miss moments like this when I'm a counselor, but I know that I'll be serving a greater purpose. What I was meant to do.

When I drop my students off in the music room for their class, I head to the teacher's lounge in hopes there's some coffee left. I could really use something stronger than watered down excuse for caffeine, but alas, drinking alcohol while at work is frowned upon.

The door to the lounge opens, and I look up. I freeze, heart beating like a wild animal, when I see Nate.

"Hey," he says.

"Hi." I look at my mug and stir in some sugar.

"How are you?" He walks toward me.

"Good and you?"

"I'm okay." He nods, shifting on his feet.

Awkward silence settles over us, and I take a drink of coffee. I hate that we're acting this way. If I didn't know any better, I'd say he's keeping his distance at work because of what Principal Sanders told us. I wish his distance was from self-restraint.

Taking a deep breath, I let my heart settle and look at Nate.

"Well, I gotta go to work."

He nods, swallowing thickly, but doesn't say anything else. I shake my head as my hands tremble with sadness. After all the terrible boyfriends I've had, you'd think I'd be used to this. But Nate felt different. He felt like forever. Like a whispered promise to my heart that I deserved more than shitty relationships.

I walk to my classroom, thankful it's empty, and sit at my desk. Dropping my head to my hands, I take a shaky breath. This situation sucks. Even if I wanted to talk to Nate again, he was quick to tell me that the situation had nothing to do with me.

Not that that's comforting.

My classroom door opens, and I curse under my breath before looking up at the intruder. Andrea freezes with wide eyes.

"Whoa. You do not look good. What's going on?" She inches closer to my desk.

"Nothing." I shake my head and push my coffee to the side. It's not going to make me feel better. If anything, it'll make me angrier that I have to drink terrible coffee.

"I was going to ask if Nate was okay, but seeing your face tells me he isn't. Did you two fight?"

I love Andrea, but I do not want to talk about this.

"No," I lie.

"Right." She rolls her eyes.

"I don't want to talk about it." Tears build in my eyes.

"Okay." She smiles softly. "I'm gonna go out to buy lunch. Do you want me to bring you anything?"

"I'm okay. Thanks, though."

GUARDED DEPUTY

"A coffee?" Her brows lift as she grins.

"If you go to the coffee shop, yeah, but don't go out of your way."

"I've got you, boo. I'll see you later." She waves and walks out of my classroom, leaving me alone for a few more minutes before I have to pick up my class again.

I cross Nate in the hallway when I'm walking back with my kids. He barely acknowledges me, which is like a stab in my heart. Walker waves at him, but he doesn't get much of a reaction either.

That's not like him at all. He lives for his nephew.

I focus on my students and get back to teaching. Anything to make me forget the pressure in my chest.

When it's lunch time, I eat in my room and thank Andrea when she brings me a Frap. I really have the best friends.

By the time the day ends, I'm ready to race home, shower, and put on sweats. If I could call in sick tomorrow, I would, but my conscience won't let me. Besides, Nate will be at the high school tomorrow. Wednesday, on the other hand, is a different story since it's the day he comes into my classroom.

"Mom!" Walker yells, running to Mrs. Lundsten.

I inch back when I see her, expecting Nate to pick him up.

"Hi, Ms. Andrews."

"Hi." I smile at her, remaining professional for the sake of my career.

"How's Walker doing?"

"He's great. He's a smart kid." I ruffle his hair playfully, and he laughs.

"I'm happy to hear that." She shifts on her feet, looking at me. She leans in, catching me by surprise. "Be patient with him."

Her lips press together, and I have a feeling she's no longer talking about Walker.

I nod, forcing a smile.

"Come on, Mom." Walker pulls her arm.

"Bye," she says.

"Bye." I wave.

"Did Nate leave?" Andrea whispers.

"Your guess is as good as mine." I shrug.

She frowns, but I shake my head. I don't want my co-workers to start talking. It's bad enough that we were the center of school gossip when word got out that we were dating. I don't want the same thing to happen when things aren't going well.

After all my kids leave, I go to my class to shut off the computer and put away some papers before leaving. I drive away feeling deflated. Not even my Frap made me feel better.

My phone buzzes, and I look down to see Nate's name across the screen. I hesitate before opening the message to see what he said. I'd love anything that would give me some insight into what's going on.

Nate: Hey, sorry about earlier.

That's it? I put the phone down and slam on my brakes right on time to prevent an accident. The car honks at me, and I lift my hand in apology.

"I know. I know. I should pay attention. Got it, dude." I roll my eyes sarcastically and focus on the road and traffic around me. It'll give me time to respond to his message with something other than, It's okay.

GUARDED DEPUTY

When I get home, I grab my phone and stare at the message, fingers hovering over the screen. I take a deep breath and lean back on the couch.

Me: Hey, I accept your apology.

That sounds so formal. Oh, well. I'm uninspired.

Nate: My mind's a mess.

Me: Why? I know you said it's not about us but you've put a ton of space between us so I can't help but wonder if you're telling the truth.

I hold my breath as I wait for his response. My hands tremble, and my legs bounce.

Nate: No, Murphy. I have no doubt about us.

Me: Then talk to me, Nate. I'm breaking over here.

Nate: Don't say that.

Me: I feel like I lost you.

Nate: You haven't. Can we talk tomorrow after work?

Me: Yea

Nate: Thanks

Me: You're welcome.

I drop my phone on the couch next to me and close my eyes, letting the tears build since I don't have an audience. They sneak through the corner of my eyes, trailing down my cheeks. My lip trembles, and I cry for the first time since Nate gave me the cold shoulder. I didn't allow myself to be weak last night, but the pressure is too much today.

I rub my chest with the heel of my hand and take a deep breath to calm my galloping heart that pounds against the base of my throat.

GUARDED DEPUTY

I lie down on the couch in fetal position, hugging a cushion and burying my face into it. Tears stain the fabric, and my body shakes with my cries. Letting it out is therapeutic.

Losing track of time, I finally sit up when my tears have dried up and take a shower. Looking around my bathtub, memories of Nate and I in here hit me like a wave of longing, and I lean my head back to let the shower wash away my sadness.

It's a good sign that he wants to talk tomorrow. Maybe we can clear the air, and I'll know what's going on so I can help him. I feel ridiculous being this sad, and it only angers me more at myself.

It's a cycle of feeling guilty and hurt.

The shower helps soothe me, and I reach for my phone, ordering a pizza. I want to eat my feelings today, and pepperoni pizza with extra cheese is the way to go. While I wait for the pizza to arrive, I turn on *Gilmore Girls* re-runs and smile at Lorelai's antics.

Sometimes I wish life was like the movies, and there was an obvious slope that builds the story, leads to a climax that drops where we know will have a clean resolution. Instead, it's messy and real. It can't be tied together with a pretty bow.

Humans are complicated, our pasts intricate and webbed. We drag issues that mold us, change us, and make us react.

Nate's life hasn't been easy from what he's told me, but I hoped that I could be a shimmer of light in his life.

Maybe I still can.

chapter 31

NATE

"WHAT IF THE PERSON who offers you drugs is your parent?" One of the sophomores asks. I'm at the high school today, which gives me space to think about what I'm going to tell Lizzy without risking running into her.

The last few days have been hell. The way Lizzy looked at me with disappointment on Friday night and then again yesterday at work is eating me up. I hate it.

But my dad doesn't stop contacting me. I already told him we weren't interested in a reunion from hell.

"Come on, man, be serious," another student says.

"I am. My cousin lives in South Florida and his stories are wild. He has classmates whose families are the ones with drugs."

"That's messed up." One of the girls speaks up.

"Regardless of who it is, it's not in your best interest to take any substance unless you wanna end up washed away, broke and alone," I tell them.

Besides, family members aren't always the best examples of morals and right decisions. No need to voice that or the kids will look at me as if I'm crazy. And I really don't want a bunch of teens dissecting my life.

GUARDED DEPUTY

I focus back on my lesson of the day. Working with teenagers allows me to be more candid and open since they know more about the world.

"Addiction is real, and the risks and consequences are not something to take lightly." I look at the students. "Do you like your life? Your friends?"

They nod silently.

"The life you currently live can disappear with the snap of your fingers. We're talking jail, abandonment, health issues, death." I stare at them intently.

"Anti-drugs campaigns aren't just a social movement to make people look good. I know how y'all joke about it because I was your age, too, but the older you get and the more you meet people outside of this small town, you'll be faced with hard decisions." I take a deep breath.

In Dallas I worked with troubled teens. Here I'm working with preventative actions. It feels nice, and these kids are funny as hell when I'm in a better mood.

A knock on the door interrupts us, and I see the receptionist peek her head in.

"Deputy Moore?"

"Yes?" I stand.

"I have someone here asking for you. Can you please come out here a moment?"

My face hardens, and I pray to all that's holy that it isn't who I think it is.

"Write out a list of reasons you'd never do drugs while I talk to Mrs. Summers," I tell the class and walk out.

I see the man who had a hand in creating me and want to punch him when I see his smug smile.

293

"I'm sorry to interrupt, but he said it's a family emergency."

"Of course. Thank you." I nod and force a smile so she doesn't think anything of it.

When she walks away, I glare at my dad. His eyes are lined with wrinkles, and he has a pudgy belly. I used to think he was so tall, and now I'm a few inches taller, making me feel like I have the power.

"What the hell are you doing here?" I hiss.

"You kept ignoring me." He shrugs indifferently.

"I'm at work. You can't just show up here." I see some of the students looking at us through the small window on the door and grab my dad's arm to shove him away from view.

"You look good in your uniform, son."

"Don't call me son." My voice sounds menacing. "You lost that privilege when you fucking abandoned us. If you haven't heard from me, it's because I don't give two shits about seeing you."

"I just want to make things right. It's never too late to be sorry. You and Brooke deserve a father you're proud of. I know I have a grandson, too. I want to meet him."

"Don't you dare." I fist his shirt. "He's better off without ever knowing you. We don't need him to feel unwanted the way we did." I'm inches from his face, my other hand clenched by my side.

I hear footsteps and step back, smoothing out his wrinkled shirt. My dad barely flinches.

"I know you're angry, and it's my fault. Let me make it up to you. Give me a chance to prove I'm determined to be a father."

"You're twenty years too late. I have to get back to work. Leave," I warn harshly. "Don't ruin this job for me. The last

GUARDED DEPUTY

thing I want is to escort you out of here." I may have that power, but I don't want people in town talking. There's no denying I'm his son when people see our similarities.

"Not until you give me a few minutes of your time."

I hear whispering and more kids looking at us. Causing a scene here is the least thing I need. I see Sheriff McCall coming down the hall with a woman, and I step back.

"Fine. Get out and wait until I call you."

"Thank you, son." He nods, smiling.

The past twenty years haven't been easy on him based on the wrinkles marking his face, but they were worst for my mother so I can feel zero compassion for this man.

"Deputy Moore," Sheriff says, eyeing my dad.

"Hi, Sheriff." It doesn't look good that I'm not doing my job if the superintendent is here to observe me. I've left the students alone to deal with my father. I swear if he ruins this for me...

"You're done with your current class, right?" Sheriff widens his eyes.

"Yup. I'll be starting my next one in ten minutes."

"Great, Superintendent Cramer and I will wait for you in that classroom. I have your schedule here." I hold up the paper.

"Okay." My jaw is tense, and I glower at my dad to get the hell out of here.

I walk back into the classroom, and the students race to their seats as if I were an idiot. I hope to hell that Sheriff drags the superintendent away from here so she won't see the kids leaving the classroom and catch me neglecting my duties.

"Was that your dad, Deputy?"

I glare at Scott.

"Obviously. They look alike," Tessa says, rolling her eyes at Scott.

"Did you write your list?" I arch a brow.

"Uhh...the thing is that we were brainstorming together." Scott smirks as if he's a genius because I know they were spying on me.

"Well, then you have homework to do." I smile.

The bell rings as they groan, and I clap my hands to get their attention.

"Bring your list of thirty reasons next week."

"Thirty?" The kids call out.

"Let's make it forty, then."

"No, thirty is fine." Rob, another student, calls out. "Right, guys?" He stares at them with wide eyes.

"Yup," they say collectively.

"Great. See you next week." I wait for them to walk out of the room before I grab my things and leave. My hands tremble with anger as I fish my phone out of my pocket and send Brooke a warning text that our father's in town.

Brooke: You're kidding.

Me: I wish, sis. In order to get him out, I told him I'd call him. I don't want to talk to him, but if it'll get him to leave town, then I'll do it.

GUARDED DEPUTY

Brooke: Yea. I can see if Walker can stay with a friend, and we can have him come to the house. I don't want to see him in public.

Me: Same

I put my phone away and get to my next class, telling myself to focus on my job and forget my personal life for a little while. I need to make a good impression on the superintendent so this program moves forward.

I can't let my dad ruin anything else in my life.

ele

"I don't know if I like that Dad is going to know where we live, but it's this or talk to him outside somewhere and risk people overhearing us," Brooke says.

"I know." I nod. "I'm just glad Walker was able to stay with a friend."

I want to avoid him hearing anything unpleasant because I can't guarantee I'll be on my best behavior. I've been fuming all day, but at least the superintendent seemed pleased with her observations and congratulated us for the work we're doing.

I pace the living room, waiting for my dad to arrive. It's a slow torture waiting to get this over with. Brooke's been nervous all afternoon, and I hate it for her. She's gone through enough to have the ghost of our father return. I walk to her and give her a side hug.

297

"It's going to be okay."

"I know." She smiles up at me. "I don't know how it's going to feel to see him again after all these years. What he did to Mom, to us..." She shakes her head, trailing off.

"It was a bastard move," I finish for her.

"Yeah." She sighs.

A knock echoes around the house, and we look at each other.

"Let's get this over with." I squeeze her shoulder and move to the front door.

I open it to find my beaming father. He whistles and looks at the porch.

"Nice place you have here." His smugness makes me furious.

"It's Brooke's place, and she's worked her ass off to have it. No thanks to you."

Brooke appears at the door, arms crossed.

"My baby girl," my dad croons.

"Save it," she bites out.

He flinches, furrowing his brows. "I deserve that." He looks down at his feet.

I don't buy his act one bit. The man is shameless.

"Can we talk?" He blinks up at us. "Like I told Nate, I just want a chance to make things right." He takes a deep breath.

Brooke nods, stepping away. I already see a few neighbors looking out their windows at the situation.

"Come in." I close the door and walk into the living room.

My dad looks around, taking in the decorated living room with photographs. He walks to a family picture of Brooke, David, and Walker on the TV stand. Grabbing the frame, he smiles.

GUARDED DEPUTY

"I have a handsome grandson. Looks just like his mother." He turns his head toward Brooke. "Is he with his dad now?"

I take a deep breath and look at Brooke.

"No." Her voice is cold.

He must notice because he places the frame back where it was and looks at us.

"I don't know where to begin." He frowns. "Leaving my family behind was the biggest mistake I've made. I know that nothing I say will be enough for you to forgive me, but I hope you'll give me a chance to at least get to know each other again." He smiles, and it almost seems genuine.

"You left us, Dad. You broke Mom's heart, and we had to struggle to make ends meet. If you cared at all, even if you fell out of love with Mom, the least you could've done was take care of us. We are your children, you know?" Brooke stands tall, arms crossed.

"You're right." He bows his head.

"You seem to have done well for yourself despite that. Both of you." He glances between us. "My two kids are grown up and professionals. Brooke with a family. Nate a man of the law." He boasts proudly.

"Don't let this view fool you. It hasn't been easy getting here, thanks to you," I tell him. "Now, if this is what you came to say, you can go." I lift my hand toward the front door.

"Tell me about my grandson. At least give me that," he tells Brooke, ignoring me.

"Why? So you can break his heart like you did to me by disappearing without a trace?" She lifts her brows.

"Right." He frowns. "Remember when I taught you how to throw a football? We watched the Cowboys every week." His eyes shift to mine.

I hate that he uses this to get to me. It's my favorite memory of him. It was our thing to play catch and cheer on our home team.

I nod silently as memories rush my mind, the first time I threw a spiral and he carried me on his shoulders like I won the Super Bowl, when he bought me my Cowboys jersey so we could match, teasing my mom about her lack of football knowledge. It all crashes over me like a wave, and I take a seat on the couch, rubbing my jaw.

"What do you want?" I ask, tired.

"I already told you. I want to start over and make up for lost time." He sits beside me, squeezing my shoulder.

I shake him off and look at Brooke for guidance. She sighs, tears building in her eyes. I crack my neck and turn to my dad.

"We need time."

"Let me treat you to dinner. I can order a pizza while we talk. I can meet my grandson. What's his name?"

"Walker," Brooke responds.

"Walker. I like it." He nods with a wistful smile.

My sister looks at me and nods. I sigh and shrug. While we have our silent conversation, my dad leans back on the sofa and looks around the living room.

"I'll go pick Walker up while you order the pizza," Brooke says.

"Thank you, sweetie." My dad stands and hugs her, catching her off-guard. Brooke's eyes widen before her arms pat his back.

GUARDED DEPUTY

"Don't mention his father," she says when she steps away from him. "He passed away a couple of years ago and we're still recovering."

"I'm sorry to hear that."

"Go on, sis. We'll grab the pizza. It'll be faster than waiting for delivery." I look at my father expectantly, but he remains on the couch. "Ready?"

"Why don't you go? I don't want any questions about who I am or our family history. This really is a small town." He stands, fishes his wallet from his back pocket, and grabs a twenty. "Like this we can leave our private life out of small-town gossipers." He presses his lips together.

I watch him carefully, unsure if I should trust him. My dad keeps holding the bill out between us. I snatch the twenty from his hand and point at him with narrowed eyes.

"Don't do anything stupid. You're lucky you're even here."

"I wouldn't dare. I'm determined to prove it to you, Nate. Your resentment is valid, but I plan to change your mind." He smiles, nodding encouragingly.

"I'll be back soon, and Brooke shouldn't be more than ten minutes." I clench my jaw, praying I'm making the right decision.

I grab my phone to call in the order before driving off so I don't have to wait long. When I hang up I see a text message notification. Opening it, I curse when I see it's from Lizzy asking what time we were going to get together.

Fuck, fuck, fuck.

I forgot I told Lizzy we'd talk today. I slam the steering wheel and pull out of the driveway, racing to House of Pies to pick up

301

the pizza. When I get to the restaurant, I step out of my car and walk in, sending Lizzy a text message apologizing.

Me: Lizzy, I'm sorry. I'll call you later tonight.

Me: Fuck. I want this.

"Hey," I tell one of the waiters and walk to the pick-up counter while I wait for my pizza.

I talk to a few people who say hello, not in the mood to socialize. My life's a mess. It's not exactly something I want to talk about. I want to stay to myself, process what's going on, and talk to Lizzy.

I stare at the screen but there's no sign that she's responding. I'll give her some time, be done with this stupid dinner with my dad, and talk to her. I can't lose her. She's become the most important woman in my life. The one I hope to have a future with.

I won't end up like my father.

My phone rings as I'm paying for the pizza, and I see Brooke's name on the screen.

"Hey, I'm heading home now," I answer and walk out of the restaurant.

"Nate." Her voice sounds panicked. "Someone broke into the house."

chapter 32

NATE

MY HEART POUNDS AS her words sink in.

"What? That can't be right. I left Dad—" I stop immediately, kicking the ground. "Fuck! That son of a bitch," I growl, throwing the pizza box and garnering the attention of people nearby.

"He..." Brooke's voice shakes. "I don't understand."

"I'll be right there. Don't touch anything."

"Okay." She cries, and it breaks my heart.

I shouldn't have trusted the bastard. I pick up the pizza box from the floor to throw out at home and race to the house. Guilt consumes me for leaving him alone at the house. The part of me that's a broken ten-year-old believed the man when all he does is leave. The boy in me trusted him enough to think he'd at least stick around for dinner, even if it was one last meal. The one we never got when I was a child since he simply never returned home from work.

But to make it seem like someone broke into the house.

What the hell happened?

I pull into the driveway and fling the door open, stepping out. I run up the porch steps and find Brooke hugging Walker as he cries.

GUARDED DEPUTY

"I'm going to kill him," I yell.

Walker squeezes Brooke tighter, and I frown.

"Sorry."

My wide eyes assess the situation a part of me breaking at the thought that our father would do this after so many years. He didn't just make it seem like someone broke in. It seems he was the intruder. Didn't he have enough abandoning us?

The couch cushions seem like they were lifted and hastily placed back down. Some of the kitchen cabinets are open.

"My bedroom," Brooke says.

I stalk that way and find her drawers open and contents spilled about. Her mattress is off-center, and the secret drawer in her dresser is open and empty. Brooke had some money saved in there. I scrub my face, tears burning my eyes.

She doesn't deserve this. Hell, I don't deserve this.

As I go into Walker's room, I pray he didn't touch it. It's the least the asshole could do. I breathe out when I see it's as it should be.

When I walk into my bedroom, some things are a mess but not as bad as Brooke's. He must've gone to hers first and run out of time.

I run a hand down my face and slam it on top of the dresser. It rattles beneath my palm. My eyes sting with emotions. For the boy who lost his dad. For the man who is angry. For the unfair world we live in.

I take a few deep breaths, not wanting Brooke and Walker to see me like this. I have to be strong for them, show them we'll overcome this. When I feel like I have strength in my legs, I go back to the living room.

305

FABIOLA FRANCISCO

"It's okay, buddy." I bend down and talk to Walker. "We're safe."

Tears trail down his face, and I hate my father more than I thought possible for doing this to Walker. For scaring him unnecessarily.

"What if they come back?" he asks.

"He won't," I promise him. "A bad man did this, but he's gone now."

"How do you know?" Walker's round eyes shine with moisture.

"Because he got what he wanted." I hug him tightly and look up at Brooke, who's trying and failing to hold back her cry.

I nod, reassuring her.

After making sure he believes us, we get Walker to go to his room. I sit on the couch with Brooke, dropping my head in my hands.

"Should we call the police?" she asks.

"And accuse our own father of stealing from us? I'll give you the money."

"No, Nate." She shakes her head.

"Yes. I'm the one who left him here alone. I should've known better." I slam my fist into my forehead. Brooke grabs my arm and lowers it.

"I thought he was being honest. I believed him." Her voice trembles.

"Me too," I admit. "Even if it was just to hear him out and then decide we wanted nothing to do with him."

"Yeah." She sighs, looking around. Her eyes are swollen.

GUARDED DEPUTY

"I fucked up. I was supposed to meet Lizzy today to talk to her, tell her what's going on. I've been shutting her out. When Dad showed up, I totally forgot."

"Go talk to her now."

I shake my head. "I don't think she wants to see me."

"Our dad fucks with our emotions. It's like we revert back to those kids again, needing to be wanted by him. Tell her that. Be honest and open instead of guarding yourself. She's a good person, and it's clear she loves you." Brooke squeezes my hand, and the air rushes out of me.

Love.

We haven't talked about that, but I love her and she doesn't even know it.

"You think I should show up at her place?"

"If a man wanted to apologize, I'd hope he'd move mountains to make it happen." She smiles sadly.

"Are you okay alone?" It's been an emotional afternoon, and I don't want to leave her alone.

"I'm okay. I'm going to make some mac and cheese for Walker, talk to him and explain our childhood. I need him to know this is a safe place for him, even if it means telling him about the ugly in life."

"I think that's a good idea." I nod. "Call me if anything, and I'll be right here." I hug her.

"Go on and win Lizzy back. I like her."

"I do, too." I smile.

Brooke shoves me with her shoulder. "Go."

"I'll be back early."

FABIOLA FRANCISCO

"Don't worry about us. He isn't stupid enough to return." Her chest rises with a breath. "I'm going to talk to Walker, maybe make cookies after dinner."

"Save me one." I stand.

"I'll think about it," Brooke teases.

I chuckle and grab my phone, heading out to my truck. I hope to God that Lizzy answers the door. Just in case, I shoot her a message since she hasn't responded to my other ones.

Me: I'm coming over.

Me: I need you.

I drive to her apartment complex and park in a guest spot. I jog to her apartment and knock on her door. I can't lose her. I've already lost so much, but if I can have this woman by my side, have her love, it'll make the pain diminish. She's my light.

ee

LIZZY

I look through the peephole although I know it's Nate based on his text message. I was so hopeful when he told me we'd talk today, but when I didn't hear from him, the sliver of hope disappeared like a magic trick. It was just an illusion.

308

GUARDED DEPUTY

I'm left with a hole in my chest, because even though his message sounded sad, I'm not sure if there's a way to fix this.

I open the door and find him leaning his hand against the frame and his head bowed. He glances up at me, and I frown. The pain in his eyes is heartbreaking. I wish I knew what was happening so I can help him, but he's completely shut me out.

"Murphy," he whispers in relief.

Nate stands to his full height, steps toward me, and wraps his arms around me. He breathes me in, and I can't help but hug him.

"Thank you," he whispers. His voice is hoarse as if he's fighting back his emotions.

I step away from the hug and wave him in. I don't want neighbors watching us. We sit on the couch, and he looks at me with a frown.

"I'm so sorry," he starts. "My dad started contacting me a few days ago,

"What?" I call out, shifting on the sofa to get a better look at him.

"Yeah. Apparently, he wanted to reconnect and apologize. And then he showed up in town, at the high school today."

"Oh my goodness, Nate." I cover my mouth in shock. From what he's told me, he hasn't seen his dad since he was a kid. "What... How did that make you feel?"

"Hearing from him again has been...hard." He shakes his head.

"I can imagine. You haven't seen him since he left, right?"

"I saw him once from far, but we didn't interact." He rubs a hand down his face. "It's been weighing on me. So many emotions resurfacing."

309

"It must've been difficult to see him again."

"But that's not an excuse for pushing you away. My dad is a sensitive topic for me. I've told you a bit about him, but the truth is that I never overcame him leaving us."

"Nate..." I rub my hand across his back.

"I'm sorry." His voice cracks and body shakes.

I wrap my arm around him and tug him to me until his face is buried in the crook of my neck.

"I wish you would've told me."

"I know. I'm an asshole."

"No, you aren't. You're hurt." I smooth my hand up and down his back, comforting him how I've wanted to do all these days.

The last thing I expected was to hear his dad showed up in his life again. I can't imagine what that would feel like. To see the man who left you when you were a child.

"What happened?" I ask.

"He said he wanted to explain why he left and make it up to us, prove he was a changed man." He snorts.

"And he wasn't?" I'm afraid to ask.

Nate sits up and stares at me. "No. We invited him to the house to talk and when I went to grab pizza and Brooke left to pick up Walker, he stole from us. He took Brooke's small savings."

I gasp, covering my mouth. What kind of father does that? Nate presses his lips into a thin line as his eyes take in my reaction.

"I'm so sorry." My heart breaks for them.

"It's not your fault. I should've known not to leave him alone while I went to pick up the pizza. We could've ordered it, but

GUARDED DEPUTY

I wanted to get it quicker to be done with the meal as soon as possible." He bows his head.

"Hey." I lift his face to look at me. "Do not blame yourself for this, Nate. The only person at fault is your father."

"He fucking stole from us, Lizzy. He stole from my widowed sister knowing she's a single mom." He shakes his head, a tear falling from his eye. "You know the worst part?"

I shake my head.

"A part of me believed him...or wanted to." He rubs his eyes with the heels of his hands.

I grab his wrists and pull his arms down. "Cry if you need to. Scream. Let it out."

He nods, swallowing thickly. He lies on my lap, and I brush his hair in silence while I gather my thoughts and he cries.

"It's normal that you wanted to believe him. He's your father, no matter how much you think you hate him. It's like a part of us is always children when facing our parents."

"Yeah," he says gruffly. "I've had to be so strong in front of Brooke and Walker so they don't worry more than they already do. I'm exhausted of keeping it all in, of acting out of anger." His body goes limp. "Don't stop brushing my hair. It feels good." He shifts his body, curling to fit as much as possible on my sofa.

"I won't."

I brush his hair and run my fingers along his forehead, just sitting with him while he breaks apart in my lap. It's so sad to watch. To see this strong man cry for his father.

"Why does he do this?" He shakes his head.

"I don't know," I answer honestly, bending down to hug him and drop a kiss on his neck.

311

Nate turns to look up at me, raising his arm to brush my face. A sad smile marks his face.

"You're beautiful."

I smile shyly.

"Thank you for letting me in."

"Of course. I only wish you would've talked to me on Friday."

"I know." He swallows. "I was processing. I've had a lot of internal struggles since my dad left us and a big fear that I'd be just like him." He frowns, looking away from me. "I've kept myself guarded for so long thinking I wouldn't be able to offer anyone what they need nor wanting to hurt anyone the way he hurt my mom. She never fully recovered."

"You're nothing like him," I say confidently.

"How do you know? I could be. He was a great dad at one point." His face hardens.

"Because I've seen your heart and it's pure." I hold the side of his face. "You're an amazing man and human, and I don't just say that because you're my boyfriend."

He sits up and tugs me to him until I land on his lap. His arms come around me, and I sigh, breathing him in. I can breathe easy for the first time in days.

"I'm still your boyfriend?" He asks against my neck.

"Yeah." I cup his cheeks with my hands and stare into his eyes. "I don't want to lose you, and I hated knowing something was wrong and you wouldn't talk to me. Please trust me."

"I do, but I didn't want to disappoint you. Hearing from him again threw me off and every emotion I held in broke loose. If you saw that part of me, you'd leave."

My brows furrow as I shake my head. "Why? I like you for who you are—the good, the bad, the beautiful, and the ugly.

GUARDED DEPUTY

All of these experiences and parts make you this wonderful person."

"I don't deserve you."

"You do." My thumbs stroke his cheeks.

"I love you."

I freeze, looking into his eyes as I tear up.

"Really?"

"Yeah." He chuckles. "Is that hard to believe?"

"We weren't on great terms, and I was afraid."

"Baby, we're going to go through a lot more rough patches. It's part of life, but I'll always love you."

My lips tremble as emotions overcome me in the best way possible.

"I love you, too."

He takes my lips in his in a searing kiss full of promise and apology. I melt into him, enjoying having him in my arms again. Nate slows the kiss and smiles.

"Are you hungry? I didn't get to have dinner with this mess."

"Oh, my God!" I leap from the couch and run to the oven, taking out the dish I left in there to give it a few more minutes.

I look at the baked pasta and breathe out in relief when I see that only the corners are toasty. A win for smart ovens that turn off when the timer ends.

"Safe!" I call out.

Nate chuckles from the other side of the kitchen, looking at me.

"What'd you make?" he asks, eyeing my food.

"Baked pasta. Do you want some?"

"Yeah, Murphy." One side of his lips lifts. "Thanks."

313

"I'm glad you're here and don't want you to leave ever again. Maybe I'll handcuff you to my bed." My eyes widen with my bright idea.

"I wouldn't mind." Nate crosses his arms, arching an eyebrow.

"My hot deputy stripper." My eyebrows waggle.

"Only for you." He winks.

"Well, of course. That's why I said *my*." I lift my brows.

His phone pings, and he grabs it from his pocket.

"Sorry, let me make sure it isn't Brooke."

I nod and plate our food while he checks his phone. I'm so happy he opened up to me and told me what was happening. I can sympathize with him. I'm not sure what trauma I'd have if my dad had abandoned us. My dad's choice to stay with us was stripped from him, but Nate's dad consciously made that decision. My heart hurts for the three of them. I can't imagine Walker's reaction.

"You've gotta be kidding me."

"What happened?" I look at Nate.

He turns his phone around, and I read a message from his dad.

Unknown Number: I owe some people money and they're looking for me. I need to leave the country. This will be the last you hear from me. I'm sorry. It was this or get killed. They don't know about you, I made sure of that. You're safe.

GUARDED DEPUTY

"Wow." All I can think about is that I'm happy these people don't know his dad had kids. If they came for them as revenge, I'd kill someone.

"Well, that's over." He pockets his phone.

"How does that make you feel?" I chew on my lip.

"Like I can heal and move on with the woman I love."

"I like the sound of that. And if you let me, I'd love to help you overcome this."

"I'm done shutting you out, Murphy." He comes around the counter and wraps his arms around my waist.

My grin breaks free. I wrap my arms around his neck and lean up on my toes, pressing my lips to his.

"I like the sound of that, Mr. Hot Deputy.

"Don't forget 'Packing.'" He winks, and I giggle, kissing him as if I had all the time in the world.

epilogue
LIZZY

I JUMP WHEN MY door swings open and then closes. Looking over my shoulder from the board where I'm writing the day's agenda, I see Nate stalking toward me with a Frappuccino.

"Uh, hi?" I lift my brows.

"Hey, Murphy. I brought you some coffee." He winks, and my face splits into a smile.

"Thanks, babe."

He places it on top of the low bookshelf by the board, wraps his hands around my thighs, and picks me up.

"Whoa." My legs go around his waist and my hands hold on to his shoulders.

Nate smirks, carrying me to my desk and setting me down. He stands between my legs and cups my face. My hands go to his hair, holding him close. He inches back to glance up at me, and I sigh happily, closing my eyes to breathe him in.

His hands skim up my knees, pushing my dress up a bit. My eyes snap open, and I find his full of desire.

"Someone can come in. We're at work," I whisper-hiss.

My eyes move from his hands on my thighs to his face. When he squeezes my legs, my breath catches. I wish we were back at my place.

GUARDED DEPUTY

"We can't, Nate." I widen my eyes.

He smiles slowly and leans in to kiss me. It's slow and lazy.

"I haven't kissed you in so long."

I giggle and shake my head. "You're incorrigible. You kissed me last night."

"That's a lifetime to me."

I laugh at his exaggeration against his lips and tug his hair. Things have been amazing between us, and every day I surprise myself with how much more I can love this man.

It's been a healing journey for him and his family, and I've been able to support him as he's needed.

"I love hearing you laugh," he says, breathless.

"I love you." I kiss his lips and inch back. "But we're at work."

"Fine." He sighs, feigning disappointment. "But I expect all your kisses this afternoon."

"I thought we were going to have dinner with Brooke and Walker?" Nate asked if I wanted to have dinner with his family. We've spent more time together, especially now that the school year is almost over and Walker will move on to second grade.

"Before and after." His brows waggle.

I laugh and shake my head.

"Now, enjoy your Frap. I got it 'specially for you. This time, if your students ask if your boyfriend got it for you, I expect you to say yes."

"Yes, sir." I salute him.

His eyes darken and he leans in. "Leave the submissive behavior for the bedroom, babe."

My lips part, and I shiver. "With handcuffs?" I smile.

FABIOLA FRANCISCO

"Whatever you want, but I'll make sure to put the key away. With your Murphy's Luck, we'll lose it and not be able to remove them."

"That would be something that would happen to me." I laugh.

Nate's hands move down my ribs to my waist, and he leans in to kiss me one more time. When the bell rings, he sighs in annoyance.

"I guess it's time to go to work."

"Yup, but I'll see you later when you come in here."

"And for lunch." He kisses my forehead. "I'm so happy to have you in my life, Lizzy." I never get tired of hearing him tell me that.

"Me, too." I hug him tightly and release him when I start to hear noise in the hallway.

Nate helps me down from the desk and fixes my dress. He winks and walks out of my room, leaving me breathless and in a daydreamy state. Grabbing the cup, I take a sip of the delicious caramel Frap and sigh happily.

"Hi, Ms. Andrews." My students start to walk into my classroom.

"Good morning." I say with a smile and finish writing the agenda on the board before we start class.

The day flies by, and when Nate walks in again, my smile grows. Until I see my uncle and a woman dressed in a suit enter behind him. I grow serious, wondering what's going on.

"Who are those people?" Paul points at them.

"Paul," I warn with a stern voice.

GUARDED DEPUTY

"It's okay." The woman laughs. "I'm Mrs. Cramer, and I'm here to watch your class. can I join you today?" The woman asks, and my students nod.

"Why?" Stephanie calls out.

"I want to see how Deputy Moore helps you."

"Do you need help with Stranger Danger?" she asks Mrs. Cramer, who laughs.

"You can never be too careful."

My uncle nods at me, and I smile softly. I'm guessing the woman is from the county to observe the mentorship program. I was under the impression that all the observations were complete, but maybe she wants to watch another lesson.

Hopefully it goes well. Nate's been counting on the approval from the county.

I stay at my desk, wanting to see Nate in action. He talks to the children about fire safety, asks them questions about what to do in an emergency, and even has them act out certain situations.

Mrs. Cramer smiles throughout and my uncle looks proud. I fall a little more in love with my hot deputy. He glances over at me and smiles.

When the class finishes, he leaves with our guests, and the children wave at them excitedly. It was a great lesson, so hopefully they get an answer soon. I know a lot is riding on this program. Uncle Roy has worked his behind off to get this pilot program approved.

elle

"Ms. Andrews, do you like Tic-Tac-Toe?" Walker asks me.

"I do." I smile at him from across the table at the restaurant.

"Awesome. Let's play." He turns his kid's menu over and makes a grip with a crayon.

Brooke ruffles his hair and smiles at me.

"Did you replace me?" Nate asks.

"Sorry, Uncle Nate, but I never get to have dinner with my teacher." He shrugs and looks at me. "What color crayon you want?"

"I'll have green."

He hands it over, and we start playing. Nate's phone rings as we're in our second game, and I see my uncle's name on the screen.

"I need to take this." He stands and goes outside.

"I won!" Walker calls out. "You suck at Tic-Tac-Toe, Ms. A."

"Walker!" Brooke chastises him. "Be polite. We don't use those words."

"Uncle Nate uses them." He shrugs.

"He's an adult and has a potty mouth sometimes."

I try to hold back my laughter.

"Apologize to your teacher."

"I'm sorry," he says glumly.

"It's okay. I'm not very good, so you're right about that." I doodle smiley faces on the O's.

"I'm so sorry." Brooke widens her eyes and shakes her head. "Sometimes I don't know what to do with him. He admires Nate so much, I'm afraid he'll be throwing curse words around to be just like him. Although, he tries to be better about it in front of Walker."

"It's understandable. They have a strong bond."

"Yeah." She sighs. "I'm glad they do. After losing my husband, Nate has been Walker's role model."

"I can't even imagine what that's like. I'm glad you have someone you can count on."

Nate returns to the table with a full smile, dimples and all.

"Great news." He sits down. "It seems like the superintendent loved what she observed. They need to make a final decision, but it looks promising that this program will be incorporated throughout the county."

"That's amazing. Congrats." I squeeze his arm.

"Thanks."

"It's wonderful news," Brooke says. "Proud of you, little bro." She grins.

"I don't get it." Walker shakes his head.

"I did a good job at work, and that lady liked it. Other schools are going to have a deputy working with them."

"But you're not leaving my school, right?" He frowns.

"I don't think so, but things change," Nate answers honestly.

I know this part of being a deputy wasn't his ideal situation, but he seems to be fully involved in the program.

After dinner, Nate takes me home. Standing by my door, he squeezes my hip and leans down to kiss me.

"Thanks for coming to dinner tonight."

"I had fun."

"I'm glad. My sister and Walker are the only family I have." He smiles sadly.

"You've got friends here now. And me." I cup his cheek. He closes his eyes and nods, moving his head to kiss my palm.

"Want to come in?"

"Always."

We walk into my apartment, closing the door behind us. I lean up on my toes, kissing Nate. His arms wrap around me, and a sense of home fills me. He's all I want, all I need. He's my forever.

"I'm going to marry you someday." He breaks away from the kiss, his breath a whisper against my lips.

"I can't wait." I smile.

Thank you for reading Guarded Deputy. I hope you enjoyed Lizzy and Nate's story as much as I did writing it! I'd love if you left a short review on Amazon and Goodreads.

Read Dani's story next! When Dani's neighbor becomes the new business consultant at the radio station, things get heated—in more ways than one. Get ready for a fun ride with her neighbor—the guy she loves to hate. Read Arrogant Neighbor now by scanning the QR code below.

If you're in the mood for a quick, holiday read, check out Kneading the Grinch, Avery and Gabe's story!

thank you!

FIRSTLY, THANK YOU FOR reading Guarded Deputy! I've been so excited to share this story.

I've got an amazing bunch to thank, who have helped me make this release happen. Thank you to ME Carter for working with me through developmental edits to make this the best version of the story and do Lizzy and Nate justice. Thank you to Victoria from Cruel Ink Editing for editing and proofing this story! Melody, thank you for bringing this cover to life in a way only you can. Your talent amazes me.

Savannah, thank you for believing in my work and all your support and encouragement.

Daniele and Andrea, thank you for reading an early copy and offering feedback. I appreciate it a ton!

Christy and Rachel, I can always count on you two, and that means the world to me.

To my review team and master list, who always come through for me. THANK YOU for being the best supporters a girl could as for!

For my author friends who continue to cheer me on, we're in this together. I appreciate you so much.

For my readers, bloggers, and bookstagrammers, thank you for all the love you show me. I'm a lucky girl.

about
Fabiola Francisco

FABIOLA FRANCISCO LOVES THE escape books offer. She writes contemporary romance, mostly small town romances with swoony book boyfriends and strong and sassy heroines.

Writing has always been a part of her life, penning her own life struggles as a form of therapy through poetry. Now, she writes novels that will capture your heart and make feel a range of emotions.

She is continuously creating stories as she daydreams. She also enjoys country music, exploring the outdoors, and reading.